Emily smiled and said to them, "We need to do the tree lighting. Lyla, you can do the honors."

"Aren't we going to do the countdown?" Lyla asked.

"Of course. Ten. Nine..." The rest of them joined in and counted down until they reached "One. Lights!"

Lyla hit the button and the lights on the dark spruce trees out front twinkled to life. The smallest tree, the one they'd planted in Coop's memory, was adorned in blue. Could Coop see his kids growing up? Did he know they all still thought of him, still loved him? What would Coop say if he knew about that flutter Emily had been feeling in Nick's presence?

She stole a glance toward Nick. He'd bent down next to Lyla, listening intently and nodding his head as she spoke. Once again Emily's heart swelled. "Stop it," she whispered to herself. She didn't have time for romance, especially with someone who would be leaving soon.

Dear Reader,

Have you ever been on the cusp of something you really wanted, just to hit a roadblock? Pilot Nick Bernardi has been offered his dream job flying in Hawaii, but during his preemployment exam he discovers he can no longer pass the vision test. Fortunately, it's just a temporary setback until he has eye surgery. And while he's recovering, he decides to help out his friend Emily Cooper, who needs a temporary nanny.

Funny thing about roadblocks—sometimes the detour can take you to wonderful places you'd have never gone otherwise. In Nick's case, delaying his dream meant he'd have the chance to find the family he never knew he wanted. I love the idea of serendipity, a "happy accident," but sometimes the accident doesn't seem happy at all at the beginning. Sometimes, it's only in looking back that we realize the roadblock was actually rerouting us to a better path.

I'd love to hear about your roadblocks and detours. You can find all my links and email details, as well as information about my books and newsletter, at bethcarpenterbooks.blogspot.com.

Wishing you serendipity always.

Beth

HIS ALASKAN CHRISTMAS

BETH CARPENTER

HEARTWARMING

If you purchased this book without a cover you should be aware that this book is stolen property. It was reported as "unsold and destroyed" to the publisher, and neither the author nor the publisher has received any payment for this "stripped book."

Recycling programs for this product may not exist in your area.

ISBN-13: 978-1-335-46014-1

His Alaskan Christmas

Copyright © 2025 by Lisa Deckert

All rights reserved. No part of this book may be used or reproduced in any manner whatsoever without written permission.

Without limiting the author's and publisher's exclusive rights, any unauthorized use of this publication to train generative artificial intelligence (AI) technologies is expressly prohibited.

This is a work of fiction. Names, characters, places and incidents are either the product of the author's imagination or are used fictitiously. Any resemblance to actual persons, living or dead, businesses, companies, events or locales is entirely coincidental.

For questions and comments about the quality of this book, please contact us at CustomerService@Harlequin.com.

TM and ® are trademarks of Harlequin Enterprises ULC.

Harlequin Enterprises ULC
22 Adelaide St. West, 41st Floor
Toronto, Ontario M5H 4E3, Canada
www.Harlequin.com

Printed in U.S.A.

Beth Carpenter is thankful for good books, a good dog, a good man and a dream job creating happily-ever-afters. She and her husband now split their time between Alaska and Arizona, where she occasionally encounters a moose in the yard or a scorpion in the basement. She prefers the moose.

Books by Beth Carpenter

Harlequin Heartwarming

A Northern Lights Novel

The Alaskan Catch
A Gift for Santa
Alaskan Hideaway
An Alaskan Proposal
Sweet Home Alaska
Alaskan Dreams
An Alaskan Family Christmas
An Alaskan Homecoming
An Alaskan Family Found
An Alaskan Family Thanksgiving
Her Alaskan Summer

Love Inspired Suspense

Alaskan Wilderness Peril

Visit the Author Profile page at Harlequin.com.

This book is dedicated to those generous souls
who keep the spirit of Christmas alive all year long.

CHAPTER ONE

HERB-AND-APPLE stuffing or sage-and-sausage dressing? Emily Cooper studied the two recipes on her laptop screen. The sausage sounded good, but maybe she was influenced by the mouthwatering smells of basil, fennel, and garlic coming from the pot of spaghetti sauce she'd left simmering on the stove. Her kids, Max and Lyla, loved Italian sausage on pizza, but would it overpower the flavor of the turkey if she made it for Thanksgiving? Her husband, Coop, had always made the cornbread dressing from his grandmother's recipe, but in the two Thanksgivings since he'd been gone, Emily had never been able to reproduce it, despite following the directions on the stained recipe card to the letter. Maybe that was the problem. Coop's cooking was always more about mood than measuring, and he was never in a better mood than when he was cooking for the holidays.

Anyway, Emily had decided that this Thanksgiving, it was time to try something new. Under the table, their golden retriever, Nala, lay her head on Emily's foot. Emily reached down to pet her before hitting the print button for both recipes. Tomorrow she would be starting her two-week hitch on the Alaska North Slope, where she worked as a production engineer, keeping the oil wells in her section of the Prudhoe Bay field maintained and producing efficiently. Her friend Gloria, who was a cook there, could give her an expert opinion on which recipe to use.

The oven timer beeped. Carefully extracting her foot without disturbing the dog, Emily went to stick a toothpick into the chocolate zucchini loaf she'd made for dessert. Done. She set it on a rack to cool, turned on the burner under the pot of water, and pulled the salad she had made earlier from the refrigerator. She always liked to make one of the kids' favorite meals the day before she left for her two-week hitch on the slope. It wasn't as though Max and Lyla didn't eat well when she was away—she always filled the freezer before she left, and her mother-in-law, Janice, was a fine cook—but Emily just liked to spread a little extra love around to tide them over while she was gone.

While she waited for the water to boil, Emily slipped into the spare room down the hall to collect the recipes. Although it had a bed and doubled as a guest room, this room had been Coop's home office, from which he'd run his structural engineering consulting business. Now, it was seldom used unless someone needed to print something. Emily crossed to the corner desk, which held two monitors, the printer, and a grow lamp that had been set up over a row of terra-cotta pots containing bean plants that were part of Max's science-fair experiment. In the printer tray, Emily found her recipes on top of a set of charts documenting the growth of the bean plants. She leafed through the papers. One displayed the title of Max's experiment—"Do bean plants grow better when they are around people?"

Emily had been skeptical when Max had announced his premise, but to her surprise, the plants in the kitchen were significantly taller than the ones here, despite identical grow lamps, water, and fertilizer. Emily tended to attribute it to the extra humidity and warmth from cooking, but maybe Max was right. Maybe plants, like people, thrived in an atmosphere of noisy conversation and love. At least that was his conclusion, spelled out in colorful letters on the next page.

As a sixth grader, this would be Max's last year at Swan Falls Elementary. Next year, he would be moving to the middle school at the other end of the building. It seemed like just yesterday, Coop had been taking video while Emily let go of Max's hands and hovered, ready to catch him while he took his first steps. Now, Max was only a smidge short of Emily's five foot five, and at the rate he was growing, he'd pass her by next summer. Lyla, tallest in her fourth-grade class, wouldn't be far behind. Emily gathered up the papers.

"Max," Emily called up the stairs. "I thought you had everything done for the science fair tomorrow."

"I do." Max stepped out of his room and hung over the railing. "I just have to glue the stuff I printed onto my display board."

"You're using the same board as you used last year, right?" Emily hadn't thought to ask if he'd located it yet.

"Yeah. It's in the garage, I think."

"Well, you'd better go find it. But first, tell your sister that dinner will be ready in about ten minutes."

"Lyla, dinner in ten minutes," he yelled while thundering down the stairs.

"Okay," Lyla yelled back.

Emily had intended for Max to tap on Lyla's door and speak in a normal voice, but whatever. She returned to the kitchen and added the spaghetti to the pot of water. Max pushed through the door to the garage, letting it slam behind him. Five minutes later, the door flew open again. "Mom! We've got to go get a new display board."

"Why? What's—" But then she saw the problem. He must have left it leaning against the wall of the garage at ground level. During the winter, enough snow melted off the car's tires in the heated garage to wet the floor on a regular basis. The water had wicked up into the cardboard, leaving the bottom five inches a moldy mess. "Oh." She glanced at the clock. Six thirty. Swan Falls Mercantile, the local grocery and whatnot store, would have closed half an hour ago. Emily had been shopping there that afternoon and could have easily picked up whatever Max needed if he'd bothered to check his supplies, but, of course, he'd left it to the last minute. She studied the stained three-section board in his hands. "What if we just cut off the ruined part?"

"That would look terrible."

"Why? If we cut it straight, I'll bet you couldn't even tell—"

"The judges will know, because everybody else's will be taller. It would be embarrassing."

This concern about embarrassment was a recent development with Max. He'd always been an easygoing and confident kid. Emily wasn't sure if it had to do with missing his dad, or just that he was approaching his teen years, but either way, she didn't want to add to it. "All right," she agreed. "Once we're done with dinner, we'll drive into Wasilla and get it." If they finished dinner by seven and spent an hour for the round trip to Wasilla, there would still be time for baths and reading time before bed. Barely.

"Ice cream?" Lyla asked hopefully as she pulled out her chair from the table. Nala scrambled to her feet to greet the kids.

"What about ice cream?" Emily took a wedge of Parmesan cheese from the refrigerator and the grater from the drawer.

"Is that what we're going into Wasilla for?"

"No. I made chocolate zucchini bread for dessert. We need to go into Wasilla to get a new display board for Max's science project."

"Oh. I need new markers, too. Some of mine are all dried up."

"Fine." Emily grated the cheese into a bowl. "We'll get markers, too. Max, could you set the table, please? Lyla, please feed the dog and pour the milk."

Lyla poured Nala's kibble into her bowl. "Where's Gramma?" she asked, as she took down the glasses.

"She and her friends went to a craft show, and then they're eating at that new tearoom in Wasilla." Emily briefly considered calling Janice and asking her to pick up the board and markers but decided against it. Not that Janice would mind, but she deserved to have this uninterrupted time with her friends before she stepped in tomorrow for her two-week shift as Max and Lyla's primary guardian.

When it came to mothers-in-law, Emily had hit the jackpot. She had heard the horror stories of in-laws who constantly snooped or meddled in a couple's private business, or conversely couldn't be bothered to spend time with their grandchildren. But Emily and Janice had felt like friends from their very first meeting. When the children were born, Janice couldn't have been more thrilled and supportive. And when Coop had died in that freak kayaking accident two years ago, Janice had immediately offered to move from Anchorage to Swan Falls, allowing Emily to keep her two-week-on-and-two-week-off engineering job on the North Slope while Janice took care of the kids.

Max and Lyla loved having their grandmother with them, and so did Emily, although she sometimes felt like she was taking advantage of Janice's generosity. Janice had been a single mom, raising Coop alone after his father left them. She'd retired from her administrative job at the university in Anchorage five years ago. This should be the time of her life for hobbies, travel, and fun, but instead she was here, helping to raise her grandchildren. But she seemed to enjoy life in this tiny town with her grandkids and her friends. Besides, Emily's only other option would be to transfer to an office position, which would mean moving to Anchorage, and she really didn't want to do that. The kids' school, their home, and their friends were all here, in Swan Falls.

The timer went off, and Emily drained the spaghetti, then fixed everyone a plate. "Did you get your math assignment finished?" she asked Lyla, although she had no doubt she had. Lyla adored school. Emily passed the salad to Max, who put a token amount on his plate and drowned it with ranch dressing before passing it on to Lyla.

"All done," Lyla confirmed. "But I need to practice my spelling words."

"Your spelling test isn't until Friday," Max pointed out, before stuffing a whole meatball into his mouth.

"Yeah, but I want Mommy to quiz me before she goes," Lyla replied.

Comments like that made Emily question her decision to keep the slope job. Even though they video-chatted every evening, she missed her kids during her two-week hitches. But in between, during her two weeks off, she was free to volunteer in their classrooms, plan special projects, and basically devote herself to them, so it all kind of equaled out. "We'll do it after dinner while Max loads the dishwasher." When Max opened his mouth to object, she continued, "Before we drive into Wasilla to get the poster board I could have picked up at the mercantile today if someone hadn't left it for the last minute."

Max's protest died away, and he put a forkful of spaghetti in his mouth instead. They spent the rest of dinner discussing Max's science-fair experiment and what kind of pie they should have for Thanksgiving. Max wanted apple, but Lyla wanted pecan. Emily was partial to pumpkin, and she knew it was Janice's favorite. They would probably end up making all three. Once they'd finished eating, Lyla ran off to get her spelling words, while Emily helped Max clear the table. Max had just put the first plates into the dishwasher when they heard the crunch of wheels on the gravel out front and the front door opened and closed.

A moment later, Janice breezed into the kitchen, carrying two shopping bags and a new white display board. She handed the board to Max. "I thought you might need this for the science fair."

"Thanks, Gramma. I'll go glue my stuff on it." Abandoning the dishes, he sailed out of the room with the folded board under his arm.

"You're a lifesaver." Emily took the shopping bags and put them on the counter. "We were about to drive to Wasilla to get one. How did you know he needed it?"

"Peggy mentioned she's a judge at the science fair tomorrow, which reminded me that I hadn't checked on Max, so I decided to pick it up just in case."

Lyla skipped into the room. "Hi, Gramma. Mommy's going to help me practice my spelling words and then we're driving to Wasilla for new markers."

"Oh, we're not going, because—" Emily began, but before she could complete her sentence Janice reached into one of the shopping bags and pulled out a box of markers.

"Here you go," Janice told her. "Better put them in your backpack so you don't forget to take them to school tomorrow."

"Thanks!" Lyla took the markers and dashed up the stairs.

At Emily's inquisitive look, Janice laughed. "She mentioned yesterday that some of her markers had dried up."

"Well, thank you." Emily smiled. Much as she worried, the truth was her kids couldn't be in better hands while she was away.

Nala padded over to Janice. "I didn't forget you," she assured the dog. She pulled a new bundle of chewy sticks from the bag and gave one to Nala, who took it politely and trotted purposefully to the rug in the living room.

Emily smiled. "How was the new tearoom?"

"Nice, but it was one of those places where they bring you this beautiful plate, but once you start eating you realize there are only a couple of bites of food there and the rest is just decoration. Any of that spaghetti left?"

"Plenty. Help yourself." Emily handed over the dish she'd been about to put into the refrigerator. "What else is new with your friends?"

"Helen is fretting, as usual. You remember she won that European Christmas market river cruise?"

"Oh, that's right. That sounds like fun."

"It really does. She was showing us the brochure. All kinds of interesting things to see, and even cooking lessons teaching how to make some of the classic European Christmas cookies." Janice set her plate in the microwave. "Helen and her sister leave in early December, but they'll be gone for more than three weeks, and even though Helen has people scheduled to cover the bookstore while she's gone, she's worried about it. You know how she is—she's convinced if she isn't doing it herself, it won't be done right. I told her I'd stop in and check on things a few times while she's gone."

"That's nice of you."

"Well, it's hardly a hardship to visit a bookstore, especially just before Christmas." Janice took the plate from the microwave to the table and sat down to eat. "Helen's nephew from Eagle River is taking over as manager while she's gone." Janice watched Emily from the corner of her eye. "Helen says he's recently divorced. Sad story. She showed us his picture. He's very good-looking."

Emily laughed. Janice had mentioned a couple of times that if Emily wanted to go out for an evening, she'd be happy to babysit. "If you're hinting what I think you're hinting, forget it. Too busy."

"Maybe that's the problem," Jan replied. "You should be dating, having fun. When was the last time you did something fun just for you?"

"Um…" Emily thought about it. "I went to a movie last week."

"A kid's movie, that Lyla wanted to see."

"I bought a new dress."

"Because you're giving a presentation at that professional meeting in January." Janice shook her head. "If you won't do it for yourself, think of the kids. It might be good for them to have a male influence in their lives."

"You managed to raise Coop without the benefit of a man in your life, and he turned out pretty good." Emily set the rest of the plates in the dishwasher.

"Yeah," Janice said, but she sighed, as though she wasn't convinced.

"But, hey." Emily grinned. "If you think it's important, why don't you make a play for Helen's nephew? You're single, too."

Janice burst out laughing. "Wouldn't that get Helen's feathers ruffled."

Emily washed out the spaghetti pot. "Ask him out. I dare you."

"I'm too old," Janice replied.

"Too old for what?" Emily dried the pot and put it in the cupboard.

Janice grinned. "Too old and wise to let myself be manipulated by a dare. Ooh, is that chocolate zucchini bread?"

"From your recipe." Emily set the loaf on the table. "Enjoy."

CHAPTER TWO

EMILY CAREFULLY PLACED THE tub containing Max's bean plants on the floor of the minivan, where they were in no danger of falling over on the short ride to school. Her own bags were already in the back seat of the small SUV she used to commute between Swan Falls and the Anchorage airport. Max carried out the new display board and put it in the back, then slung his backpack onto the seat.

"Is that everything you need for the science fair?" Emily asked him.

Max grunted in the affirmative.

"Including those little folding cards you made to set in front of each pot?"

"Oh. Just a sec." He ran into the house and came back with the cards, which he set in the bin with the plants.

"Everything looks good," Emily said, taking one last look at his display board. "Gramma will help you carry your stuff in. And she said she'd take pictures after the judging and send them to me so I can see everything."

"I know."

"I'll call you from the slope tonight so we can talk about it."

"Yeah, Mom, I know." Max didn't quite roll his eyes, but he clearly thought about it. "It's not like this is your first hitch on the slope. We know the routine."

"Okay." She restrained herself from reminding him she would be home in two weeks, the day before Thanksgiving. He knew her schedule, and besides, it was on the big calendar in the kitchen.

Lyla came skipping into the garage and tossed her backpack onto the seat. "*D-i-s-a-p-p-e-a-r.* Disappear."

"Nice." Emily smiled at her daughter. "You've got those spelling words down. Now, come give me my hugs."

Lyla threw her arms around her mother and hugged her tight, then pulled her down and gave her a big smacking kiss on the cheek. "'Bye, Mom. Have fun on the slope."

"Thanks, honey. You have fun in school, too. Max? Hugs?"

Max glanced around as though making sure there were no witnesses other than his sister before allowing an awkward hug. "'Bye, Mom. Talk to you tonight."

"For sure. I love you guys."

"Love you, too." Their voices were almost in unison.

Emily checked her watch. She needed to hit the road. "You two get in the minivan, and I'll go say 'bye to your gramma and Nala before I leave." Emily stepped into the kitchen and poured the last of the coffee into her travel mug. She could hear Janice's voice coming from her room at the back of the house. She must be on the phone. Nala padded over to Emily from her spot under the table. Emily bent down to ruffle the dog's ears. "You take good care of the family while I'm gone, okay, girl?"

The big dog wagged her plumy tail in agreement.

Janice came down the hall, holding her phone to her ear. "That's a shame. Yes, it sounds amazing, but you know I can't go. I'm taking care of the kids. You'll just have to find someone else." There was a pause. "Well then, I'm sure you'll meet some nice people on the boat. Listen, I need to take the kids to school now. I'll call you later. Okay, 'bye."

Janice ended the call and smiled at Emily. "You heading out?"

"I'm just about to. But what was that about?"

Janice shook her head. "Helen. You know she and her sister were going on this European Christmas river cruise." At Emily's nod, she continued. "Well, the sister fell off a ladder getting her suitcase down from the attic, and broke her leg, so now she can't go."

"That's terrible. So Helen asked you to take her place?"

"Yes, but I don't know why. She knows you work two-and-two, and she'll be gone for a month. I told her there was no way."

"Such a great opportunity for you, though." History, food, and crafts were right up Janice's alley. Emily hated for her to miss out. "Maybe I can find someone temporary. I could call an agency—"

"No, I wouldn't want to leave the kids with strangers. Don't give it another thought. Helen will be fine without me." Janice glanced at the clock. "You'd better get going. I know you like to get to the airport early. Come here." She enveloped Emily in a hug. "You go do your engineering thing and don't worry. Everything is under control here. We'll talk tonight."

"Okay. Thanks, Janice. I love you."

"Love you, too, sweet girl. Now, get out of here." Janice made shooing motions with her hands.

Laughing, Emily carried her coffee to the little SUV, waved at the kids one more time, and pulled out of the driveway. Fifty-five minutes later, she was stepping onto the shuttle bus that would carry her from the off-airport parking lot to the terminal. Her favorite driver lifted her bag onto the rack. "Hi, Em."

"Hi, Fin. How's school going?" From their brief conversations every two weeks, Emily had learned that Fin was studying engineering at UAA, in the same program she'd graduated from seventeen years ago.

"Not bad, although physics is kicking my butt. Was Professor Johnson there when you were?"

"He was! I can't believe he's still there. He's tough."

"Yeah. I've got a midterm next week, and if I don't get at least a B, I'm sunk." Fin turned to help another passenger, and Emily found a seat. Traffic had been uncharacteristically light on the highway, and she'd arrived earlier than usual. Two more passengers climbed aboard, and the bus made the short trip to the terminal. Fin handed over Emily's small suitcase with a daisy decal on the front and accepted her tip. "Thanks. See you in two weeks."

"'Bye, Fin. Good luck on that physics midterm. When you study, focus on the thermodynamics section. Johnson loves thermo."

"Okay. Thanks for the tip!" He glanced at the bill in his hand. "Tips, rather."

She laughed and hitched the strap of her satchel more securely on her shoulder before rolling her bag into the airport. She had no luggage to check, so she was heading toward security when someone called, "Emily!"

She turned. "Nick!" Nick Bernardi was one of Coop's oldest friends. He'd been best man in their wedding, and a frequent visitor to their home, although less frequent after Coop died. Last time she'd seen him was in September, at Lyla's birthday party in a bowling alley in Anchorage. He'd led Lyla's team to victory, let Max beat him at air hockey, and given Lyla a stuffed giraffe so big it had to ride home on the roof of the car. Lyla insisted on keeping it in the corner of her room, where it got in the way every time she opened or closed her closet door, but she loved it so much she didn't care.

"What are you doing here?" Emily asked. "Oh, duh. You're a pilot." Although instead of his pilot uniform of a navy polo shirt with company insignia, he was wearing jeans and a faded blue shirt over a white T-shirt and dark-rimmed glasses instead of his usual contacts. The start of a beard covered his jawline.

"Yeah, well, not a pilot at the moment." Nick's usually cheerful face seemed glum.

"What do you mean?" she asked.

"Long story." He ran his fingers through his hair, pushing it away from his face. Emily had never decided exactly what color Nick's hair was. The summer sun rendered it blond, but now, in the winter, the loose waves were a shade darker, with a definite hint of red, like a bronze statue. "You on your way to the slope?"

"I am, but the security line looks short, and I have a little time. Let's grab a cup of coffee and talk a minute." They ordered coffee at the nearby kiosk and carried their cups to an empty row of chairs near the front window of the terminal. Emily sat next to Nick and leaned forward. "What's going on? Did something happen to your job with Puffin Flying Service?"

"You could say that. I just finished my exit interview with Puffin. I resigned to take a new job with Nene Airlines. They fly interisland in Hawaii."

"Hawaii? That's great. You've always wanted to move there." Nick would visit Hawaii two or three times a year sometimes. She used to wonder if he might have a girlfriend there, but Coop didn't think so.

"Yeah, but there's a snag," Nick explained. "At my pre-employment physical, I found out I can't pass the eye exam with my contacts anymore. I went to the optometrist yesterday for a new prescription, but he can't get me to 20/20, which means I can't fly."

"Oh, no. Can you drive?"

"Oh, sure. You can drive with 20/40, but if I want to fly, I'm going to have to do laser surgery."

Emily blew out a breath. "That's not so bad, then. I'm surprised you waited this long. I had the surgery years ago."

"Yeah, I know. Coop kept telling me I ought to do it, but the idea of lasers cutting into my eyeballs..." Nick shuddered.

Emily laughed. "Yeah, it sounds horrible, but the laser part lasted less than a minute per eye, and there really wasn't any pain to speak of, just a gritty feeling. It's been so nice not to have to mess with glasses or contacts. Once it's done, you'll wonder why you waited so long."

"I hope so, because I made the appointment. That's also why I'm wearing glasses, because they said to skip the contacts until the surgery. Unfortunately, I can't get in until after Thanksgiving, and I can't fly until four weeks after surgery, so it looks like I'm grounded for a while. But Nene says they'll hold the job for me until the end of the year."

"Too bad about the grounding, but it sounds like it will all work out in a few weeks."

"You're right, but you know how I hate sitting around, twiddling my thumbs." Nick waved his hand. "But enough about me. What's new with you? How's the family?"

"The kids are great. Max grew bean sprouts for the science fair at school today. Lyla has recently taken up bracelet making." Emily held up her wrist to display the purple-and-turquoise paracord bracelet she wore.

"Cool." Nick leaned closer to examine the knotted bracelet. "I wonder if she'd make me one."

"I'm sure she would. Just let her know what color you want. Janice is good, too. Sometimes I feel guilty, though, like this morning, when her friend Helen invited her along on a trip to Europe to see the Christmas markets, and she can't go because I'll be on the slope during that time. Sometimes I think I ought to hire a nanny, so Janice isn't tied down."

Nick tilted his head. "I can't imagine it would be easy to find a nanny in Swan Falls. What's the population now, about two thousand?"

"Not quite." Emily grinned. "But Melanie at the diner is pregnant with twins, so we might get there soon. You're right, though. I'd have to go through an agency in Anchorage, and I'm not sure any of their nannies would want to move to Swan Falls. Especially since it's such a weird schedule, basically all day and night for two weeks, then off for the other two. Even if I could find somebody, I'd hate to hurt Janice's feelings, make her think we don't want her there. She's been so great. I can't imagine what we would have done without her after Coop died."

"Yeah, Janice has always been like that. When we were kids, Coop and I always hung out at his house. Janice made me feel like I was part of the family."

"She did that with me, too, even before Coop and I were married. But she deserves time off. Hey, since you're not piloting for the next few weeks, maybe I ought to hire you to take care of the kids." She changed her voice to sound like an infomercial. "Have you ever considered an illustrious career as a nanny? Or, what's the new term for guys—a manny?"

Nick laughed. "A manny, huh? That probably doesn't require laser eye surgery."

"No, just lots of feeding and chauffeuring. And

laundry." She sighed. "Sometimes, based on the number of loads I do, I think there must be at least three people living in our house that I've never met." She took the last sip of her coffee and stood. "I'd better go, but I'm glad I ran into you, Nick. The kids would love to see you. If you don't have plans, why don't you come for Thanksgiving?"

"I might just do that, since I won't be working."

"Great! Okay, see you then, and if not, good luck on that laser surgery." She touched his shoulder and turned to go, but just before she stepped into the line for security, she looked back. Nick was still standing where she'd left him, staring out the front window, but she got the impression he wasn't looking at the cars dropping off passengers, or even at the Chugach Mountains in the distance. He was looking at the sky, itching to be flying once again. Poor Nick. It was going to be a long six weeks for him.

NICK FINISHED HIS last sip of coffee and crumpled the cup. He turned to look for a trash can, but his eyes were drawn toward Security, where he could just make out a dark ponytail swaying like a silken tassel as Emily set her steel-toed work boots on the conveyor belt and stepped into the scanner, out of his line of sight. Despite the heavy khaki work pants and hoodie, she looked almost as pretty now as she had in her wedding dress the day she married Coop.

Not long afterward, Emily and Coop had purchased a sprawling fixer-upper in Swan Falls, a tiny town northeast of Anchorage. For the first couple of years, they spent most of their time off on home renovations, until the house was hardly recognizable as the dilapidated wreck Nick had advised Coop not to buy. Nick had gotten dragged into a few of those renovations and was surprised to discover he rather liked hanging drywall and building decks. Or maybe he just liked being around Coop and Emily. Once the house was done, Coop and Emily went to work filling those bedrooms. Emily took a few years off work after Max was born, and didn't return to her job on the slope until Lyla started kindergarten. Meanwhile, Coop had started his own home-based engineering consulting business, arranging projects so that he was always home with the kids while Emily was on the slope. Everything was going great, until Coop's accident.

Nick still felt a pang of regret whenever he thought of the accident. He should have been there. He and Coop had made plans to take their kayaks down that stretch of white water, the same stretch they'd done a dozen times before. But someone had called in sick, and Nick had to take an extra flight that day, so he hadn't been able to make it. Ordinarily Coop wouldn't have kayaked alone, but he knew that river so well, he must have felt safe. Only he wasn't. The strong current had pushed

Coop's kayak into a strainer, a newly fallen tree, and with no one to rescue him, he'd drowned there, leaving Max and Lyla fatherless.

Emily had been crushed, but with two children to care for, she hadn't stayed that way for long. Nick was in awe of her strength. He was sure she'd never counted on being a single mom, but she had stepped into the role with courage and confidence. And, of course, Coop's mom had been there, too. Max and Lyla may have lost their father, but between Janice and Emily, they were well loved.

Nick crossed the street to the short-term parking garage, found his truck, and headed home, still thinking of Emily and the kids. He did what he could to help. On birthdays and Christmas, he would shower Max and Lyla with gifts. He called them periodically and would occasionally take them for a day of junk food and fun. It was no hardship for him—Max and Lyla were great kids, and he enjoyed his role as the "fun uncle." But he knew that Emily and Janice did the real work, staying up all night with the kids when they were sick, making sure they ate their vegetables and did their homework, cheering on their successes, and listening when they needed to talk.

All those things Nick had seldom experienced as a child, and never really learned how to do. There was a good reason Nick was single, and why he intended to remain that way. Nick was no family man. Not like Coop. And now, he wasn't even a working pilot. But Emily was right—in six weeks, assuming the surgery went as planned, his eyesight would be up to specs, and he would be flying in Hawaii, something he'd aspired to since he was a kid. This was just a blip, not a major life reset like she'd been through. Maybe it was even a good thing. He could spend the next six weeks doing those things he never seemed to get around to, like cleaning his oven and getting his oil changed.

Three hours later, his self-cleaning oven had completed its cycle, his car maintenance was up-to-date, and he'd rescheduled with the car auction and moving companies for after Christmas. He'd already donated the stuff he didn't need and packed everything he planned to take to Hawaii, other than what he used every day. No use unpacking all that kitchen stuff—although he enjoyed cooking, it hardly seemed worth it for one person. He had one more call to make. "Hi, Mark. I know I gave notice that I'd be out of the apartment by November fifteenth, but it turns out I'll be in Alaska a little longer than I thought. Can I change that move-out date to the end of the year?" He didn't expect a problem. His landlord had always been accommodating.

But apparently not this time. "Sorry, Nick. I can't. I've already got new renters lined up for your apartment. They're moving in December first."

"Can't you cut me a break? I've been a good tenant for what...six years now? No loud parties, no pets, never late with the rent. I even let you show prospective tenants my apartment."

"I know, and I appreciate it. I would let you stay, but they've already put down a security deposit and signed a contract, and I don't have any other vacant apartments. I can give you a few extra days, but I'd need you out by, say, the Monday before Thanksgiving to give us time to paint and clean the carpet. Does that help?"

"Not a lot, but thanks, anyway. I'll figure something out." Nick hung up the phone. On Monday, he'd been grounded. Tuesday, scheduled for a surgery he was dreading. Today, Wednesday, he'd found out he'd be homeless for the holidays. This was not shaping up to be a good week.

CHAPTER THREE

"Hey, Em. Got a second?" Brant, the production engineer from the Anchorage office who had flown up on the same plane as she had yesterday to supervise a workover, asked as she stepped into the building for her midday meal. "I have a question about those production logs."

"Sure." Emily shrugged out of her enormous arctic-weight parka and went to look at his computer screen. After answering his question, she stopped by her room to drop off her parka, pants, and gloves. Standard arctic gear took up an entire duffel bag and most of her storage locker, but with temperatures occasionally as low as forty below zero at Prudhoe Bay, it was necessary. She changed her super-insulated bunny boots for steel-toed leather work boots, washed her hands and slathered them in lavender-scented lotion to counteract the dry air in the building, and made her way toward the cafeteria for a well-deserved lunch break. She'd long ago learned to pace herself over the twelve-hour workdays on the slope.

But before she arrived, her cell phone rang. Nick? She stepped to the side of the hallway to pick up. "Hi. You're not having second thoughts about that laser surgery, are you?"

"Nah, that's still on the schedule. I need your advice on something else. I've looked and looked, but I can't seem to find the store that sells those giant magical purses and flying umbrellas. Any ideas?"

It took her a second to get the reference, and then she snorted with laughter. "You've decided to become a nanny."

"Your nanny, anyway, if the offer is still open. My landlord is eager to have his cleaning team in to get my apartment ready for the next tenants. Any chance I could start right away?"

She'd only been half-serious, but why not? Max and Lyla loved Nick, and he loved them. The trip Helen had invited Janice on didn't start until after Thanksgiving, so that gave him a little time to get up to speed. "You're in luck. The position hasn't been filled, and I don't require my nanny to have a flying umbrella or a British accent."

"That's a relief. You're the best, Emily."

"No problem. I'll call Janice and let her know you'll be coming. You okay staying in Coop's old office? It's a little crowded, but you can move the desk and computer equipment to the living room if you want, and it does have its own bathroom."

"It will be fine. Thanks. I really appreciate this."

"You're the one doing me a favor. Now, we just

have to convince Janice to put herself first, for once, and go on that trip."

"I'll do my best. 'Bye, Emily. I'll text you once I'm there."

"Sounds good. 'Bye." She started to return the phone to her pocket, but if Nick was really moving in right away, she'd better give Janice a heads-up before she went to lunch.

"Hi, Janice. It's Emily."

"Hi, sweetie. Can you believe Max got a blue ribbon for his bean-growing project?"

"I know. He even beat out the potato clock and the baking-soda volcano. Thanks for all the great pictures, by the way."

"You're welcome. I think the judges gave Max extra credit because he started growing the bean seeds six weeks ago," Janice said. "The volcano was obviously a last-minute panic entry. The papier-mâché was still damp."

Emily laughed. "Kind of like Max's solar-system model last year, when all the stores were out of Ping-Pong balls by the time he remembered the assignment, and he had to use fruit?"

"I still think Lyla's idea of using a tomato for Mars, the red planet, was quite original."

"That's for sure." Emily switched the phone to her other ear. "Say, I was calling about Nick."

"Nick Bernardi?"

"Yes. I ran into him at the airport. He's going to be moving into Coop's study for a while." Emily explained about the eye surgery and the delay before he could take the job in Hawaii.

"Goodness. I hope the surgery goes well. I don't know what Nick would do if he couldn't fly anymore."

"I know. He was really feeling down when I talked to him at the airport yesterday, but I'm sure he'll be flying soon. In the meantime, Nick and I were thinking…since he's going to be at the house, anyway, he can take care of the kids, and you can take that trip with Helen."

"Oh, I couldn't do that," Janice protested.

"Sure you could." Emily lowered her voice to a conspiratorial tone. "You know Nick. He never lets anyone do him a favor. The only way I convinced him to stay with us was if he's doing *us* the favor, taking care of the kids while you travel. Otherwise he'll probably just hole up in some generic hotel all by himself until the end of the year."

"Oh, that would be sad, stuck in a hotel, especially with the holidays coming up. But you can't really mean to leave the kids with Nick. He's never even taken them overnight, much less for two weeks while you're on the slope."

"When does your trip start?"

"Helen flies out December first, and doesn't get back until Christmas Eve," Janice replied. Emily noticed she still wasn't including herself in the plan.

"Today is November 14th, so that gives you a little time to train Nick. Hey, if anyone can do it, you can."

"Maybe," Janice allowed.

"Let's give it a try," Emily urged. "You teach Nick what he needs to know, and if you feel comfortable, you'll take the trip. When do you need to make the final decision?"

"Helen already had the tour company issue new tickets in my name, even though I told her I wasn't going. She says there's no one else."

"Well, then, better dig out your passport and order some lederhosen or whatever you'll need for the trip."

Janice laughed. "I think lederhosen are for Oktoberfest, not Christmas."

"Whatever you'll need, then. Good walking shoes for sure. I'd better get some lunch. Talk with you more tonight."

"Okay. 'Bye, honey. Love you."

"Love you, too." Emily pocketed her phone and rubbed her hands together. That bit about Nick holing up in a hotel was inspired, if she did say so herself. Janice would never allow Nick to be alone and homeless over Thanksgiving or Christmas. Now, it fell to Nick to convince Janice he was capable of keeping her two precious grandchildren alive and well for two weeks while she traveled. Emily just hoped he could pull it off.

NICK WAS UP early on Friday, determined to beat Janice into the kitchen. He had arrived yesterday afternoon, bringing flowers for Janice and a big box of doughnuts for the kids, and that, the doughnuts at least, may have been a mistake. A serious nanny would have brought something practical and healthy, like a fruit basket.

They'd all welcomed him with excitement and hugs, but for the rest of the evening, Janice had treated him like a guest—a guest in need of comfort. She'd even made what had been his favorite dinner when he was in middle school: cowboy meat loaf, mashed potatoes, corn, and rocky road ice cream for dessert. He had to admit, the meat loaf, with its tangy barbecue glaze, was probably still in his top ten favorites. But she had refused to allow him to help with the cooking or cleanup. How was he going to convince her he could take care of the kids, when she wouldn't allow him to lift a finger?

This morning, he dressed quickly and slipped into the still-dark kitchen before anyone else was up. Nala rose from her bed in the laundry room and stretched, her plumy tail wagging a greeting. Nick ruffled her ears and let her outside before washing his hands at the big farmhouse sink he'd helped Coop install. He checked the refrigerator and pantry for supplies. By the time he heard sounds coming from the rest of the house, he'd already made coffee, sliced oranges, set the table, and whipped up a bowl of blueberry-pancake batter. He glanced at the clock over the kitchen table, which featured a picture of a bicycle ridden by a cat printed on the clear acrylic case, with the clock gears visible behind the wheels of the bicycle so that it looked like they were slowly turning. Definitely Emily's choice. It was just on seven thirty.

A few minutes later, Janice appeared in her blue bathrobe, her usually tidy hair flat on one side of her head and her mouth open in a yawn. "Oh. Good morning. I was going to make coffee."

"Already made." Nick filled a mug printed with the slogan If Mom Says No, Ask Grandma and passed it to Janice.

"Thanks." She yawned as she took a jar of pumpkin-spice creamer from the refrigerator and added it to her coffee. "What's all this?"

"Breakfast. Do the kids usually take their lunches, or do they eat in the cafeteria?"

"Cafeteria, generally." She took a sip of coffee. "You shouldn't have gone to all this trouble."

"No trouble. After that wonderful dinner last night, you deserve a break. How much are school lunches now? Do I need to set out some money?"

"No." Nala scratched on the door, and Janice moved to let her in. "Things have changed since you and Coop were in school. It's all online now, and Emily set up autopay for school lunches. Lyla takes her lunch every other Wednesday, though, because she doesn't like chili dogs, and Max takes his on the opposite Thursday when they serve chicken nuggets. They'll make their own lunches if I remind them the evening before."

"I thought Max loved chicken nuggets." Nick opened a drawer, looking for a pen to take notes on the kids' lunch preferences.

"Only with sweet-and-sour sauce. He won't eat them with just ketchup."

"Oh. How do you keep track of all these details?" Nick asked in admiration.

"It's all on Emily's calendar." She nodded toward the bulletin board over the desk in the corner.

Nick went to look. The school menu for the month had been printed out, with chicken-nugget and chili-dog days highlighted in yellow. Below were grid calendars of November and December, printed on legal paper. Blue bars across the top highlighted which days Emily was at Prudhoe Bay. Lyla's after-school craft class was in pink on Tuesdays and Thursdays, and Max's indoor soccer on Mondays and Thursdays were in green, with Saturday games in darker green. Today had a red note, "whole school field trip," and also a handwritten comment, "10:30 shopping with PN."

"What's PN?" Nick asked.

"Peggy Newell," Janice told him. "A friend of mine. She's been the cook at Swan Lodge forever. She and I are running into Anchorage today for a little early Christmas shopping. We'll be back in plenty of time to pick up the kids after school, though."

"I could do that," Nick pointed out. "Per Emily's instructions, I'm already fingerprinted and cleared to volunteer at the school, and I'm on the approved pickup list."

"It's nice of you to offer, but I'll be back in time." She set her mug on the table. "I'd better go check on the kids and make sure neither of them crawled back into bed." She patted Nick's shoulder as she passed by. "I'm glad you're here with us and not in some stuffy hotel."

Nick suppressed a sigh. She was glad he was here, but she didn't seem to trust him to take care of Max and Lyla. Maybe she still saw him as the kid who used to come home with Coop after practice and hang out in the kitchen, ostensibly to help, but in actuality to bask in the attention of an adult who was genuinely interested in his life. He turned on a burner and set the griddle on to preheat.

He'd just flipped the first batch of pancakes when Max barreled into the kitchen, making a beeline for the pantry, where he pulled out a package of whole-wheat bagels and a jar of peanut butter. Lyla followed, skipping over to the refrigerator.

"Wait," Nick told them. "I'll have blueberry pancakes in two minutes."

"Oh, no thanks," Max replied as he expertly split the bagel and popped it into the toaster. "I need protein for concentration."

"Okay." Nick moved the first four pancakes to a plate. "How about you, Lyla? Pancakes?"

"I usually have yogurt for breakfast before school," she said, waving a container of strawberry-banana. She must have sensed his disappointment because she added cheerily, "But I guess I can have a pancake today."

"Only if you want to," Nick replied. Lyla was a sweetheart, but he was supposed to be taking care of her. "Yogurt is probably more nutritious." Nick poured out another four pancakes. No use wasting the batter.

Lyla smiled. "Okay." She grabbed a spoon and pulled off the lid.

At least both children ate the orange slices along with their preferred breakfasts, Nick noted as he added another four pancakes to the plate and poured the last of the batter onto the griddle. Janice returned, now dressed in jeans and a dark green sweatshirt with a picture of pumpkins on the front. "Save me one and I'll eat it after I drop off the kids."

"Sure." Nick flipped the pancakes.

"Let's go, kids. Lyla, don't forget your hat." Janice glanced at the calendar. "Do you both have your permission slips for the field trip?"

"I do," Lyla sang out.

"Oh, I left mine upstairs." Max galloped out of the kitchen and up to his room, returning a moment later waving a slip of paper which he crammed into his backpack. After a flurry of coat zipping and backpack gathering, the three of them piled into the minivan, leaving the house feeling unnaturally quiet.

Nick finished cooking the last few pancakes, washed the dishes, and cleaned the kitchen, and then poured himself another mug of coffee and sat down at the table, staring at the untouched pile of blueberry pancakes in front of him. Nala came to stand next to the table, sniffing the air and wagging her tail hopefully.

"Nice try," Nick told the dog. "That many pancakes would make you sick." But at least someone wanted his cooking.

A small rumble signaled that the garage door was opening. A minute later, Janice came in, pulling off her coat. "Those smell good." She slid the top pancake onto a plate and put it into the microwave. "If you put wax paper between them and wrap them in foil, we can have the leftovers tomorrow for Saturday brunch. Max likes to carbo-load before a soccer game."

"Okay." Feeling better, Nick helped himself to a pancake and waited his turn for the microwave. "When are you leaving for Anchorage?"

"Peggy should be by in about fifteen minutes."

It was more like ten, and Nick was about to heat up a second pancake when he heard a car pull up outside. Janice stuffed her plate into the dishwasher and grabbed her coat. "See you this evening. Have a good day."

Through the kitchen window, Nick watched her slide into the passenger seat of an ancient Subaru.

He turned to Nala. "I guess it's just you and me, kid."

The old retriever wagged her tail politely before returning to her bed in the laundry room. A second later, she was snoring.

"Just me then," Nick muttered to himself as he sat down to finish his breakfast. Why should eating alone bother him? He'd lived alone since he moved back to Alaska after college, and he'd never had a problem filling his days. But that was when he was working. Although his job for the last five years had been flying a Cessna 207, a reliable workhorse of a plane, either with tundra tires or floats, he made sure to fly enough hours to keep proficient in several other models. And when he wasn't flying, he was reading up on new technologies, or networking with other pilots. That's how he'd found out about the opening in Hawaii. Someone he'd gone to flight school with mentioned a friend who was leaving a job in Honolulu because she wanted her kids to live closer to their grandparents. Not something Nick had to consider.

He finished his breakfast, wrapped up the leftover pancakes as Janice had suggested, and was trying to decide how to fill the day when the phone on the desk rang. Nick had almost forgotten landlines existed. He looked at it for a second before answering. "Cooper residence."

"Hello. This is Ms. Englund, Lyla's teacher. Is Janice there?"

"No, sorry, she's gone to Anchorage for the day. Is Lyla okay?"

"Oh, Lyla's fine. Sorry, didn't mean to worry you. It's just that one of the parent chaperones for the field trip today had to drop out, and now we're short a driver. I know Emily's working, but I was hoping Janice could sub in." She paused momentarily. "Say, you're Coop and Emily's friend, the pilot, right?"

"That's right. Nick Bernardi."

"Ms. Susanna, our school secretary, mentioned you were cleared for volunteering. I don't suppose you'd be willing to fill in for the field trip?"

"Me?" Emily had mentioned he might volunteer by running copies or sorting papers for teachers, not chaperoning.

"If you're available. I assume you drive and have liability insurance."

"I do," he replied, warming up to the idea. Maybe if Lyla's teacher trusted him, that would encourage Janice to follow suit. "When do you need me there?"

"You'll do it?" Ms. Englund sounded thrilled. "Terrific. The sooner the better. The plan is to head out in thirty minutes, and you'll need to do some paperwork in the office first."

"On my way." Nick hung up the phone and went to collect his jacket. Today was shaping up, after all.

CHAPTER FOUR

"LYLA, PAISLEY, ELI, you're with Mr. Bernardi." Ms. Englund continued to assign the rest of the class to drivers while Lyla and the two other kids went to stand next to Nick. "We'll all meet up next to the main deck at Swan's Marsh. Remember to stay with your adult. No taking off alone." She glanced toward Eli as she said it. "Okay. Let's head out."

After waiting for the kids to put on their jackets and hats, Nick shepherded them to the parking lot, glad he'd thought to drive Emily's minivan rather than his own pickup. He got them buckled up without incident. The two girls chatted happily during the drive, but Eli stared straight ahead with his arms crossed.

Ten minutes later, they'd parked at Swan's Marsh. Nick had been here many times with Coop, Emily, and the kids. He'd always liked the marsh, a private bird sanctuary run by the people at Swan Lodge. The biggest draw was a pair of trumpeter swans that nested there each year. Nick waited while the kids climbed out of the car. The first snow of the season was yet to fall, and they'd lucked into an unseasonably warm November day, with the sunshine pushing temperatures into the midforties.

"Hey, Uncle Nick," Max called, walking by with a group of kids. "What are you doing here?"

"Lyla's class needed an extra driver," Nick explained.

"Cool." Max moved on without greeting his sister, but Lyla didn't let that fly.

"Hi, Max," she yelled out as she climbed out of the car.

Her brother looked back and acknowledged her with a little wave. Lyla and Paisley giggled. Eli finally climbed out of the minivan and Nick pressed the fob to close and lock the doors. "Okay, let's go find your teacher." The two girls immediately started toward the deck, but Eli dragged behind. "Lyla, wait," Nick called.

The two girls looked back. "Hurry up, Eli," Lyla called.

Muttering to himself, the boy caught up with them and the whole group joined the rest of the class.

Ms. Englund handed out bags holding folded sheets of paper, tiny golf pencils, granola bars, and water bottles to each adult. "This is a list of the most commonly found birds at Swan's Marsh this time of year. See if you and the children can identify at least one bird from each category." Nick opened the sheet to find the birds, each with a thumbnail photo, listed under headings of shorebirds, land birds, waterbirds, raptors, and waterfowl. He wasn't sure he understood the difference between a waterfowl and a waterbird, but whatever.

"You can stop and have a snack at some point during your walk. Marissa Allen, a wildlife biologist, will be here to talk with us at 11:30," Ms. Englund continued, "so we'll need to meet back in one hour. Any questions?"

One of the boys raised his hand. "Will whoever finds the most birds get a prize?"

"No, Aiden. It's not a competition. Just try to find as many as you can."

"I still bet we find the most," the boy said to the group around him.

"Nuh-uh," a girl in another group challenged. "We will."

Ignoring them, Ms. Englund said, "Let's go!"

Nick turned to find only the two girls standing there. Eli, meanwhile, had eased over to the group with Aiden and was following them down one of the boardwalks that zigzagged through the marsh. "Hey, Eli," Nick called. "Over here."

Eli ignored him, but Ms. Englund went to the boy and turned him around. "Stick with your group, Eli."

With a dramatic sigh, the boy returned to Lyla and Paisley. Nick chose a different boardwalk and took the group down it. "Keep looking for birds."

"There's one." Paisley pointed at a tiny bird that flitted by.

"Great. What was it?" Nick asked, holding the paper where they could see the pictures.

Paisley looked at the paper. "I think it was a chickadee."

"No, it had a red spot on its head," Lyla claimed. "It was a redpoll."

Nick tried to get Eli involved. "Eli, want to weigh in?"

The boy shrugged. "If you can't tell, it doesn't count."

Lyla put her hands on her hips. "You're just trying to help your friend Aiden win."

"Ms. Englund said it's not a competition," Nick pointed out.

All three kids gave him a pitying look. The bird, or one just like it, flew back into view. "It does have a red spot," Paisley acknowledged. "It's a redpoll."

Nick checked off the bird and they moved a few more steps down the boardwalk. "There's a duck."

"It's a mallard," Lyla said confidently.

Eli scoffed. "It's a merganser."

Nick checked his paper to see if he could tell the difference. Naturally, the only two ducks listed were the mallard and the common merganser, and they looked a lot alike in the photos.

"It has a red bill," Eli pointed out. "Mallards have yellow bills." Another duck swam into view, this one with a more blunt, yellow beak. "That one's a mallard," Eli said, crowing.

Nick marked them both. "Great. We've already got two categories covered. I wonder why swans aren't listed under the waterbirds."

"Because they've already migrated," Lyla told him. "They always leave in October."

"And they come back the third week in April," Paisley added.

"Always?" Nick asked.

Paisley nodded. "Every year but two. My great-great-aunt Eleanor kept track."

"We usually take this field trip in September before the swans and other summer birds fly away, but it got rained out and that's why we're doing it now," Lyla explained.

Meanwhile, Eli had wandered on ahead. "Hey, Eli, wait up." Nick hustled the other two up to him. "We need to stick together."

"There's an eagle," Eli said in a disinterested tone, looking at the bird soaring in front of the mountains in the distance.

"A bald eagle," Lyla clarified.

Two smaller black birds appeared and swooped close to the eagle, harassing it. "Those are ravens chasing the eagle," Lyla told him.

"Got them." Nick checked them off. They continued to make their way farther into the marsh, identifying birds as they went. By the time they reached the end of the boardwalk, they had nineteen birds and all five categories covered. Nick was feeling pretty good about his first time as a field-trip chaperon. Maybe this would buy him credit with Janice. "Good work, you guys. Are you ready for a snack?" Nick took the granola bars from his pocket.

"Yeah." Eli practically grabbed one from his hand, then sat cross-legged on the boardwalk, and tore open the package.

"Thank you," Paisley said, accepting the second one.

"Thanks, Uncle Nick." Lyla gave Eli a pointed look before unwrapping her bar and biting it.

Eli's eyes narrowed. He obviously wasn't going to let Lyla goad him into politeness.

"Is that another merganser?" Nick asked, to change the subject. "Never mind, it's gone." He gave the kids time to eat their bars and then looked at his watch. "We'd better be heading back. Ready?"

Both girls stepped forward, but Eli remained sitting on the boardwalk.

"Eli, it's time to go."

"I'm tired," the boy replied.

Nick didn't see how a quarter-mile stroll could have been so exhausting, but he nodded. "Okay. We'll give you another minute to rest but then we need to head back if we want to make it in time." The girls spotted two more types of birds while they waited. "All right, Eli. It's time to go."

The boy remained seated. "I don't want to."

"Well, we have to. Your teacher said we need to be back for the biologist."

Eli shrugged.

"Get up, Eli. We're going to miss the talk!" Lyla insisted, but the boy just smirked.

Now what? It was tempting just to throw the kid over his shoulder in a fireman's carry and haul him back, but the training video they'd had Nick watch in the office mentioned he shouldn't touch the kids. He couldn't leave Eli alone, and he couldn't send Lyla and Paisley for help, because they were all supposed to stay together. Unfortunately, none of the other groups had chosen to follow this boardwalk, so he couldn't send Lyla and Paisley back with another group. He gave it another ten minutes and then declared, "Last chance, Eli. Let's go."

The boy shook his head.

Nick took out his phone, found the number for the school, and explained his predicament to the office secretary who had helped him with the forms.

"I understand," she told him in a calm voice. "Stand by."

Shortly after, his phone rang. "Hello, it's Ms. Englund. Could you please give Eli the phone?"

Nick turned to him and held out the phone. "Eli, your teacher wants to talk to you."

Eli scrambled to his feet. "I'll come."

"First, talk to Ms. Englund."

Reluctantly, he took the phone. After listening

for a few seconds, he replied, "I was tired." After another pause, he seemed resigned. "Yeah. Okay. I'm coming."

He dragged his feet the entire way, but several minutes later, the entire school watched as Nick and his group returned to the main deck. Nick caught a few sympathetic looks from other parent volunteers. They joined Ms. Englund and the rest of the class. "Take a seat, please, everyone," the principal announced, and all the students sat down on the deck while most of the parents took advantage of the benches around the perimeter of the space.

Nick found a spot beside one of the dads, who whispered, "What happened?"

Fortunately, the biologist began speaking and Nick didn't have to answer because he was embarrassed to admit that a stubborn ten-year-old had held him hostage. Maybe Nick was just bad with kids, and Emily shouldn't trust him to care for Max and Lyla. Should he confess and bow out? But that would mean Janice couldn't go on her trip, and nobody wanted that.

It wasn't long before the biologist had finished her surprisingly interesting presentation, which included a couple of rescue birds, and most of the parents seemed to have forgotten all about Nick and Eli, for which Nick was grateful. Maybe none of this would get back to Janice, or to Emily.

Nick could only hope.

Once he'd delivered the kids back to school, Nick returned home and collapsed onto the couch. It was only mid-afternoon. How could he feel so exhausted? Nala padded over and lay her head next to his, breathing hot doggy breath in his face. He reached over to pet the dog. "Hi. How's your day going?" She sniffed around the hem of his jeans, wagging her tail. "Yeah, took the kids to Swan's Marsh. Sorry we couldn't take you, but you know, no dogs allowed on the boardwalk."

Nala's sudden snort could have been coincidence, but it made Nick laugh. He sat up and ruffled the dog's ears. "Maybe I'll take you and the kids on a hike this weekend." He went to look at the calendar. "Max has a soccer game tomorrow, but we could go Sunday afternoon if the weather holds." Yeah, that could work.

A glance at the school-lunch menu had him thinking about dinner. His breakfast plan had failed, but he could try again with the famous five-alarm Crock-Pot chili recipe he always made for poker nights with the guys. Modified, anyway—he'd leave out the beer and cut the number of jalapeños way down. But he'd better check with Janice first, to make sure he wasn't stepping on her toes.

He texted: Okay if I make chili for tonight?

After a moment, the row of dots came up indicating she was typing a reply, but then he got a phone call from her instead. He picked up. "Hi, Janice."

"Hi. Don't feel like you have to cook. I was just going to bake one of the casseroles Emily left in the freezer."

"I want to," he told her. "I have plenty of time."

"All right, then, if that's what you want. I heard you got roped into driving for the school field trip this morning."

"How did you know about that?"

"Lyla's teacher had left a message on my phone asking if I could drive. When I called back to tell her I was in Anchorage, she said you'd volunteered to take my place. So how did it go?"

How much should he say? Less was probably more. "All three kids they assigned me survived the trip alive and well."

"Mission accomplished, then. It's a shame they had to cancel the September field trip when they could have seen the young swans learning to fly. Did you find lots of birds?"

"We did, and the biologist who talked to the kids had pictures of the swans and their story. I didn't realize they weren't the same two swans as the ones that were here when Coop and Emily bought this house."

"Sadly, we lost Victoria a few years ago. We were afraid we wouldn't see any more cygnets, but then Albert brought home a new bride, and they've settled right in. Let me think—what is her name?"

"Alison," Nick supplied.

"Right. Oh, got to go. Peggy's ready to move on.

Thanks, Nick. Chili sounds great. I'll make cornbread after I get home. 'Bye." She hung up before he could offer to make the cornbread himself.

But at least she'd allowed him to make the chili. Hopefully, that would be a point in his favor when she was deciding whether he was capable of watching the kids while she traveled. Suddenly energized, he grabbed his keys and headed over to the mercantile to pick up what he needed.

Janice arrived back home before the end of the school day, as promised. By that time, the aroma of chili, cumin, and peppers filled the house. "Smells good," she told Nick. "We usually eat at six unless we have a conflict. Will it be ready by then?"

"Yes, ma'am." Nick folded the last of the towels he'd washed earlier and set it in the basket to take upstairs. "How was your shopping?"

"We got a lot crossed off our lists. I left a bunch of bags on the porch. I could use a hand getting them in and put away before I pick up the kids."

"No problem." Nick chose the three heaviest-looking bags, leaving the fourth for Janice, and followed her to her room, where she instructed him to put everything on the highest shelf in her closet and drape a blanket over it.

"Max pays no attention, but Lyla notices things, and she's been wanting this particular brand of boots for a long time. If she sees the label, it would kill her not to open them before Christmas."

"Christmas isn't for more than a month."

"That's why we need to hide it." Janice checked the time. "I'd better get to the school. The rest of this stuff is wrapping paper and decorations. Could you put it in the storage area behind Emily's closet for me, please?"

"Sure." After she left, Nick carried the bag upstairs to the master bedroom. This house had started out as a small bungalow, but several additions and remodelings over the years had made it a sprawling home with quite a few quirky components, one of which was the door at the back of the master-bedroom closet that led through a short hallway to another storage area tucked behind the sloping roof.

Coop had been gleeful when he'd discovered the hidden attic area while converting a bedroom adjacent to the master bedroom into a bathroom and his-and-her closet space. Nick had helped him and Emily wire the space and install flooring, insulation, and drywall. They also lined the back of Emily's new closet with cedar, allowing the door to disappear into the wood. Only the doorknob gave away the door's location, and just for kicks, Emily had mounted several matching doorknobs on the wall around it to hang handbags and scarves, making it even more invisible.

They'd had lots of fun coming up with crazy ideas for the hidden room. Emily had suggested a laboratory for Coop, where he could work up secret spice formulas. Coop said it could be a reading room, where Emily could disappear when she was on the final chapter of a book so that no one would disturb her until she'd reached the end. Nick floated the idea of soundproofing the walls and one or the other of them taking up the bagpipes. But since the space had no windows and connecting it to the ventilation system would have been prohibitively expensive, the space had ended up as extra storage.

Nick walked through the master bedroom, filled with colorful quilts and family photos, and approached the two closet doors. He avoided looking at the left one, the one that had been Coop's, and opened Emily's. Inside, the cedar still gave out a woodsy scent. Emily's clothes were neatly hung and arranged by color, except for her slope clothes, which had their own section. At the back of the closet, he located the hidden door. He crouched down to get through the low ceiling of the connecting hallway, and entered the storeroom, flicking on the light as he went. It had been years since Nick had been inside, so he wasn't entirely prepared for what greeted him. Shelves about two feet wide lined the taller wall, each shelf stacked with red and green boxes with labels like Rustic, Traditional, Red, Gold, and Avian. More bins and baskets with labels like Autumn, Easter, and Halloween filled the space under the sloping ceiling on the other side. It looked like the entire room had been dedicated to the holidays, especially Christmas.

A simple wooden table on casters stood in the center of the room. A rack mounted on the far wall held rolls of wrapping paper and spools of ribbon on dowels. More rolls, still encased in plastic, stood in a hamper nearby. Gift bags and several pairs of scissors hung from pegs, and a shelf held a basket labeled Tape and Gift Tags. Wow, he knew Emily loved Christmas, but he doubted even Santa's workshop held a candle to this.

He unpacked Janice's shopping bag, wondering what she could possibly have found that wasn't already there. The roll of wrapping paper had pictures of a golden retriever that looked an awful lot like Nala wearing a Santa hat and frolicking in the snow. Okay, that was pretty cool. And the five ornaments had the year stamped on the boxes, so maybe Janice collected new ones each year. Nick put the wrapping paper in the hamper and left the ornaments on the table, since he didn't want to disturb Emily's system, and returned downstairs to set the table.

The kids loved Nick's chili, and he had to admit, Janice's cornbread was better than his. Over dinner, the kids told Janice all about the field trip, with no mention of Nick's difficulties. Nick was beginning to believe he was home free. That is, until that evening.

The kids were at the kitchen table, on their nightly video call with their mom, while Nick loaded the dishwasher behind them. Peggy was in the living room. Emily entertained Max and Lyla with a story about a young grizzly bear that someone had videoed climbing a ladder to the top of one of the tanks that held crude oil before it went to the processing facility and down the Alaska pipeline. "And once he got to the top, he couldn't figure out how to get down. He sat up there and bawled until his mother went up after him. The guy said he's going to post it online. I'll send you a link once I get it. So how was today's field trip?"

Max shrugged. "Fine. Better than math."

"It was fun!" Lyla declared. "We had this really cool lady who told us all about the birds and we met a hawk and a raven. A rescue place saved them after they got hurt, but they still can't fly, so they live there when they're not visiting schools and stuff. Somebody's mom was sick, so Uncle Nick drove."

"Did he?"

"Yeah, but Ms. Englund put Eli in the group with Paisley and me, and he was a pain. Right, Nick?"

Nick put in the last spoon and shut the door. "Um, he wasn't the most cooperative."

Lyla continued, "Eli was mad because he wanted to be in Aiden's group, but he had to be with us. We found lots of birds, but when we got to the end of the boardwalk and it was time to go back, Eli wouldn't go. Nick kept saying we had to go now, but Eli just sat there. Nick had to call Ms. Englund and let her talk to Eli before he would move. And when we got back, everybody in the whole school was waiting on us!" Rather than embarrassed, Lyla seemed delighted by this.

"The whole school?" Emily said doubtfully, but Max confirmed the story.

"We'd all been waiting for, like, twenty minutes so the biologist could start her talk, but they said the last group hadn't checked in. People were saying they must have been eaten by a yeti or something."

Lyla jerked her head back and stared at her brother. "There's no such thing as a yeti, at least not at Swan's Marsh. Mrs. Swan has been keeping records of every kind of bird there for, like, forever, and she never saw a yeti."

Max rolled his eyes. "They were joking."

Peggy came into the kitchen. "Joking about what?"

"Max says people thought we got ate by a yeti when me and Paisley and Eli and Nick were late getting back from our bird walk because Eli sat down and wouldn't move."

Peggy gasped. "She gave you Eli? On your very first field trip?"

On screen, Emily was laughing. "Talk about throwing you into the deep end. Sounds like you handled it well, though."

"I guess." Nick shrugged. "Basically, I punted."

"Which was exactly the right move," Emily assured him.

"Nick made supper tonight, too," Lyla told her. "Chili."

"Ooh, Nick's famous five-alarm chili," Emily said in a teasing tone. "I'm jealous."

"Only about two-alarm tonight," Nick said. "And if you want, I'll freeze you some leftovers."

"I want." Emily smiled. "Thanks, Nick."

CHAPTER FIVE

EMILY MENTALLY REVIEWED her meal preparation schedule for Thanksgiving dinner tomorrow as her headlights picked out the familiar landmarks along the Glenn Highway. It was only four thirty in the afternoon, but the sun had already set without fanfare. Winter was late in coming this year, and with no snow on the ground, everything was darker than it should be. But none of that mattered because Emily was on her way home.

As usual, Janice was on top of things. When Emily called yesterday, Janice had assured her that all the necessary grocery items were ready for the big day tomorrow, including locally grown apples and fresh sage for the herb-and-apple stuffing Emily had decided on. Janice was playing it close to the vest, though, about whether she would go with Helen on the Christmas river cruise. While she'd admitted privately that Nick had been helpful, she still didn't seem ready to leave him in charge of the kids, and time was running out.

She'd also hinted about some surprise for Emily.

Maybe she was making Emily's favorite sourdough dinner rolls for the big meal. Last winter Peggy Newell, the cook from Swan Lodge, had given Janice some sourdough starter to experiment with, and Emily had loved the results. Unfortunately, around February, they got so busy that she and Janice both forgot to feed the starter, and that was the end of the experiment. But Janice had mentioned something recently about trying again.

Emily took the Swan Falls exit and a few minutes later, was pulling into the garage. The minivan was already there, and Nick's truck was in the driveway. She grabbed her bag from the back of the car and stepped inside, passing through the laundry room into the kitchen.

"Mommy!" A warm missile slammed into her and her daughter's arms wrapped around her waist.

"Lyla!" Emily squeezed Lyla close. Nala came to lean against Emily's leg.

Max hovered nearby, trying to pretend like he'd just happened to wander into the kitchen and wasn't waiting his turn. But when Emily greeted him and pulled him in for a hug, he hugged her back. Three pies were cooling on a wire rack near the stove and, yes, bread dough rose in a basket next to the oven. Emily ran a hand over Nala's soft head. "Where are Gramma and Nick?"

Max shrugged. "Upstairs somewhere."

"I helped with the pumpkin pie," Lyla told her.

"Gramma made the crust, and me and Nick made the filling."

Emily stopped to admire the pie. "It's beautiful. They all are."

Footsteps sounded on the stairs. While they waited, Emily said, "I've got a Thanksgiving joke. Want to hear it?"

Max shook his head, but he was smiling. Lyla grinned and said, "I do!"

"What do you call little turkeys made of glass?" She waited.

"I give up. What?" Lyla asked, as Janice arrived in the kitchen, with Nick behind her carrying the turkey platter and a large soup tureen.

"Wait," Janice said. "I have to hear the setup."

"What do you call little turkeys made of glass?" Lyla repeated, for Janice's benefit.

Janice shook her head. "I don't know."

Emily grinned. "Goblets."

Lyla laughed, Max booed, and Janice chuckled as she came in for her hug. "That's just terrible."

Behind Janice, Nick was trying not to laugh, but his lips were twitching.

Emily hugged Janice and released her. "Looks like you've been busy." She nodded toward the pies and dough.

"Just getting a head start on tomorrow's feast."

Nick set the platter on the island and looked at Emily, as though he wasn't sure how this greeting thing worked. A blue-and-tan paracord bracelet encircled his left wrist. She opened her arms. "Everybody gets a hug when I come home."

Nick grinned and strong arms enveloped her. "Welcome, home, Emily." Mmm, had he always smelled so good, like leather and spice?

"It's good to be home. Nice bracelet."

"It's great, isn't it?" He lifted his wrist to admire it. "It's a Lyla original."

Emily chuckled as Lyla wiggled with pleasure. "Lyla says she helped you and Janice with the pumpkin pie, too."

"She read the recipe and measured everything," Nick claimed. "I just worked the mixer. Max made the bread dough."

"Oh, yeah? Thanks, Max." Emily smiled at her son, who ducked his head, but not before she caught a little smile.

"Peggy gave me more sourdough starter and her no-fail recipe for rolls," Janice confirmed. "And Max said he'd heard kneading bread was good for muscle building. The dough can rise overnight in the refrigerator, and tomorrow we'll make it into rolls."

"You know how much I love sourdough. That's a wonderful surprise."

"Oh, that's not your surprise," Janice said, her eyes crinkled up in mischief.

"No?"

Janice reached for Emily's suitcase and handed it to Max. "Max, would you take this up to your mom's room, please?" Janice said. "And Lyla, why don't you hang up her coat?"

Emily shed her jacket and handed it to Lyla. As soon as the kids were out of the kitchen, Janice said, "Helen's nephew, Peter, is staying with her so that he can learn how to run the shop while she's gone, and he'd like to get to know some of the local people. So—"

"Please say you didn't set me up," Emily begged. "I told you I don't date."

"It's not a date, exactly. I just told him you would be home from the slope soon, and he mentioned that he plans to eat at the diner on Friday while Helen, Peggy, and I are at that cable knitting class we signed up for in Wasilla. So I said maybe you would meet him there about six."

"If you're going to be in Wasilla, I'll need to stay home with the kids," Emily said, surprised that Janice had left her such an easy out.

"Why? You've been telling me how responsible Nick is. He can stay with the kids," Janice countered. "Okay, Nick?"

"Um—" Nick scratched the back of his head. He obviously didn't want to take sides. Emily took pity on him.

"I'll tell you what. If Nick doesn't mind watching the kids on Friday, I'll go, but only if you agree to go with Helen on that trip to Europe."

"That's hardly—"

Emily held up a hand in a stop gesture. "Nick, do you mind watching the kids Friday evening?"

"No, of course not," he answered.

"Okay then. Janice, here's the deal—I have dinner with Helen's nephew, and you go with Helen on the river cruise. Take it or leave it."

"You drive a hard bargain." Janice twisted her mouth to one side, then finally said, "Okay, deal. But you have to promise to give Peter at least an hour. No making up an excuse and dashing home ten minutes after you arrive."

Janice knew her too well. She had been considering exactly that. "I promise," Emily agreed. She figured if she could survive being in a minivan with Lyla, Max, and four of his more obnoxious teammates on the five-hour drive to the tournament in Fairbanks every summer, she could survive an hour's conversation with anyone.

Janice grabbed a pen and paper from the door. "I'll make a note to set up my cell phone with international calling, in case Nick has any questions while I'm in Europe."

Nick opened his mouth, and Emily suspected he was about to point out that Janice would be ten time zones ahead of them, but Emily caught his eye and gave a little headshake. He winked so that only Emily could see. "Thanks, Janice. I appreciate that. Now, where did you say you kept the extra leaf for the dining room table?"

николаевич watched Emily remove a shaggy yellow mum from the bouquet he'd grabbed at the mercantile on impulse yesterday and replace it on the other side of the vase, next to a peachy orange rose that almost matched the color in her cheeks. Her glossy brown hair was pulled back from her face, part of it caught in a clip and the rest cascading past her shoulders. Helen's nephew was going to thank his lucky stars when she walked into the diner tomorrow. "Perfect." She smiled at him. "They're beautiful. Thanks, Nick."

"You're welcome." Nick wasn't sure how he felt about her dating. On one hand, Coop had been gone for two years. Coop had loved Emily with every fiber of his soul, and he would want her to be happy. But Emily deserved the best—not some random guy who happened to be related to Janice's friend. And what was the deal with Coop's mom setting her up, anyway? Wasn't that weird?

Emily set the vase on the china cabinet and grabbed the yellow tablecloth she'd left there. She gave it a shake and it snapped open. It floated for a moment before settling on the dining table. "How much overlap is at that end?" she asked.

Nick estimated. "About six inches."

"I've got at least fourteen at this end. Give it a tug." Together they got the tablecloth centered. Nick reached into the china cabinet for plates, but Emily shook her head. "Not those. The Thanksgiving plates are behind the lower left door."

"You have Thanksgiving plates?" Nick opened the door to find a stack of plates bordered with autumn leaves and berries.

"You've seen them—or maybe not. Coop got them for me four years ago. I don't think you've done a Thanksgiving with us since then."

Nick had gotten into the habit of volunteering to cover flights on holidays so that the other pilots could spend them with their families, which wasn't as altruistic as it sounded. The first couple of years after he'd returned to Alaska, he'd tried to placate his parents by eating two Thanksgiving meals, one with each of them, but that had turned out to be a disaster. His dad's new wife obviously resented Nick's presence, glaring at him if he so much as opened his mouth to comment on the weather. Then at his mother's house, the entire conversation would be her digging for dirt. "Did she make the turkey, or did she get one of those premade dinners?" or "he was late on child support every month while you were growing up, and now he's driving a Lincoln? What's up with that?" After that, Nick started spending holidays with Coop and his mom, and later Emily and the kids, but then his mom would protest that "you can't be bothered to celebrate Thanksgiving with your own mother, but you'll spend it with strangers?" As if Janice and Coop were strangers. His mom hadn't had a problem with him practically living at Coop's house when he was a kid, so why this sudden jealousy when he was grown? All the same, he'd found it was easiest just to say he was working. Nobody could argue with that.

He arranged the plates while Emily centered the flowers in the middle of the table and placed candles that matched the plates on either side of it. He'd never realized how much work went into a Thanksgiving meal. All five of them had been at it since early this morning, preparing the turkey, chopping apples and onions for the stuffing, making the rolls. But the funny thing was how much they all seemed to love it. Lyla voicing silly conversations between the turkey-shaped salt-and-pepper shakers while she filled them. Max looking up tips on the internet for cool ways to shape the sourdough rolls. Janice humming as she peeled sweet potatoes. And Emily, darting from place to place, assigning tasks, admiring the results, making jokes, touching shoulders. Just making sure everyone was part of the effort and that they all felt appreciated, including Nick. Was this how families were supposed to work? He'd seen the dynamic between Janice and Coop, but being a kid, he hadn't given a lot of thought to parenting and what went into raising good kids.

Not that Max and Lyla were perfect. After Max shaped his rolls and set them to rise, he'd walked out of the kitchen to turn on football, leaving a floury mess all over the kitchen counter, and grumbling when Emily made him clean it up. Lyla had decided the brown cloth napkins that matched the plates were too dull and proceeded to create napkin rings from neon-colored pipe cleaners and beads, completely ruining the elegant vibe of Emily's table setting. But none of it seemed to phase Emily. She teased Max out of his mood, approved Lyla's table contribution with only the smallest shudder, and taste-tested Janice's smoked salmon dip. "Nick, try some of this. It's amazing!"

"We went dip netting last summer, and I tried smoking some of the sockeye," Janice explained. "There's a bunch more in the freezer."

Nick spread some of the dip on a cracker and bit into it. Cream cheese flavored with smoky fish, tangy green onions, and savory flavors melted on his tongue. "Oh, wow, that is excellent," he told Janice. "Better than any restaurant in Anchorage."

Janice smiled and transferred the dip from the mixing bowl into a pottery dish that matched the tray where Lyla had arranged circles of crackers. "Just something to hold us over until the turkey is ready. We'll eat the main meal around four."

A little after noon, Emily came downstairs carrying one of the red-and-green bins he'd seen up in the secret closet. He went to intercept her at the bottom of the stairs. "Let me take that."

"It's not heavy," she said, "but if you want to grab the other one at the top of the stairs, I'd appreciate it."

"Sure." Nick brought down the second bin,

crossed the living room, where Lyla and Max were watching a halftime show, and deposited the bin next to the first one by the front door. In the kitchen, he found Emily basting the turkey once again.

Janice covered a casserole dish with foil and set it in the refrigerator. "The stuffing is ready to bake."

"Good." Emily shut the oven door and picked up a clipboard with a paper featuring a turkey design across the top of a printed checklist. If she was this organized at home, Nick could only imagine how she was at work. "Let's see, the table is set. Pies and cranberry sauce are done." She checked off appropriate boxes as she went. "Potatoes are mashed and in the slow cooker. Stuffing, green-bean casserole, and sweet potatoes are ready for the oven. Rolls are rising. The turkey is on schedule." She set down the clipboard. "We've got almost two hours until everything else needs to go into the oven." She untied the leaf-print apron she'd been wearing over her sweater, and called, "It's time, kids. Grab your coats."

"Yay," Lyla called, and even Max turned off the television without protest.

"Time for what?" Nick asked as Janice handed him his jacket from the coat closet.

"It's tree-light time," Lyla told him as she pulled on a hat with cat ears. "I want purple lights this year. What color are you doing, Max?"

Her brother gave a casual shrug. "Probably green."

Everyone spilled out the front door. Janice carried two long poles, each with a U-shaped hook screwed into the end, while Nick and Emily carted the bins to the three spruce trees in the front yard. Wait, weren't there only supposed to be two? Coop had planted the first tree the week Max was born. It was now close to twelve feet tall. Lyla was born in May, three years later. Her tree was only about two feet shorter than Max's. The third tree was shorter, only about five feet tall.

"That's Daddy's tree," Lyla said, confirming Nick's suspicions. "We put blue lights on his tree, because blue was his favorite color."

Nick wouldn't have been able to name Coop's favorite color, but it made sense. Blue was the color of the sky, of the ocean. The color of the rivers Coop had loved to kayak. But the river had stolen his life, and now, all that was left of Nick's best friend was this memorial tree. Man, he missed that guy.

The kids rummaged through the bins. Nick's Christmas lights, which he'd donated when cleaning out his apartment, had been wadded up and stuffed in a box. In contrast, these strings of lights had been neatly wound around individual spools. Each spool was labeled according to color and length in Emily's neat handwriting, along with a note stating the last date tested. "Uncle Nick, could you help me with my tree?" Lyla asked, as she unwound the purple lights.

"Sure." He walked around the tree, unspooling while he went, while Lyla tucked the lights in among the branches. As they got closer to the top of the tree, where Lyla couldn't reach, they switched jobs. They had to use the pole to place the last few feet of lights at the top of the tree.

Meanwhile, Emily and Janice were working with Max and his larger tree. "Hard to believe it's Thanksgiving and we still don't have snow," Emily said. "Usually we have at least a foot by now."

"I just hope we get some before the deep cold comes," Janice replied. "Without snow cover, the frost can get so deep into the ground that pipes start freezing."

Max tucked a loose strand of lights into the branches of his tree. "Last year we had a whole week of cross-country skiing at school before Thanksgiving."

Nick checked his phone. "There's a forty percent chance of snow on Saturday."

Emily held up both gloved hands with her fingers crossed. "I hope it does."

Once both of the kids' trees were done, they all converged on the smallest tree. Max got out the blue lights and handed them to Emily. The five of them formed a circle around the tree, unwrapping the lights and passing them to the next person as they wound them around and around.

"Remember when Daddy got that inflatable Christmas moose?" Lyla giggled. "And one night the wind blew it away and he couldn't find it anywhere?"

Max laughed, too. "And when we went to school, it was on the field, stuck against the goalpost."

"And Daddy said—" Lyla was laughing so hard she could barely get words out. "Daddy said the moose wanted to try out for the football team."

"As a kicker." Emily snorted.

By now, Nick and Janice were laughing, too. Nick had never heard that particular story, but it sounded exactly like something Coop would say. It felt good, laughing together and sharing memories. It still hurt that Coop was gone, but Nick had been wrong earlier—Coop had left behind so much more than a memorial tree. He'd left fond memories for the people who loved him, and most importantly, he'd left two amazing kids. The world would be a better place because those kids were in it. What finer legacy could a man hope for?

They finished wrapping the tree. "I'll get the extension cords." Max headed for the garage. Nick went with him to help, and together they laid the cords out along the edge of the driveway from the trees to the outlet on the side of the garage.

Emily held up a plastic box. "I've got something new. It's a smart plug. I can program the lights to come on at a preset time or turn them on and off with my phone." She plugged the box into the garage outlet.

"Cool." Max plugged the extension cords into the box.

"Yeah. Nick, remind me to give you the password later, so you can manage it through your phone, too. Okay, let's go inside. It's about time for the turkey to come out and the other stuff to go into the oven."

"Aren't we going to turn on the lights?" Nick asked.

Max looked at him like he'd said something shocking. "You can't turn on your Christmas lights until after Thanksgiving."

Lyla gave a vigorous nod. "It's a rule."

"I see." Nick exchanged looks with Emily.

Her eyes danced with mischief, but she nodded solemnly. "Tradition."

"Of course." Nick followed them back to the house, an unaccustomed feeling of warmth in his chest. There was a lot to be said for tradition.

CHAPTER SIX

THE NEXT DAY, Emily spread out the leftovers on the kitchen island, while Nick played a video game with Max and Lyla that seemed to involve a lot of hooting and giggling. "Nick, do you want cranberry sauce on your turkey sandwich?" she called.

"You bet," he called back.

"Ew." Max made a gagging sound. "Cranberry sauce on a sandwich?"

"Turkey and cranberry is a bestseller at the deli by the airport in Anchorage. You ought to try it," Nick answered. "Ooh, watch out for that booby trap."

"I see it," Max said. Moments later, Lyla cheered, and a fanfare announced that they had successfully completed a level.

"Don't start another level," Emily called. "Lunch will be ready by the time you've washed your hands." Janice had gone to Anchorage with Peggy and Helen for the day. Their plan was to hit the Black Friday sales until their energy ran out and then take in a movie before attending the craft class they'd signed up for in the evening.

Emily set a tray of veggies and ranch dressing in the center of the round kitchen table. Next, she arranged each plate with a sandwich and a few chips. Everyone got a pickle except for Lyla, who got apple slices instead. Nick and the kids trooped in after washing up, carried their plates to the table, and sat down. Nick took the chair nearest the window. Coop's chair.

Not that there was anything wrong with that. Max, Lyla, Janice, and Emily had already staked out four of the six chairs, and the last one was in an awkward corner that required squeezing past a ficus tree, so, of course, he would have chosen the chair he did when he moved in week before last. And it wasn't that she resented Nick being in Coop's chair. No, the disconcerting thing was that she kind of liked it. It felt right, Nick joshing with the kids about the video game, pretending to steal a potato chip from Lyla's plate, thanking Emily for the sandwich. Like he belonged.

"Great sandwich." Nick looked at Max. "Want to try a bite with cranberry?"

Max wrinkled up his nose. "I guess."

Nick broke off a corner of the sandwich and passed it to Max. Max studied it with suspicion before popping it into his mouth. As he chewed, his eyebrows rose. "Not bad."

"Told you." Nick grinned at Emily, and she felt a little flutter in her stomach.

Whoa, what was that about? Granted, Nick was good-looking—obviously, with those soulful dark eyes and easy smile. But in all the years she'd known him, she'd never felt any sort of physical attraction before. For several months now, Janice had been gently encouraging her to date, but Emily wasn't interested. She'd lost the man she loved, and it felt like that part of her, the romantic part, had gone dormant. So why now? Why Nick? Could she possibly have picked a more inappropriate man? Good grief, he was Coop's best friend. And he was a confirmed bachelor, a complete cynic when it came to marriage and family. Not to mention, he would be moving to Hawaii before the end of the year.

Nope, nope, nope. She'd better nip this in the bud. She'd told Janice she didn't have time for dating, and it was true. The kids came first, and since she was away half the time, she needed to devote herself completely to family when she was home. She would keep her bargain with Janice and go on this "nondate" tonight, but that was the end of it.

Nick finished his sandwich and checked something on his phone. "They've raised the chance of snow tomorrow afternoon to seventy percent, predicting six to eight inches. What would you say to one last hike before the snow flies?"

"To Swan Falls?" Lyla asked eagerly.

"Sure, why not?" He turned to Emily. "Unless you had other plans? Sorry, I should have asked first."

"No, a hike sounds nice. I have to get back early, though."

"Oh, right." Nick nodded. "For your date."

Lyla's eyes widened. "You're going on a date?"

"No, not a date," Emily assured her. "Gramma just asked me to have dinner with someone who's visiting Swan Falls and doesn't know anyone."

"Who? A man?" Lyla asked.

"Yes, Helen's nephew." What was his name again? She couldn't remember. "He'll be running Birdsong Books for Helen while she's traveling."

Max hadn't said anything, but his eyes had narrowed. Lyla tilted her head. "You're not going to marry him or anything, are you?"

Emily laughed. "Highly unlikely. Come on. Let's clean up this table and get ready for our hike. Nick's staying with you guys while I'm out this evening, so I'll get a casserole out of the freezer. What kind do you want, lasagna or chicken and rice?"

Max raised his head. "Can we go for pizza instead?"

"Pizza sounds good," Nick agreed.

"That's fine with me." The kids loved the pizza at Raven's Nest, so at least that would distract them. "But be sure to get a salad, too. And eat it."

"We will," Max and Lyla chimed.

"Okay, then. Go put on your thermals and wool socks. Let's get a move on."

Max dipped the last carrot in ranch and munched on it while he carried the tray to the island. "I'll get my backpack."

THE HIKE HAD gone well. Although Nick had hiked to the waterfalls many times before, he'd never done it in the winter, and even though the weather had been in the forties a week and a half ago, temperatures had fallen, and the freezing process had begun. At the edges of the falls, icicles dripped from the ledges, growing ever larger, while along the splash zone, ice crystals covered the stones and glittered in the pale winter sunlight. It was brisk, but layers of clothes and exercise kept them warm. Emily seemed to enjoy it as much as the kids, snapping photos and leading the kids in hiking songs in her clear, if off-key, voice.

It was four o'clock and the sun had just sunk behind the horizon when they returned to the trailhead. Already, snow clouds bunched together in the east, turning a soft pink in the twilight. A few autumn leaves still clung to the trees. Tomorrow, after a blanket of snow, everything would look completely different.

They all piled into the minivan and drove home. Max announced that he might die of starvation if he didn't get an immediate infusion of popcorn, so Nick put a bag in the microwave while Lyla and

Emily went upstairs. Something about a new bracelet design. During the two minutes it took for the popcorn to pop, Max ate peanuts, a banana, and a container of strawberry yogurt, some of which dribbled onto his sweatshirt. The kid was definitely going through a growth spurt.

"Don't forget, we're getting pizza later," Nick warned as he poured the popcorn into a bowl.

Max waved him off. "I'll be hungry."

He and Max took the bowl of popcorn into the living room and settled in for another round of video games. They'd been at it for about an hour when Emily came downstairs, dressed in a lacy sweater, slim corduroy pants, and leather ankle boots. She'd pulled the front of her hair back into a clip, and silver teardrops dangled from her ears. She always looked great, but in that outfit, she took his breath away. There was no way some random guy who had a month free to run his aunt's bookstore was good enough for her.

Nick struggled to keep his voice casual. "You look nice."

"Thanks." She laughed. "I figure Janice will hear all the gossip tomorrow, and I don't want her to weasel out of our deal by saying I didn't try."

Lyla came skipping down the stairs after her. "Are we lighting the trees now?"

"No," Emily told her. "We'll do it later tonight, after Gramma gets home."

Lyla studied her mother. "You look pretty."

"Thank you." She took her wallet from her purse, pulled out three twenties, and handed them to Nick. "For pizza."

Nick shook his head. "I've got this."

"No, they're my kids. And this one—" she ruffled Max's hair "—is a bottomless pit. Sometimes I think he must have a pet mastodon hidden in his closet that he's secretly feeding."

"M-o-om," Max protested, squirming away from her hand. He grinned at Nick. "I am starving, though. Can we go soon?"

"Sure. You might want to change your shirt first." The kids went upstairs, and Nick accepted Emily's money. "Thanks."

"No, thank you for watching them this evening." Emily took a wool coat from the closet, then took a deep breath and straightened her shoulders as though she was about to face Goliath. "Well, I'm off. See you in a bit."

Nick had a sudden urge to beg her to cancel this date and come with them, but instead he managed a smile. "Have fun."

Emily waved on her way out the door.

Fifteen minutes later, Nick parked the minivan in the lot behind Raven's Nest Pizza. They started for the restaurant, but Lyla stopped. "Wait. Can we go by the bookstore first?"

"I'm hungry," Max moaned. "We can go after."

"But the bookstore closes at six thirty," Lyla

said, "and the new *Adventure Kids* is supposed to be in this week."

Max perked up at the mention of the book. "Okay, but just that one book. No looking around." Both kids looked at Nick.

"Fine with me." They walked the half block to the bookstore.

Sleigh bells jingled when they opened the door, but the place appeared empty until a young woman with a blond ponytail popped up like a meerkat from behind a table in the middle of the store. She couldn't have been more than seventeen. "Welcome to Birdsong Books. Oh, hi, Lyla. Hi, Max."

Lyla skipped forward. "Hi, Jenna. Do you have the new *Adventure Kids* book yet?"

"We sure do. Let me show you." They scurried off toward a painted moose with a cutout hole for photo ops in the back corner.

Nick went to wait beside the table where Jenna had been working. Several stacks of books were arranged around a New sign, and a half-empty carton of books sat on the floor beside the table. Nick recognized one of Emily's favorite authors, who wrote mysteries set in Scotland. *Wonder if she's read it yet.*

Lyla came back, book in hand. "We got it!"

Nick picked up one of the Scottish books. "Are these just out?"

"Yes." Jenna straightened one of the books. "It

released Tuesday, but our shipment didn't arrive until today."

Nick took a chance that Emily wouldn't have this one yet. "I'll take it." Carrying their new purchases, they walked back to the diner. He held the door open, and the kids went straight for a booth next to the front window. Nick followed.

A stack of menus and some paper placemats with games and puzzles were wedged between a jar of ketchup and a napkin dispenser, next to a shaker of red-pepper flakes and a cup of crayons. A guy a few years younger than Nick brought water glasses. "Hi, Max, Lyla. Who's this?"

"This is Uncle Nick," Lyla told him.

"He's not really our uncle," Max explained. "Just my dad's friend."

Lyla pulled out a placemat and chose a crayon. "He's taking care of us while Mommy goes on her date."

Max shook his head. "She said it's not a date."

"Nick Bernardi." Nick offered his hand, forestalling any more discussion about Emily's personal life in front of the pizza guy. Not that the whole town wouldn't know by tomorrow.

"Mike Donovan. Nice to meet you." He shook hands with Nick. "So root beer for Max and lemonade for Lyla, right? Nick, what can I get you?"

"Root beer sounds good."

"Okay, I'll give you a chance to look at the menu and I'll be right back with those drinks."

Nick took a menu. "What's good here?"

"The Blizzard pizza," Max said immediately. "And the Santa Claus. Let's get two larges."

Nick looked up. "Really, two large pizzas for three people?"

"We can always take the leftovers home," Max pointed out.

"Touché." According to the menu, the Blizzard was a white pizza with garlic sauce, onions, mushrooms, olives, and three kinds of cheese. The Santa Claus had tomato sauce, green peppers, and reindeer sausage. "Sounds good."

"I don't like olives, though," Lyla said.

Mike returned with their drinks and turned to Nick. "Did you decide?"

"The Blizzard—"

Mike nodded. "Half without olives, right?"

"Right," Nick said.

"And a Santa Claus?" Mike asked, guessing. "Both large."

"Exactly. Oh, and—"

"Salads for everyone. Ranch dressing, okay?"

Nick gave him a thumbs-up and Mike disappeared into the kitchen. Nick raised his eyebrows at Max. "You must come here a lot."

Max shrugged. "There are only two places to eat in the whole town. And this is really good pizza."

"Look, it's Mommy!" Lyla pointed at the window.

Sure enough, there was Emily, at the table in

front of a window across the street. Nick hadn't thought about the diner being directly across from the pizza place. The bright lights inside the diner spotlighted her, catching the glossy sheen of her hair and highlighting the shape of her gorgeous face. Despite two kids and a career, she really didn't look much different than she had when Nick had first laid eyes on her—could it really be fifteen years ago?

He remembered it like it was yesterday. Coop had been working on a big project up at Prudhoe Bay that summer, so Nick hadn't heard much from him until one day when he'd called and asked, "Nick, do you believe in love at first sight?"

"Definitely not." Nick wasn't sure he believed in love at all. His parents certainly hadn't provided much of an example. They'd spent the first twelve years of his life making each other miserable, and the next eight years passing him back and forth like a hot potato neither of them really wanted. It had been a relief for everyone when he went away to flight school in Arizona, and after his return, he seldom saw them. The only reason he'd come back to Alaska at all was because of Coop. "You can't fall in love with an illusion," he'd advised his friend. "Whoever she is, I suspect with a little time, you'll discover that she's not nearly as perfect as you think."

"You haven't met her," Coop had insisted. "She's

one in a million. Smart, beautiful, and she has a great sense of humor."

"You mean she laughs at your terrible jokes?" Nick teased.

"Exactly, and I laugh at hers. She's in the middle of a shift up here at Prudhoe, but we're both off next week. I'm going to throw a barbecue in my backyard the Saturday after next, invite a few friends and neighbors, and her. Can you come?"

"Of course."

When Nick had pushed through the gate into the backyard of Coop's rental house, the party had been well underway. Conversation buzzed against the background of Jimmy Buffett. A dozen or so adults milled around, plus a few small children, a baby or two, and a couple of dogs. Nick recognized some of the people, but most were strangers. Over at the grill, Coop had been talking to a pretty blond woman—so his type. Nick navigated around the crowd to reach the back porch. He deposited the case of craft beer he'd brought into the cooler, and then turned to make his way down the steps to meet this woman Coop was so excited about.

But at the bottom of the steps, another woman with a curtain of dark hair had bent over to pet one of the dogs, blocking his path. He'd cleared his throat. "Excuse me."

"Oh." The woman straightened, and the most amazing pair of cobalt-blue eyes looked back at him. She pushed the glossy strands of hair behind her shoulder. "Sorry."

"It's okay. I'm Nick. An old friend of Coop's." He offered his hand, noticing there were no rings on her fingers. Could such a gorgeous woman really be unattached? Man, he hoped so.

"Emily." She'd smiled, and it was almost like she'd flipped on the high beams in those amazing eyes. She took his hand in a firm grasp and shook it. "I work with Coop on the North Slope."

"Oh." The sinking feeling in Nick's gut was confirmed when Coop appeared at her elbow.

"Nick, glad you could make it. I see you've met Emily…"

The blonde at the grill turned out to be a neighbor, mother of one of the toddlers playing in the flowerbed. Nick had met several people that day, but the only one who mattered was Emily, the woman who had captured his best friend's heart. It seemed that Coop was right—Emily was perfect. Not objectively, of course. She snorted when she laughed, which was often, because she really did have the same corny sense of humor as Coop. She preferred diet soda to craft beer and couldn't be persuaded to try one of Coop's famous jalapeño poppers. And, as she demonstrated when she led a chorus of "Happy Birthday" after one of the other guests admitted he'd turned thirty the day before, she was clearly not meant for a professional singing career. But she had been perfect for Coop.

And now, there she was, sitting across the table from some other man. He wasn't visible from this angle, but he must have been saying something funny, because Emily was laughing. It looked like more of a polite laugh, though, not the sudden snort that meant something had tickled her funny bone. That alone told Nick he didn't have to worry about her falling for that guy, whoever he was. Not that it was any of his business whom Emily spent her time with. He just wanted the best for her. Because she deserved it.

Deliberately, he turned away from the window and picked up Lyla's book. "*Adventure Kids*, huh? What's it about?"

Lyla pointed at the picture on the cover. "These three kids live in Alaska, and they go to different places—"

"Their parents are adventure guides," Max interrupted. "And they take families out on adventures, but something always goes wrong—"

"And the kids save everybody," Lyla said, shooting Max an annoyed look. "This one is at Independence Mine at Hatcher's Pass."

Mike arrived with their food. Nick moved glasses, crayons, and books out of the way so he could put the pizzas on the table. "Anything else I can get you?" Mike asked.

"I think we're good, thanks." Nick distributed slices of pizza to the kids' plates and his own. He took the first bite. "Hey, this is really good pizza."

Max smirked. "Told you."

Nick took a second bite and looked out the window again, watching Emily flash another smile. Suddenly, she turned her head toward the glass and Nick quickly looked down at his pizza. Could she see them as clearly as they could see her? Would she think he was deliberately spying on her? He resisted the temptation to look again until the end of the meal, but when he'd paid the check and was standing up, helping the kids get their jackets on, he chanced one last glance. Emily was still there, talking to the server, who was writing something down. Dessert? Maybe the date really was going well. After all, she had three types of pie left over from Thanksgiving in her own kitchen.

Nick shrugged on his coat. "Okay, guys. Let's go home."

CHAPTER SEVEN

EMILY YAWNED AS she pulled into her driveway and hit the button to open the garage door. How could spending an hour with someone feel so exhausting? It wasn't as though Peter wasn't a perfectly nice person. He owned a computer-repair and tech services shop in Eagle River, but business was slow this time of year, so he'd agreed to leave one of his employees in charge and manage Helen's store while she was in Europe. Which was nice of him. And Janice was right—he was good-looking, tall, with dark hair and an attractive clef in his chin.

But they couldn't seem to move the conversation past small talk. Weather, work, family. He'd mentioned a recent and stressful divorce, but to Emily's relief, hadn't gone into the details. When she'd said she had two kids, he said he liked kids, but didn't show any interest in knowing more about them. She'd kept her promise to Janice, staying for over an hour, even ordering a dessert that she didn't really want because he said he was trying the cheesecake. But when it came down to it, there wasn't a single spark between them.

She parked, closed the garage door, and went inside through the laundry room, feeling herself relax as she reached the kitchen, lit by the automatic outside light shining through the bay window. Through the archway into the living room, flames crackled in the fireplace and Nick was talking. She tiptoed into the room. There was her family gathered around the fireplace. Janice sat in a swivel chair on one side, her hands busy working knitting needles. Max was on the floor, leaning against the couch and staring into the flames. Nick had settled into the corner of the couch and was reading aloud, with Lyla leaning against his shoulder, completely caught up in the story.

"Raven cried, 'Where could they be?'" Nick said in a falsetto voice and then switched to a low menacing growl. "'I don't know,' Mr. Whither replied, 'but they'd better not have gone into that mine alone.'" Nick was really getting into it.

For the second time that day, Emily's stomach gave a little flutter. There was just something so appealing about Nick reading to the kids from their favorite series, doing the different voices to make it more entertaining for them. He loved those kids.

Janice looked up and spotted her. "Oh, Emily, you're home. We didn't hear the garage."

"I guess you were too invested in the story."

Emily shed her coat and crossed to the closet to hang it up. "How was the class?"

"Good. I think I've got the basics down." Janice lifted the knitted teal square she'd been working on. "Although I'm afraid I might have dropped a stitch. I'll look for it later." She set the knitting down on the table.

Lyla twisted around to face Emily. "We went by Birdsong Books and got the newest *Adventure Kids* book before we went for pizza. Nick got one for you, too."

"A pizza?" Emily asked.

Nick laughed. "No, a book." He picked one up from the coffee table. "It's the newest Elsbeth Carberry mystery."

"Oh, wow." Nick remembered her favorite author? Gosh, she hardly remembered anymore. "I haven't read a mystery in forever."

"Really?" Nick handed her the book. "You used to read all the time. You even had a book with you at the cookout at Coop's place the day I met you."

It's true, she had. Back then, she'd gotten into the habit of carrying around her current book to read whenever she had a minute to kill, like when she was waiting in lines. Coop used to tease her about it. "Yeah, well, life got busy. I mostly read technical journals these days. But thank you. This will be a treat."

"So," Janice said, breaking in to the conversation. "How was your dinner?"

"Good," Emily replied. "Not as yummy as that Thanksgiving feast yesterday, but Roger's chicken potpie is always delicious. And I had a fudge brownie for dessert."

"And the company?" Janice persisted.

"Fine." Emily shrugged. "I think Birdsong Books will be in good hands while you and Helen are traveling."

Janice looked disappointed, but what could Emily say? Peter just didn't do it for her. No flutter in the tummy. Not like...okay, she wasn't going there. Instead, Emily clapped her hands together. "I almost forgot. We need to do the tree lighting."

"Yay!" Lyla jumped up and ran for the coat closet. The others followed. Once they had on coats and shoes, they all trooped outside onto the porch.

Emily pulled up the smart plug app on her phone. "Here, Lyla. You can do the honors. Tap that button right there."

"Aren't we going to do the countdown?" Lyla asked.

"Of course. Ten. Nine..." The rest of the crew joined in and counted down, until they said in unison, "One. Lights!"

Lyla hit the button and the lights on the dark spruce trees out front twinkled to life. Max's tree, the tallest one, on the left in green. Lyla's tree covered in purple. And the smallest tree, the one they'd planted two years ago in Coop's memory, adorned in blue. Could Coop see his kids growing up? Did he know they all still thought of him, that they still loved him? What would Coop say if he knew about that flutter Emily had been feeling in Nick's presence?

She stole a glance toward Nick. Lyla was talking, and he'd bent next to her, listening intently and nodding his head. Once again, Emily's heart swelled. "Stop it," she whispered to herself. She'd been honest with Janice when she said she didn't have time for romance, especially with someone who would be leaving soon. Her family came first. First, last, and always.

THE NEXT DAY just after lunch, Nick carried Janice's luggage to the minivan. "Got your passport?"

"Right here." Janice patted her carry-on bag.

"Travel documents?"

"Check."

"Euros, cell phone, chargers, and adapters?"

"Check, check, and check." She glanced toward the door she'd just come out of. "Maybe I shouldn't go. What if something happens?"

He grinned. "Are you wearing clean underwear?"

Janice burst out laughing. "I meant to the kids. I'll be fine."

"I know you will, and you're going to have a great time. Max and Lyla will be fine, too. I'm not entirely useless, you know."

Janice patted his arm. "I never thought you were.

I just didn't think you were up to taking care of the kids for two weeks, but you've changed my mind. You're good with them."

"I appreciate that."

The door opened, and Max and Lyla spilled out. Max wore his jacket unzipped over his blue soccer jersey, shorts, and knee-high socks. His feet were thrust into untied sneakers. Max threw his soccer bag into the back of the car and climbed in through the sliding door. "Take the back seat," Janice told him. "We're picking up Helen."

"Why?" Max asked as he and Lyla climbed into the back seats.

"Because your mom is dropping Helen and me at the airport before your soccer game in Anchorage." Janice took the passenger seat. "Where is she, by the way?"

Max shrugged. "I don't know. She was right behind us."

Nick closed the tailgate and took a seat in the second row. A moment later, Emily came into the garage, her phone against her ear as she got into the driver's seat. "Which school is that? Oh, the one off Rabbit Creek Road? Got it. Thanks. We'll see you there." She hung up. "That was your coach. Apparently, there's a roof leak at the gym where your game was scheduled, so they've moved the game to Goldenview."

"Is Goldenview the gym with the climbing wall?" Lyla asked.

"Yes, but you're not allowed to climb on it," Emily warned. "We're just there to watch Max's game."

Lyla sighed. Emily opened the garage door and started to back out. "Got your passport?" she asked Janice.

Janice and Nick laughed. "I have all the essentials," Janice assured her. "Nick already checked."

Five minutes later, they pulled up in front of a blue cottage directly behind Birdsong Books. A man opened the front door and carried out two suitcases. This must be Helen's nephew, whom Nick hadn't been able to spot through the window last night. He waved, and Emily rolled down her window. "Hi, Emily," the man called.

"Hi, Peter." She pressed the button to open the tailgate.

Nick got out of the minivan and went around. "Here, let me help you with one of those."

"I've got them," Peter replied, making a show of carrying both suitcases down the steps and across the yard, which was completely unnecessary, since they both had wheels, and he could easily have rolled them on the sidewalk. Nick stifled a laugh. Did Peter really think Emily would be impressed? She was an engineer. Applying mechanical advantage to make tasks easier was one of her favorite topics.

Nick reshuffled Janice's suitcase and Max's duffel so that Peter could lift Helen's luggage into the car. A minute later, Helen came through the door, carrying a tote bag with a U-shaped pillow, a pair of headphones, and a pink sleep mask attached to the strap with purple carabiner clips. Nick returned to his seat, leaving the one nearest the door open for Helen. She climbed in, and Pete came to stick his head inside the car. "Got everything? Your passport?"

Helen huffed. "Of course. It's right…" She unzipped the outer pocket of her bag, frowned, patted the pocket of her jacket, then rummaged through the inside of the tote. Then, she muttered, "Travel documents, wallet, phone, book." She sat up and gasped, "Oh, my goodness. It's in that travel belt with the secret compartment I didn't wear because it's too wide to fit through my belt loops."

"I'll get it," Peter offered and trotted off into the house.

Helen shook her head. "This is so embarrassing."

"Not as embarrassing as driving all the way to the airport before you figured it out," Janice pointed out.

Soon, Peter was back. "Here you go, Aunt Helen. Enjoy your trip."

"Thank you." Helen carefully zipped the passport into the pocket and accepted a kiss on the cheek. Peter stepped away so Emily could shut the door.

"Thanks, Peter. 'Bye." Emily rolled up her window. "And we're off."

Helen was shaking her head. "I can't believe I almost forgot my passport."

"No harm done." Janice said. "Every trip has something that goes wrong. You've just gotten it out of the way early, so it's not hanging over our heads anymore."

Helen chuckled. "And that's why I wanted you along on this trip. Always positive."

At the airport, Emily pulled up to the curb. "Nick, if you'll help them with their luggage, I'll wait in the cell-phone lot."

"You don't need to do that," Janice said as she reached over to give Emily a quick hug. "We can manage. 'Bye, kids. Be good for Nick. Good luck on your soccer game, Max."

"'Bye, Gramma. Have fun," Max and Lyla chimed.

Helen laughed as she got out of the car. "We can manage, but why should we when we have a strong man available to lend us a hand?"

"It would be my pleasure." Nick lifted all three bags out of the back of the minivan and onto the curb. "Hey, what's in this one, feathers?" he asked Helen.

"Just a sweater and an extra pair of shoes." Helen extended the handle. "I mostly brought it so we'll have a way to get our shopping home."

"Good thinking," Janice said, extending the handle on her own bag.

Nick took the third bag and followed the women into the airport to help them with the process, but it was clear they knew exactly where to go and what to do. Once they had their luggage checked and boarding passes in hand, Janice gave Nick a hug. "Thanks for the help. We can get through the security line on our own. If you need me for anything, just call. Or text. I'll be sure to keep my phone charged."

"I will," Nick told her, although he had no intention of disrupting her trip. Helen stepped up, so he hugged her, too. "Have a wonderful time."

"We intend to," Helen promised, and the two ladies gripped their carry-on bags and headed toward the security line.

Nick texted Emily, and by the time he'd made it back outside, she was pulling up to the curb. He climbed into the front seat that Janice had recently vacated. "They're all checked in. Hope they have a great trip."

Emily pulled forward. "They'd better." Her voice was low enough that only Nick could hear. "I don't want that date I suffered through at the diner to be in vain."

Nick laughed. "Was Peter that bad?" Why did the thought of Peter striking out with Emily make Nick so happy?

She made a face. "He was fine. It just felt weird.

Maybe I've forgotten how to have a normal conversation."

"Your conversation skills seem fine to me," Nick assured her. If Peter couldn't hold her interest, Nick figured that was on him.

Not long after, they pulled up to Goldenview Middle School. While Max grabbed his soccer bag from the car, Nick stopped for a moment to take in the scenery. It was obvious how the school had gotten its name. Autumn-colored hills rose up to the east, with the spectacular backdrop of the snow-covered Chugach Mountains behind. To the west, the land fell away toward the ocean. Lyla grabbed his hand. "Come on, Nick. This way."

He and Lyla followed Emily and Max to the gym. As soon as they passed through the door, Max spotted some of his teammates and trotted away. Nick recognized Ian, Max's best friend, who had tagged along once when he took the kids to drive go-carts. The players straggled onto the gym floor, where they started passing around a soccer ball while waiting for the team to assemble.

Emily led the way to the bleachers, greeting people as she passed them, and sat down on the third bench, with Lyla next and then Nick.

"Hi, Em." A woman in front of them half turned, exposing blond bangs under a cap with a soccer ball patch above the rim. "Good to see you. Did you make it home for Thanksgiving?"

"Hi, Dina. I did. I'll be here next week, too."

"Next week is a bye week," Dina told her. "Remember, some scheduling conflict or something, which is why the season is a week longer than usual."

"Oh, that's right. Unfortunately, I'll be back on the slope for the final game and the party. Dina, this is Nick. He'll be taking care of the kids while I'm out. Nick, this is Ian's mom, Dina."

"Nice to meet you, Nick," Dina said, her eyes running over him from head to toe. "I hope Janice's okay."

"She's traveling," Emily said, "and Nick offered to step in while she's out of town."

"That's great. Nick, I'm happy to help if you need anything. Why don't I put my number into your phone, in case of emergency or—" she gave a little half smile "—whatever?"

Nick didn't feel like he had any choice but to hand over his phone. Dina punched some buttons and handed it back. "There. I texted myself, so I'll have yours, too. Maybe we can get the boys together while Emily is out of town."

Nick glanced toward Emily. She didn't say anything, but her mouth seemed a little tighter. Fortunately, before he had to reply, Ian rushed up to his mother and handed her a rope-and-bead bracelet. "The ref says I can't wear it."

She tucked it away and, much to Nick's relief, turned to watch the kickoff. When Nick had gone to a couple of Max's games this summer, he'd been playing right midfield, but now he was back on center defense, the white number five on his chest in sharp relief against his dark blue jersey. "When did Max start playing stopper?" Nick asked Emily.

"Last month. Most of the kids don't want to play defense, so the coach put him in."

"It's a key position," Nick said, "especially for indoor soccer." A few minutes into the game, Ian dribbled past two defenders, sidestepped the goaltender, who came rushing at him, and kicked the ball squarely into the upper right corner of the goal for the first score. Nick added his cheer to all the parents and siblings sitting around him. Max ran up to slap his friend on the back before returning to his position in front of the goal.

The other team's goalie kicked it to his own winger, who passed it to the center forward, but Max cut in and stole the ball, passing to his own wing.

"Yeah, Max!" Lyla yelled.

Unfortunately, the player wasn't expecting the ball and it bounced off his ankle and out of bounds. The opposing team's player threw it in to his own forward, who dribbled toward the goal. He was a good dribbler, not quite as skillful as Ian, but he managed to get past the first defender, and once again, Max went up to meet him. He got off a shot, but Max stuck out a foot and deflected it, sending it up and over the net. A corner kick set up a nice shot opportunity, but Max threw himself in the way and the player had to shoot around him, resulting in a lob straight into the goalie's hands.

"Max looks really good out there," Nick murmured to Emily. Summer before last, Max had been a second stringer, but by last summer he was starting.

"He's been working hard," Emily replied.

"It shows."

By the end of the game, Max's team was winning 5-3, and two of those three goals were scored while Max was on the bench. Since this was a recreational league, rather than competitive, all the players spent more or less equal time on the gym floor. Max had made several nice steals and saves. As the last few minutes ticked off, Max stole the ball, looked up field, and called Ian's name. Ian looked back and then took off toward the goal, and Max kicked a long overhead pass that landed right in front of him, allowing Ian to blow past the last defender and poke the ball into the net, bringing the final score to 6-3.

"All right!" Dina yelled and turned to Emily. "That puts us at the top of the league, tied with the yellow team."

"Great," Emily said as they all climbed down from the bleachers. "Like I said, I won't be here for the final game, but is there anything you need for the party that I could do in advance?"

"Let me see." Dina opened a folder and looked inside. "Do you want to order the cake?"

"Sure, I can do that. Nick, you don't mind picking it up, do you?"

"No problem," Nick assured her. As long as he didn't have to make decisions about flavors and decorations, he was good. By this time, the boys had finished congratulating the other team and were ambling off the court as the two teams for the next game assembled. Max came to stand near them.

Emily waggled her fingers at Dina. "Okay, we'll see you next week."

"'Bye." Dina flashed a smile in Nick's direction. "Remember, Nick, don't hesitate to call if you need me."

"Thanks. Goodbye." Nick brushed past her to walk next to Max and placed a hand on his shoulder. "Great job out there. You're quite an asset for your team."

Max shrugged. "Ian scored most of the goals."

"Yeah, but you prevent the opposition from scoring and that's just as valuable. Not to mention, that full court pass was awesome."

Max grunted, but he walked a little taller as they exited the gym.

AFTER THEY GOT home from the game, Max went up to take a shower. Emily went to work in the kitchen, opening and closing cabinet and refrigerator doors, setting things on the countertop. Nick put away coats and returned to the kitchen. "Need any help?"

"I've got it, thanks. I'm just going to make a triple batch of lasagna and freeze two of them for you to use while I'm on the slope. Reheating instructions are here." She pointed to a binder opened to a page with the lasagna recipe printed out and footnotes at the bottom of the page on reheating. "It's handy because you don't have to thaw it first."

"You don't have to spend your two weeks off premaking meals. I can cook."

She waved away his protest. "I always do this. It makes it easier for Janice."

In the time he'd spent here before Emily returned from the slope, he'd noticed Janice taking food from the freezer, but he'd assumed she'd been the one to put it there. Janice was an excellent cook, as Nick could attest to, since he'd spent a good portion of his childhood in her kitchen. There was no need for Emily to prepare and freeze everything. But maybe it made her feel connected to the family even when she couldn't be there.

The phone rang. Emily answered and then put down the phone and walked to the bottom of the stairs. "Lyla, telephone."

"Okay," Lyla's voice called down. Lyla must have answered on the extension upstairs because Emily listened a moment and then hung up.

"I think you're the only one I know who still has a landline," Nick observed.

Emily shrugged and lit the burner under a cast-iron Dutch oven. "I've told the kids they can't have cell phones until they're thirteen. But most of their friends have them, so this is a compromise. Max finds it annoying to be excluded from text chains, but it keeps him away from some of the drama, too." She pushed two casserole dishes and a roll of aluminum foil across the island toward him. "Could you line these pans with foil for me, please?"

"Sure." He pressed the foil into the bottom of the pans while Emily cooked, measuring, stirring, browning the meat, and boiling the water for pasta, her movements quick and confident.

Lyla came running down the stairs. "Paisley has a new dog. Can I go over and see it, ple-e-e-ease?"

"I'm cooking right now," Emily told her. "I can take you over after dinner."

"But that's so lo-o-ong," Lyla protested.

"I could take her," Nick offered. Presumably, Paisley lived somewhere nearby.

"Yes!" Lyla squeezed her hands together. "Okay, Mommy?"

"All right, if Nick doesn't mind. Dinner should be ready around six thirty."

"We'll be here," Nick assured her. "Come on, Lyla, let's get our coats."

It turned out that Paisley lived at Swan Lodge, about five miles out of Swan Falls. "She moved here from New Mexico," Lyla told him as they drove over. "She says it's way greener here. They had mountains and snow where she used to live, but the snow goes away in a day or two and doesn't last all winter like it does here."

"Interesting." Nick supposed once he'd lived in Hawaii for a while, it would seem normal that the only snow would be on the tops of the volcanoes. Wearing shorts in the winter would be a novelty. They took the turnoff at the sign and drove along a gravel driveway to the lodge.

Nick had heard about Swan Lodge, but he'd never had a reason to visit before. The log building stood two stories high, with a tall gable overhanging the front porch. Nick followed signs to a parking lot on one side. From there he caught a glimpse of a tree-lined lake in the back, already forming a crust of ice despite the lack of snow. He and Lyla took the path to the main entrance and stepped inside. On the left, a large reception desk displayed a rack of local interest brochures, while straight ahead, a stone fireplace soared to the second-story ceiling. On one side was an area with several dining tables, and on the other, a living area with comfortable-looking chairs and couches. Glass doors and windows lined the back wall, which opened onto a porch overlooking the lake. Somehow it managed to be airy and cozy at the same time.

"Lyla!" Paisley called from near the window. "She's over here. Come see!"

Lyla shed her coat, kicked off her shoes by the

door, and ran across the room. Nick hung their coats on some hooks and put their shoes on a tray beside the door before going after her. Paisley sat on a rug, holding a blond fur-ball of a puppy in her lap. A man was perched on the edge of the couch behind her, smiling.

"She's so cute!" Lyla gushed as she dropped down beside Paisley. "What's her name?"

"Willow or Nugget. We haven't decided."

The man stood as Nick got closer and offered his hand. "Hi. I'm Nathan Swan."

"Nick Bernardi." Nick shook hands with him. "Nice to meet you, Nathan. I didn't realize Swan was a family name. I'd always assumed Swan Lodge was named after Swan Falls."

"It was named for both. My great-uncle, Harry Swan, and his wife, Eleanor, noticed Swan Falls on the map and planned to hike over to see the waterfall, but when they saw the land here was for sale, they decided to buy it and build a lodge. This was all way before the town of Swan Falls." While he spoke, a woman with red hair had come into the room carrying a tray with an insulated pot, stacks of mugs, and a plate of cookies. "Here, let me get that." He took the tray from her and set it on a nearby end table. "Nick, this is my wife, Amanda. Amanda, Nick Bernardi."

"Nice to meet you." Nick shook her hand as well.

"Hello, Nick. You're Emily's nanny, right?"

"I am," Nick replied. "Just while Janice's out of town."

"Everybody was so relieved that Janice was able to go with Helen after Helen's sister broke her leg," Amanda told him. "Helen has never traveled overseas before, and she wasn't sure she could do it alone. So thank you for stepping in to take care of Max and Lyla."

"We heard about your little problem during the field trip to Swan's Marsh," Nathan said, with a laugh.

Did everyone in this town know about that? "Yeah, that didn't go so well."

"From what Paisley told us," Amanda said, "you handled a difficult situation with grace."

Nick shrugged, but he felt better about the incident. Lyla squealed happily as the puppy tugged on one of her socks. Nick laughed. "Cute puppy. Golden?"

"The rescue thinks golden and husky mix," Nathan replied.

"Sounds like a good Alaska dog. Nala, Emily's golden retriever, has always been great with the kids."

"Yeah, Nala was a big factor in our choice," Amanda said. "We've been waiting for a golden mix to come up on one of the rescue sites. Would you like some hot chocolate?"

"Sure. Thanks."

Amanda poured and distributed the mugs, but

the girls were busy playing with the puppy, so she set their cups on the table and passed the plate of cookies. Before she sat down, she pulled a card from her pocket and handed it to Nick. "If you need anything, especially once Emily goes back to the slope, feel free to call us. We're fairly new in Swan Falls, too, but we're settling in."

"Thank you. I appreciate that." Nick accepted the Swan Lodge business card, which had Amanda's and Nathan's cell-phone numbers written on the back. "Lyla mentioned you moved here from New Mexico. What brought you here to Swan Falls?"

"Nathan and I met when we all came up this past summer for my aunt Eleanor's memorial service. Eleanor was married to Harry, Nathan's great-uncle, who passed away several years ago. Anyway, we were both surprised to discover we had inherited this lodge jointly." Amanda reached for Nathan's hand. "And then…we discovered we're meant to be together. We were married in September."

"Oh, congratulations." Marrying that fast sounded risky, but Nick had to admit they looked happy together.

"Thanks." Nathan smiled at Amanda before turning back to Nick. "So how long have you been a nanny?"

"Oh, I'm not a professional nanny." Nick laughed. "I'm a pilot. But I had a little time off, and Emily needed someone to be with the kids, so it all worked out."

"How long have you and Emily known each other?" Amanda asked.

"Oh, let's see. Fifteen years, I guess. Her husband and I grew up together."

Amanda glanced at the girls. The puppy licked Lyla's face, and Paisley giggled. Amanda said softly, "I never met Emily's husband, but from what I've heard, he was a wonderful man."

"Yeah, Coop was great." He wondered if Amanda had been a widow, too, but he didn't like to ask. Whatever her story, it was clear from the way Nathan looked at her that he was besotted, and she looked pretty happy, too. Maybe a quick marriage wasn't such a bad idea. After all, his own parents had dated for five years before marriage, and now they absolutely despised each other. Maybe it wasn't the length of the relationship, but the strength of the commitment that made the difference.

The puppy broke away from Paisley and ran to Nick's foot, biting the toe of his sock and growling. Nick laughed and reached down to disengage the pup's teeth from the wool. "You sure are a cutie."

The pup yipped, as though she was offended that her growling hadn't scared him, and everyone laughed. Nick passed the puppy back to Lyla.

Nick chatted with Nathan and Amanda for almost an hour. During that time, a few guests came and went, with Amanda and Nathan calling cheerful greetings to them. One couple stopped to admire the new puppy for a few minutes before heading to town for dinner, which reminded Nathan to check his watch. "Lyla, we need to go. I promised your mom we'd be home for dinner at six thirty."

Lyla sighed. "Okay." She hugged the puppy once more before they put on their coats and shoes and said their goodbyes.

"Come back anytime," Nathan told him.

"Thanks," Nick replied. "See you around."

He and Lyla stepped outside and walked toward the parking lot. The air had changed while they were indoors. A few skiffs of white clung to trees, and more flakes were drifting from the sky. "It's snowing," he told Lyla.

She gasped and looked up at the sky, a huge smile across her face. "Snow!"

CHAPTER EIGHT

SNOW! EMILY BARELY noticed the first few flakes as they drifted past the kitchen window, but by the time Nick and Lyla drove into the garage, big, fluffy flakes, like downy feathers, danced and swirled in the pool of light from the porch fixture.

The kids would be ecstatic. The first snow of the year was icing on the cake, after Max's team had won the soccer game. Emily hadn't missed the look on Max's face when Nick praised his performance today. No matter how many times she might compliment him, it meant more coming from Nick. One, because in high school Nick had played soccer well enough to get an offer for a college scholarship, which he didn't take because he went to flight school, but still, he was that good. Two, because "moms have to say that." On the drive home, Nick and Max had rehashed all the key moments of the game.

Maybe Janice had a point, not about Emily dating, but about a masculine presence in the kids' lives. Nick's availability wasn't just convenient because it allowed Janice to take the trip—it was also good for the kids, giving them a different perspective. Max was surrounded by women—herself, Janice, his teacher. Even his best friend, Ian, had a single mom. And speaking of single, what was up with Dina, blatantly flirting with Nick like that? For all she knew, Nick could be married, or engaged, or in a relationship. Not that Nick had shown any more interest in Dina than Emily had felt for Peter, but still. Hey, that was an idea. She ought to introduce Dina to Peter. Maybe then she'd leave Nick alone.

Lyla burst through the door from the laundry room. "Mommy, did you see the snow?"

"I did!" Emily told her.

"Can we do the birdfeeders today?"

"Well, of course. It's the first snow. We'll do it after dinner."

Nick came in and Lyla announced, "Mommy says we can do our first snow day today."

"We put up all the birdfeeders," Emily explained to Nick. "And then we take the sleds over to Johanson Hill, but we'll have to wait until there's enough snow on the ground to do that. At the rate it's coming down now, we'll be able to go tomorrow."

"I was beginning to think it was never going to snow," Max said as he walked into the kitchen and started to rummage through the pantry. He pulled out a bag of cheesy popcorn.

"Put that away," Emily told him.

"But—"

"We're literally eating dinner in ten minutes." She opened the oven, removed a casserole dish, and set it on a rack on the counter. "You can set the table while I make garlic toast."

"All right." Max managed to control his appetite until she could get the bread toasted and put the salad on the table, but as soon as she gave the go-ahead, he served himself a huge portion of lasagna. Good thing it was full of vegetables and not just meat and cheese.

Nick laughed. "Can you really eat all that?"

Max seemed to take it as a challenge. "Watch me."

It felt cozy, eating dinner while the snow accumulated outside the window. Lyla told them all about Paisley's new puppy. "Can the puppy come over and have a playdate with Nala sometime soon?"

"We'll see," Emily answered. "They might want to keep the puppy at home for a while, until she gets all her shots."

When they'd finally finished eating, there was at least an inch of snow carpeting the ground. "Can we do the birdfeeders now?"

"Okay. If you and Max will clear the table and put the dishes in the dishwasher, Nick and I will get everything together." She went through the laundry room to the garage, with Nick right behind her. "I take it setting up birdfeeders for the first snow is another family tradition."

Emily nodded. "Coop started it when Max was about four. We stopped putting up birdfeeders in the summer because they attract bears, so this was a way of reminding us to set them up in the winter, when the snow makes it harder for the birds to find food." She opened a storage cabinet and pulled out three bags of various seed mixes, a funnel, and two birdfeeders, one a tall tower and one shaped like a UFO, which she set on the floor. "We always do it on the first day it snows, or if I'm working, my first day home after the first snow."

"Makes sense. And the sledding?"

"Because it's fun." She grinned. "When was the last time you went sledding?"

Nick thought for a moment. "I can't even remember."

"Then it's high time." Emily opened the second door of the cabinet and handed Nick a package of suet and a basket, and then a feeder shaped like a mushroom, and another with shiny hexagonal tiles, followed by a resin bluebird holding an umbrella over the tray and a mesh cow wearing a Santa hat.

"Just how many feeders do you have?" Nick asked with awe in his voice.

"I'm not sure. We usually pick up an extra one or two every Christmas." She removed a tower with a copper pagoda roof and shut the cabinet door. She hit the garage-door button. While the door opened, she lifted one of the kids' plastic sleds down from the rack and carried it out to set on the snow. "Just put all those feeders in here." It took a second sled to hold everything, but once they were done, she closed the garage door and went back inside, where the kids were watching the snow through the window. "I've got the feeders out. Everybody, get on your snow gear. It's time!"

They all put on snow boots and jackets and made their way outside. Emily grabbed the towrope for one of the sleds, Nick took the other one, and they dragged the feeders and birdseed to the spruce trees out front. She let the kids choose which feeders they wanted for their trees first, then helped them fill the feeders with birdseed before hanging them from the branches. Meanwhile, she handed Nick the suet block and nodded toward Coop's tree. "Hang this close to the truck."

"To attract woodpeckers?" Nick asked as he unwrapped the block of suet, and put it in the mesh basket.

"Exactly." They were Coop's favorite bird.

Once the kids had chosen their favorites, Emily and Nick hung the last two, the copper pagoda and the UFO, from hooks above the railing on the porch. Nick looked back toward the spruces, where birds had already begun to gather. "How often do you refill the feeders?"

"Once or twice a week, usually. Next time I'm in Wasilla, I'll stock up on birdseed."

Nick's phone rang. "Huh, it says it's Lyla's teacher, Ms. Englund. Why would she be calling me?"

"And on a Saturday night?" Emily added.

Nick took the call. "Hello. Yes, this is Nick… Uh-huh." He paced as he talked, or rather listened, mostly, so Emily could only get the barest hint of what the call was about. "All right, I'll see you Monday… You, too. 'Bye." He hung up. "It seems someone had to drop out, and the school needs a new volunteer for the—let me get this right—Winter Jubilation Pageant." He shrugged. "I figured after the fiasco at the marsh, they wouldn't want me anywhere near the school."

"You handled that situation just fine," Emily assured him, "but that doesn't mean you have to volunteer for the pageant, especially while I'm in town. I'll call Ms. Englund and tell her I can do it until the tenth, when I go to the slope."

"No, I don't mind, and besides, practices don't start until December eighth. Monday is just to meet with the other volunteers and assign roles."

"Still, I asked you to be my 'manny' when I'm out of town, and you already babysat yesterday. Not to mention, you have surgery coming up Tuesday."

"Don't remind me." He winced. "Seriously, I'm enjoying spending time with the kids, and I'm happy to help with the winter pageant or whatever it's called. And it's probably good to have something to think about on Monday besides surgery." He shuddered.

She put a hand on his arm. "The surgery will be fine, and the school is very lucky to have you as a volunteer." She smiled at him. "And we're lucky to have you, too."

AFTER SPENDING MOST of Monday night staring at the ceiling, conjuring up one disaster scenario after another, Nick gave up on sleep and wandered into the kitchen. He would have liked a cup of coffee, but according to the pre-op instructions, he wasn't supposed to consume caffeine the day of his surgery. It would be at least an hour before Emily and the kids were awake, so he left the lights off and went to sit at the kitchen table, and gazed through the window.

It was amazing how bright it became once snow covered the ground, clearly illuminating the birdfeeder hanging from the shepherd's hooks outside the window. In the clear tower of the pagoda birdfeeder, the volume of birdseed had already fallen to the halfway mark. All the birds in the area seemed to know to show up here for a free meal. Another six inches of snow had fallen, and it clung to the top of the two feeders, making the flying saucer appear to be descending from a cloud. That feeder must have been Max's choice about three years ago, when he'd gone through his space-alien phase. For a while there, every time he saw Nick, Max would ask hopefully if he'd seen any UFOs from his plane. When Nick denied it, Max would nod and say "They must have activated their cloaking device" in such a serious tone Nick almost believed him.

Nala came padding out of the laundry room and rested her head in Nick's lap. He stroked the soft fur on the top of her head. "You didn't have to get up. You're probably tired from all that sledding." The kids had had so much fun sledding on Sunday afternoon, they'd insisted on doing it again after school yesterday, and, of course, Nala had come along, climbing up the sledding hill alongside them and running after them, barking, when they glided down. She'd even ridden in the sled with Nick once, but she'd jumped out halfway down. Emily teased him that Nala was afraid of his driving.

Yesterday had been a full day. First, the meeting at the school, where he'd met the other adult volunteers and learned a little about the pageant, sort of a musical play, with kids in the sixth grade performing speaking parts, while the lower grades sang songs between scenes. Or maybe it was during the scenes—Nick wasn't quite clear. He'd returned home for lunch with Emily and gone with her to the feed store in Wasilla for dogfood and birdseed, and to the grocery store for a major shop before returning home to pick up the kids from school. Then came the sledding, and after that, since Max had soccer practice on Mondays at six, that meant another trip to the school to drop him off. Nick had helped her put together chicken enchiladas. Then it was back to school to pick Max up before dinner a little after seven, followed by homework, baths, and bed for the kids. Supposedly Emily was teaching Nick the routine, but he got the feeling she was mostly dragging him along so he wouldn't have time to worry about this surgery.

And for the most part, it worked. It was fun watching the kids revel in the new snow, and streaking down the hill on a plastic saucer was still a thrill, even for a pilot. He'd actually missed flying less than he thought he would, probably because he didn't have that much time to think about it. But flying was who he was, and he couldn't imagine never going up in a plane again. In fact, it was the only reason he was going in for this surgery today.

The stairs creaked, and a moment later Emily came into the kitchen, backless bear-paw furry slippers slapping against her feet. She flipped on the lights and jumped when she saw him there. "Oh, you startled me."

"Sorry." Nick stroked Nala's head.

Emily came to rest a hand on his shoulder. "Nervous, huh?"

"Oh, yeah."

"I was, too, but it's been great. Just wait until the

first time you wake up and everything is in focus. It's awesome."

Nick nodded. He would be fine with blurry mornings if it meant he didn't have to go through with this worry. But he wasn't willing to give up flying, so...

Emily squeezed his shoulder and then started the coffee brewing. "You can eat, right?"

"Yes, they said no caffeine, but to eat a healthy breakfast."

She opened the refrigerator. "How about an omelet? I've got mushrooms and that smoked Gouda you like. With bacon and whole wheat toast?"

"Sounds great, but I can make it."

"No, let me take care of you today. You'll be in charge of everything soon enough."

Despite the butterflies in his stomach, Nick managed to eat the omelet, bacon, and most of the toast. At Emily's urging, he went off to shower and dress while she got the kids up and moving. By eight, they'd dropped the kids off at school and were on the highway to Anchorage.

Nick stared straight ahead, trying not to think about lasers or needles. Emily glanced his way. "It will be okay."

"Yeah," he said. "Except what if it's not?"

"The complication rate for this surgery is less than one percent," Emily said, "and for your particular surgeon only three tenths of one percent."

He looked at her. "You checked out my surgeon?"

"Of course." She patted his knee. "And he has an excellent reputation."

"That's good," Nick acknowledged.

"Very good." They rode in silence for several minutes. Then Emily said, "Oh, I meant to tell you, I got an email from Janice this morning."

"Oh, yeah? Is everything going all right?" Nick asked, glad for the distraction.

"So far, so good. They cleared customs and made their connecting flight to Amsterdam with no problems. She sent a picture of people ice skating at an outdoor rink in front of a museum. She says Helen has absolutely no sense of direction, so it's a good thing she went along."

Nick laughed. "Janice always has to be taking care of somebody."

"So it seems. The cruise company will pick them up at the hotel and take them to the ship tomorrow. She sounds excited. I'm so glad you agreed to stay with the kids so that she could go."

"Me, too. They're a lot of fun."

She glanced his way. "You mean that, don't you?"

"Of course. I've always enjoyed taking them for fun days, but I didn't realize how much I like just being around them. Getting their take on things. Seeing how creative they can be. And the perks." He held up his arm to show off his bracelet.

They reached the clinic and went inside. New age music played over hidden speakers somewhere. A waiting area with chairs filled the front room, with a few potted trees near the door, restrooms on the right, a desk with a window in the back, and an ominous pair of doors to the left. A young woman in brightly printed scrubs stepped through the doors. "Susan Martin?"

"Right here," a middle-aged woman replied in a bright voice. Together they vanished through the doors, the patient chattering excitedly.

Emily touched his arm. "Come on. You need to check in."

"Right." They went to the window and Nick gave them his name and ID. The receptionist asked a few questions and then returned his driver's license. "I see you filled out the questionnaire online, so you're all set. Please take a seat. It shouldn't be too long."

Nick and Emily found two empty chairs farthest from the door. Nick's stomach churned, and he began to regret that hearty breakfast. Emily looked through a brochure she'd picked up. "It says you just have to wait two weeks after surgery before swimming, so you'll be good to hit the beach when you get to Hawaii. Although you should wear goggles if you play beach volleyball."

"I'll keep that in mind." Nick stared at the brochure, which showed an illustration of an eyeball.

He couldn't stop thinking about that laser. "Excuse me," he muttered as he rushed into the restroom.

Fortunately, the room was empty, because he had just enough time to get into the stall before throwing up. He took a minute of deep breathing to make sure it wasn't going to happen again, but his stomach seemed okay now. He washed his hands and face. A pale replica of himself looked back at him from the mirror. His heart was racing. How was he going to do this?

He took a deep breath and returned to Emily. She took his hand. "Hey, you okay?" she asked softly.

"Not really," he admitted. "I lost my breakfast."

She nodded without judgment and squeezed his hand. "I get it. Eye surgery is scary."

"You've done it, and I'll bet you didn't toss your cookies."

"Maybe not, but I came close when I had to give a presentation to a whole auditorium of people at a conference last summer. We're all scared of something."

"I guess," he muttered, deliberately slowing his breathing.

After a moment, Emily said, "You know you don't have to do this if you don't want to."

"Yeah, I do. At least if I ever want to fly again." And he couldn't imagine life without flying. He shook his head in frustration. "I don't get it. Remember when that goose collision took out my engine five years ago, and I had to land the plane with no power?"

"How could I forget?" Emily shuddered.

"Well, I wasn't nearly as scared then as I am now."

"That's because you were in control," she said without hesitation. "You knew what needed to be done and you did it. You can bet the four passengers with you were petrified. But you knew what you were doing, and you got that plane down safely."

He managed a little smile. "So you're saying this eye surgeon knows what he's doing?"

"That's the rumor. He's supposed to be as brilliant a surgeon as you are a pilot."

Nick let out a long, slow breath. As his panic subsided, his embarrassment increased. He tilted his head to look at Emily. "You sure you trust your kids to a chicken like me?"

"Stop that," Emily said. "It's easy to do things that don't scare you. Courage is moving forward even though you're scared. And as for my kids, how many nannies can say they've kept their cool and achieved a dead-stick landing on a village airstrip in a single engine plane?"

"Probably not a whole lot," Nick admitted.

"Nicholas Bernardi," the woman in scrubs called from the doors.

Nick forced himself to his feet. "I guess it's time."

"Want me to come with you?" Emily asked.

"Would you?" He hated to ask, but her steady presence was the only thing making this bearable.

"You bet." She took his hand again and they walked toward the doors.

The nurse, or whoever she was, didn't offer any resistance to letting Emily in. "Right this way." She led him to a small room and had him sit in a chair while she shined a light into his eyes and made some notes. Emily sat quietly in the corner. "Everything looks good," the woman said, and reached for a hypodermic needle on a nearby tray. "I'm just going to give you something to help you relax."

"Excellent idea," Nick replied, trading smiles with Emily.

The nurse gave him the injection and left the room. Emily scooted her chair closer and once again took his hand. "How are you feeling?"

"A little better," he told her, and it was true. The meds couldn't have taken effect yet, so it must be because of her. "I'm glad you're here."

"Me, too."

As they sat for a few minutes, the walls of the room seemed to soften. The soft background music swelled and filled the room. He looked at Emily, at the soft curves of her face, the deep blue of her eyes, and the way the light caught the color of her hair. "You're so pretty," he murmured.

She snorted. "Those meds kicking in?"

"No, really." For some reason, his words slurred

a little. "The first day I ever saw you, at that barbecue, I thought you were the prettiest woman I'd ever seen. I was going to ask you out, until I figured out you were the girl Coop had told me about."

"That was a long time ago."

"And you're more beautiful now than you were then." He touched her face. Her skin felt velvety beneath his fingers.

"Thank you." She gave him the same sort of smile as she might have given Lyla for bringing her a bouquet of dandelions.

The nurse returned. "It's time." She led them to another room and got him settled in a reclining chair.

The surgeon breezed into the room. "Hello, Nick. Nice to see you again."

"Hello." Nick's tongue felt thicker than usual.

"Let's get this show on the road," the doctor said. "If your wife wants, she can watch the whole operation through closed-circuit TV in the observation room."

It seemed like too much effort to explain that Emily wasn't his wife, so Nick just nodded.

"That would be great," Emily said, following the nurse out.

Nick didn't really remember much about the operation itself, other than the smell of something burning and the horrible realization it must be his eyes. But there was no pain, and the whole thing only took a few minutes.

"All done," the surgeon said, removing the device that had been holding his eyes open.

"That's it?" Nick asked.

"That's it," the surgeon confirmed. While he taped clear shields over Nick's eyes, the nurse brought Emily back to the room.

"That was amazing to watch how the whole thing works," Emily said. "Thanks, Doctor."

"Glad we could entertain you," Nick said, except it came out garbled. But Emily's laugh told him she understood.

"Make sure he uses these shields whenever he sleeps for the next five days," the nurse told Emily.

"It's best if he keeps his eyes closed for a couple of hours, so try to get him to nap on the drive home," the doctor added. "He did well. I don't expect any problems. You have the post-op instructions?"

"I do." Emily held up some papers.

"Okay then. I'll see you tomorrow, Nick." He turned to Emily. "Take good care of him."

"Oh, I will," Emily promised.

CHAPTER NINE

MORE SNOW HAD fallen overnight, and the plows had only cleared two eastbound lanes, so the drive to Anchorage took a little longer than it had the day before. Emily glanced toward Nick, but the giant sunglasses they'd given him to protect his eyes from snow glare made it hard to read his expression. Still, just from the way he sat, she could tell he was much more relaxed than he had been yesterday before the surgery.

She and Coop had spent a lot of time with Nick over the years, and they'd experienced some frightening situations, like the time the three of them were in sea kayaks near Homer, and a whale breached right beside them. But she'd never seen Nick truly scared, not until yesterday, and somehow his vulnerability made her like him all the more. The shot the nurse had given to relax him had helped a lot. Her cheeks grew warm when she thought of the way he'd called her beautiful and touched her cheek. Did he remember saying those things? If so, he hadn't mentioned it. Probably just the meds talking.

He looked over at her. "I really appreciate you taking all this time to drive me back and forth to Anchorage. Hopefully, this will be the last time."

"I don't mind. In fact, if you're up to it, I thought we might do a little shopping in Anchorage after your appointment."

"Fine with me. What are we shopping for?"

"I want to drop by the warehouse club and stock up on stuff like paper towels and tortilla chips, and they always have fresh poinsettias this time of year. But first, there's a store downtown that sells locally made arts and crafts, and they always have wonderful Christmas decorations. I want to get the tree up and the house decorated this weekend."

"The kids will love that. Should we stop by the Chugach National Forest office to pick up a tree permit while we're in town? Or do you need a permit?" Nick had gone along to help cut the tree the first year after she and Coop were married, and maybe once or twice since then, but not in recent years.

Emily shook her head. "We switched to an artificial tree."

"Why? You love cutting your own tree."

She really did, but it wasn't practical. "I'm not at home for half the month, and it's not fair to make Janice crawl under the tree to water it every day.

Not to mention sweeping up all the fallen needles. It's just easier and safer to use a fake one."

"Makes sense, I guess."

They arrived at the clinic and had only a short wait before the nurse called Nick's name. He stood. "Aren't you coming?"

"Did you want me to?" Emily had assumed he would prefer his privacy.

"Unless you'd rather not—"

"No, I'll come." Emily stood and they followed the nurse to an exam room.

The nurse asked a few questions and got out a blood-pressure cuff. Nick pushed up his sleeve, exposing two bracelets on his arm. The new one was yellow-and-orange.

The nurse chuckled. "Nice bracelets."

"Thanks. This one—" he pointed to the yellow one "—is my get-well bracelet. It's supposed to give me 'healing energy,' according to the artist."

Emily smiled at that. Lyla hadn't even mentioned that she'd made Nick another bracelet, although when she and Max came home from school and found him lying on the couch, wearing eye shields, they'd been very sweet, asking how he was feeling and offering to bring snacks and drinks. Max was fascinated with the concept of eye surgery using lasers "like a light saber."

A few minutes later, the doctor came breezing in, and glanced down at a file folder. "So, Nick, how are you feeling? Any problems?"

"Not really. My eyes feel a little gritty, like you said they would."

"Yes, that's normal." The doctor shined a light into Nick's eyes. "Any light halos?"

"Yeah, some."

The doctor nodded. "They'll most likely go away within a few weeks. Let's check your vision." He put a headset in front of Nick's eyes. "What's the smallest line you can read clearly?"

"The fourth one," Nick said.

"Read it for me."

"H, Z, Q, R, T," Nick replied with confidence.

"Good. Now try the next line."

This time Nick answered more slowly. *"E, S, F*... No, that's another *E*... *Z, G, N."*

The doctor nodded and made a note. "I'm clearing you to drive. You're at 20/25."

Nick frowned. "I need 20/20 to fly."

"I understand that, and you'll get there most likely. Just keep using the drops we gave you and make an appointment to come back in a week. Any questions?"

"What if I don't get to 20/20?"

"If you haven't achieved 20/20 in three months, we'll consider doing a touch-up surgery."

Nick leaned forward. "I don't have three months. I'm supposed to report for work in Hawaii on January second with 20/20 vision."

"And there's every probability that you will," the doctor told him in a soothing voice. "You're only one day out from surgery. Give yourself a little time to heal. We'll check again in a week." The doctor patted his shoulder and walked out of the room.

Nick and Emily stopped at the front desk, where he made his next appointment. Once they were back in the car, he asked, "How long did it take for your eyes to get to 20/20 after surgery?"

Emily thought back. "As I remember, it was the next day, but I've read that it often takes a few days. No need to panic."

"Not panicking, just concerned. If I can't fly in January, they might withdraw the job offer." He blew out a breath and sat back in his seat, buckling his seat belt. "But there's not much I can do about it except using my eye drops and following orders. So let's go hit that craft place you were talking about."

"Actually, it's an antique shop downtown, but they have a local arts section." Before she started the car, she rubbed his shoulder. "It will be okay, Nick. You'll get there."

He didn't answer, but he gave her a little smile.

How unfair it would be if Nick went through all that and still couldn't fly. Piloting was his whole life, his whole identity. This had to work. Nick deserved to have his dreams come true. To be eligible to fly and make that move to Hawaii. But when he did, she and the kids sure would miss him.

The rest of the week went by in a flash. Despite Nick's urging to leave it to him, Emily spent much of the time when the kids were at school preparing and freezing meals for when she was on the slope. She did allow Nick to help her clean house, run errands, and walk the dog. He'd also installed snow tires on all the cars, saving her a couple of trips to the tire center, so he felt like he'd paid her back a little for all her help and hospitality. After-school activities, homework, dinner, and small bursts of Christmas decorating, like hanging stockings and wreaths, filled afternoons and evenings.

Nick woke at his usual time the next Saturday and removed the shields from his eyes. According to the instructions, he could quit wearing them now. Presumably, that meant his eyes had healed to the point they were no longer especially vulnerable to injury. The grittiness he'd felt the first couple of days had gone away, but when he turned on the lamp beside the bed, he still saw halos around the light. Hopefully, they would be gone soon, and at his next appointment his vision would test 20/20.

He threw on a flannel robe and went to the kitchen to make coffee, but Emily was already there, dressed for the day in a gray sweatshirt displaying a gnome with a red-and-green tartan hat tying a bow on a package with a tag that read Gnome for the Holidays. Her hair was pulled back into a ponytail and jingle bells dangled from her ears. "I'll be Home for Christmas" played softly, and she stood at the island, stirring something in a slow cooker that smelled of cinnamon and oranges. She looked up and smiled. "Good morning."

"Morning. What are you making there?"

"Mulled cider. We always have it while we're decorating the tree. Mostly because it smells so good." She gave it a stir and covered the pot just as her cell phone rang. She picked it up from the counter. "Hi, Janice!" She pushed a button and set the phone on the counter. "I'm putting you on speaker. Nick's here, but the kids aren't up yet. How's Germany?"

"Wonderful! Overflowing with history. And the Christmas markets are so much fun. Hi, Nick."

"Hi, Janice."

"Yesterday we went to a castle with towers and turrets and everything. I climbed the hundred and one steps to the top of the tower, but Helen said her feet were already sore, so she skipped that part. Parts of the castle date back to 1100. Can you imagine?"

"Amazing."

"I know. And this afternoon, after touring the old town, we went to a cooking demonstration where they taught us to make traditional *kekse*, which means cookies. I emailed you the recipe for *spitzbuben*, jam cookies. Really good. So how are things there?"

"Just fine," Emily told her. "Nick won his soccer game, and they're tied for first in the league. Paisley got a new puppy, and so Lyla has gone to visit her several times. And Nick got his eyes done."

"And how did that go?" Janice asked.

"The doctor says it all looks good," Nick told her. "I'm not up to 20/20 yet, but he thinks soon." No use mentioning the halos and giving Janice something to worry about.

"We're putting up the tree today," Emily told her.

"Fun. What theme are you using?"

"I haven't decided yet," Emily replied.

"Well, be sure to send me a picture," Janice said. "Oh, and I left you some new ornaments. Nick put them in your Christmas closet."

"Aw, that's sweet. Thanks. I'll look for them."

"I've picked up some things you'll love in the Christmas markets. I can't wait to show— Oh, hold on just a sec." In the background, someone said something unintelligible, and Janice replied, "I'll be right there." Then she returned to the phone. "I've got to go. Helen is ready to go to dinner. We're having sauerbraten tonight. Have a wonderful time with the tree and give the kids my love."

"I will. Enjoy your dinner. 'Bye, Janice."

"'Bye, Janice," Nick echoed.

"Goodbye." Janice ended the call.

"Sounds like we were right to encourage her," Emily said with satisfaction. "Would you mind bringing the tree downstairs for me after breakfast?"

"I'd be happy to." Nick got out a mug and filled

it with coffee from the pot. "But what do you think about cutting a tree, like we used to do? I checked, and we don't need a permit as long as we follow the guidelines, and I'll be here to keep it watered until Christmas."

She tilted her head and looked at him, an odd little smile on her face. "You looked up the rules on cutting a tree?"

"Yeah. Why?" Nick asked.

"Because you used to tease Coop mercilessly about our Charlie Brown Christmas trees."

That was true. The native spruce trees in this area of Alaska tended to have wide spaces between the rows of branches, and the branches themselves were irregular, not neatly pyramidal like the ones from Christmas tree farms. But he also remembered the fun they had together on their tree-cutting expeditions. "I had to give him a hard time whenever I got the chance. But that doesn't mean I didn't like them. And the kids are old enough for a short snowshoe trek. It'll be fun."

"What'll be fun?" Max asked as he came into the kitchen, yawning.

Emily set a trivet on the countertop. "Nick was thinking we might want to cut a fresh tree this year."

"Cool!" Max opened the pantry door.

"I've got a cheddar, bacon, and egg strata in the oven," Emily warned. "It will be ready in five minutes."

"Okay," Max replied, but he came back from the pantry with a bagel and a jar of peanut butter. He reached into the drawer for a butter knife. "When are we going to cut the tree?"

Lyla skipped in. "We're cutting a tree?"

"I guess we are." Emily pushed a bowl of oranges closer to Lyla. "We should probably go right after breakfast, so we'll have time to set it up and decorate it this afternoon."

"Yay!" Lyla sat at one of the stools beside the island and peeled an orange.

The timer went off, and Emily pulled the dish from the oven. The aroma of bacon mingled with the cinnamon, apples, and coffee.

"Can we get a really, really big tree?" Lyla popped a section of orange into her mouth.

"We only have eight-foot ceilings," Emily pointed out. "Between the stand and the angel on top, we can't go much over six feet."

"We could put it in the middle of the stairs," Lyla suggested. It was true—there was a landing halfway up where the stairs made a ninety-degree turn and the vaulted ceiling above the stairs was easily twelve feet higher than the landing. But the landing was only about four feet square.

"If we did that, we'd have to install a fireman's pole for you to get down from your bedroom," Nick said.

"Fun! But how would we get up again?" Two cute little lines appeared between her eyebrows, miniature replicas of Emily's concentration lines. "Oh, we could hang rope ladders from our windows."

Max rolled his eyes. "He's joking."

Nick chuckled and ruffled her hair. "Yeah, probably best not to block the stairs. But don't worry, we'll find a good tree that fits in the living room."

An hour later, they'd all finished breakfast and gotten dressed. Emily filled a thermos with hot chocolate, while Nick collected four pairs of snowshoes from the garage along with a folding shovel, a sled, and some straps to attach the tree to the rack on top of the minivan. He debated taking Coop's chain saw, but if no one had used it for the past two years, it was unlikely to start easily. Instead, he threw a bow saw and a pruning saw in the back of the minivan, next to the emergency kit that always lived there. Emily, Nala, and the kids came into the garage just as he closed the tailgate. He reopened it to let the dog jump in and closed it again. Everyone else piled into the car.

"Where are we going?" Emily asked Nick, who was in the front passenger seat.

"Head toward Palmer," Nick said, consulting his phone.

Emily punched a button, and "Sleigh Ride" poured through the speakers of the car as she pulled out of the driveway. The glittery snowflake ornament that hung from the rearview mirror must have also been an air freshener, because the car smelled like pine and peppermint. Nick wouldn't have been surprised to see a sleigh pulled by reindeer at the side of the road, despite the fact that wild caribou were at least three hundred miles north of them. On the other hand, they would be driving not too far from a farm in Palmer that raised European reindeer, so maybe that wasn't such a far-out possibility.

Emily followed Nick's directions to a parking lot that served several trailheads in the foothills. This higher area had a lot more snow on the ground than Swan Falls, so it was good he'd thought to bring snowshoes. Lyla had a little trouble getting hers on, but Nick helped her and soon they were tramping along the trail into the woods. Emily carried the saws while Nick pulled the sled. Nala quickly learned that the walking was easier when she let the snowshoers go first and tamp down the snow. They'd only gone about fifty feet before Lyla stopped in front of a tree. "This one's pretty."

"We need to leave the pretty trees next to the trail for everyone to enjoy," Emily told her. "Once we get a little farther from the parking lot, we'll go off trail to find a tree." She led the way, with Lyla behind her, then Max, Nick, and Nala. Before long, Emily branched off from the main trail and onto a narrow game trail into the woods. It was tricky to get through because the brush and twigs grabbed at their snowshoes, but they walked on. Nick eventually picked up the empty sled and carried it under his arm to avoid tangling it in the twigs. Emily stopped in front of a five-foot spruce. "How about this one?"

Max went to stand beside it. "Nope. Not tall enough."

"Okay." Emily continued onward.

"That one!" Lyla called.

But when they examined it, Max nixed it as well. "Too many broken branches. We can find a better one."

Emily led them around a big mound of snow, probably hiding a boulder, and stopped so suddenly that Nick stepped on the back of Max's snowshoes and almost sent both of them tumbling. A fallen tree was blocking the game trail. "Oops, let's head back," Nick said, but Emily shook her head.

"No, look." She pointed to the other side of the fallen tree, where a seven-foot white spruce stood. "Can we get to it?"

Nick came forward and pushed on the fallen birch. It seemed solid. He took off his snowshoes and vaulted over the trunk, landing and sinking up to his knees in the snow. "Next," he called.

With a little boost from her mother, Lyla managed to climb onto the tree trunk. Nick lifted her down. Max followed, and jumped down without Nick's help, creating a poof of snow as he landed. Emily passed all four pairs of snowshoes to Nick and then encouraged the dog. "Come on, Nala. Jump."

The old dog tried, but she fell back. "You can do it," Emily encouraged her, and this time, when Nala jumped, Emily gave her a push from the back and Nala scrambled to the top of the downed trunk and over the other side. Emily followed, pushing herself on top of the tree and then throwing her legs over so that she was sitting on the trunk. Nick reached up and lifted her by the waist to deposit her gently onto the snow. For a moment, their faces were only inches apart, and when their eyes met, he felt the oddest thing—like a connection that he didn't want to break.

Then she blinked and turned toward the spruce tree. "Is it as pretty from the back?"

Max, who had put on his snowshoes, tramped around the tree. "It looks good."

"I love it," Lyla said.

"Sounds like we have a winner." Nick took the shovel from his pack and assembled it. There was already a well under the tree where the branches had prevented the snow from getting to the ground, but he and Max took turns digging out around the tree until the well was big enough for Nick to get in close and cut the tree off just a few inches above ground level with his bow saw. When he was about three-fourths of the way through, he stopped. "Everybody back on the other side of the fallen tree, please." He helped them all climb over, including the dog, passed them their snowshoes, and went back to finish felling the tree.

"Ti-im-be-e-rr," Emily called as it began to sway.

With a crack, the last inch of wood broke and the tree fell. Nick used the saw to neaten up the trunk before dragging it to the fallen birch. It took a couple of tries to get a good hold before he could lift it, but then he was able to push it up and over the fallen tree. Emily dragged it out of the way, so that he could join them on the other side. They set the spruce on the sled, but when they tried to drag it, it kept catching on brush and falling off the sled.

Emily laughed. "I'd forgotten when I came this way that we'd have a tree with us going out."

"No problem. You take the sled, and I'll get the tree." Nick grabbed it by the trunk and dragged it through the woods until they were back on the main trail, where they could use the sled to pull it to the car.

"'O Christmas tree. O Christmas tree,'" Lyla sang, and Emily joined in, off-key, but with great enthusiasm. Nick couldn't help but join them, and even Max sang along, at least until he spotted a couple of teenagers skiing up the trail toward them. Max immediately stopped singing and stepped off to one side, pretending fascination with the bark of an alder tree and distancing himself from the rest of the group until they had passed on by.

Nick hid a smile. He had the strongest urge to break into a song-and-dance routine loud enough to make the teenagers look back, but that might have caused Max to actually die from embarrassment.

They made it to the parking lot, and with Emily's help, Nick got the tree positioned onto the roof and strapped it in place. They continued singing carols all the way home. As they arrived in Swan Falls, Emily said, "What theme should we go with this year for the tree?"

"Your tree has themes?" Nick asked. Wasn't Christmas theme enough?

"Sure." Emily flashed him a grin. "We could do nature, or *Candy Land*—"

"Last year we did snowmen," Lyla told Nick.

"Let's do candy with lots of real candy canes," Max suggested.

"We can use candy canes whichever theme we choose. You'll just eat them all before Christmas, anyway." Emily pulled into the driveway and pushed the garage button. "I was thinking maybe rustic—"

"Stop," Nick commanded.

Emily instantly hit the brakes and looked at him in alarm.

"What? You don't like rustic?"

"Don't drive into the garage. The tree is tied on top of the car and it's too tall."

"Oh, wow." Emily thunked her hand against her forehead. "I totally would have wrecked the garage door."

"And the tree," Lyla added.

"Too many things on your mind," Nick said,

as Emily put the van into Park and turned off the engine.

"You're right," Emily said as they all climbed out. "I need to focus on one task at a time. I'll get lunch going if you three will unload the tree and bring it in."

"Sounds like a plan," Nick agreed.

By the time they'd wrestled the tree into the house and managed to get it standing up straight to Lyla's satisfaction, Emily had tomato soup and grilled cheese sandwiches ready. Over lunch, the kids and Emily continued their good-natured argument over the theme, landing on woodland birds. Once they'd finished cleaning up the kitchen, Emily took Nick upstairs to the storage room behind her closet. From the shelves under the worktable, she took three bins. The candy-stripe-bordered labels on the ends read Max, Lyla, and Mantel. Then from the shelves against the wall, she selected bins labeled Traditional, Rustic, Avian, Red, and Greenery, piling them high on the table. She moved to the other side of the room. "White lights or colored?" she asked.

"Um, white?" Nick really had no idea how this was all going to work, but he figured if they were going woodland, white lights would look like stars.

"I think so, too." She piled another bin on top of the stack. Finally, she opened the shopping bag Janice had asked Nick to leave there. "Oh, cute! The kids will love these."

Nick stacked three of the bins. "Lyla and Max have their own ornaments?"

"Yeah, they get a couple of new ones every year. The plan is that when they're old enough to move out, they can take their ornaments with them and have a starter set."

"I like that idea." Nick picked up the stack. "These all need to go downstairs?"

"Yeah. I'll call the kids to help us."

It took several trips, but eventually they had all the bins downstairs. Nick and the kids had put the tree in front of a window at one end of the living room, and while it was true that the tiers of branches each had several inches of trunk in between, they were full, green, and fragrant. Nala must have liked it, because she'd dragged her bed from the laundry room and was now sleeping next to the branches.

Emily pulled a step stool from the closet and placed it near the tree. "Now, to set the mood. Nick, could you please build a fire?"

"Sure." He crossed behind her to get to the fireplace, but not before he'd gotten a glimpse of something called Tree Decorating Playlist on her phone. Of course, Emily would have her own playlist all ready for the occasion. The only question was, did she use the same list or make a fresh one every year? She pressed Play and a hidden speaker piped "Deck the Halls" into the living room. While he placed the logs and kindling, she disappeared into the kitchen for a few minutes and came back with a tray holding four red-and-white mugs of mulled cider, which she set on the coffee table between the couch and the fireplace.

Nick struck a match, lit the fire, and closed the screen. He turned. "Okay, what's first?"

"Lights," Emily declared. After moving Nala and her bed to the rug in front of the poinsettia on the hearth, they formed a circle around the tree and passed strings of lights from hand to hand, wrapping as they went, until the whole tree was covered. Max started to plug them in, but Emily stopped him. "Wait. I got a smart plug for this, too." She retrieved it from the kitchen drawer and plugged the lights into it. Then she pulled up something on her phone and handed it to Max. "Okay, touch the button." He did, and the tree lit up, the white lights twinkling like a million stars against the dark needles.

"Pretty," Lyla exclaimed. "I like the real tree."

"Me, too," Emily said. "Oh, I've got a joke for this. What did the beaver say to the Christmas tree?"

"What?" Lyla demanded.

"It was nice gnawing you." Emily grinned at the groans and opened Janice's shopping bag. "Gramma got us each a new ornament before she left. Let's see, this must be Max's." She passed him a soccer ball wearing a Santa hat. "And Lyla's."

Hers was a singing angel. "And this one must be for Nick." She handed him a blue floatplane.

"Wow." Nick looked at the ornament. "I don't think anyone has ever given me my own ornament before."

"Then it's overdue," Emily said. "Look at this. She got me a snowman made of gears. Isn't that clever? Okay, let's hang them. One. Two. Three!" On three, they all found a branch and hung their ornaments on the tree. Then Emily opened the bins, and everyone went to work hanging the rest of the ornaments. It seemed that the bird theme wasn't as rigid as Nick had assumed. They still hung red balls, keepsake ornaments, and all kinds of hand-crafted ornaments the kids had made over the years, and then Emily and the kids tucked a dozen or so birdhouses in among the branches. But the best part was when they wired fake cardinals, jays, owls, and chickadees to the ends of branches, so that it looked as if they were perched all over the tree. It was the perfect theme for a wild spruce tree.

When they'd attached all the birds, Emily stepped back. "It looks amazing, but we still need a topper. Star or angel?"

"Angel," Lyla said, but Max shook his head.

"We need a raven. They always sit at the very top of trees so they can see everything."

"You're right," Emily said. "Hey, you know what? I think we have one in with the Halloween decorations. I'll get it." She ran upstairs.

Nick sipped his cider. The kids turned a couple of the ornaments so that they were facing out. Emily came trotting downstairs, holding an almost life-size raven. "Nick, can you reach?"

Nick climbed onto the step stool and set the raven in place, using the wire on the plastic feet to anchor it. Before he climbed down, he noticed a miniature Santa hat ornament and perched it on the raven's head, earning a snort from Emily. He went to stand behind Emily and the kids while they admired their handiwork.

"It's perfect," Lyla declared.

Nick couldn't have agreed more.

CHAPTER TEN

MONDAY AFTERNOON WAS the first day of pageant practice. Nick was there, along with a half-dozen parents, in the school's multipurpose room that served as a cafeteria as well as an assembly room, with a stage up front shielded by dark blue curtains. Students milled around, making more noise than Nick would have thought possible. And this was just the fourth through sixth graders. The younger students wouldn't be joining the rehearsals until later in the month, according to Lyla's teacher.

The door opened and a couple of people wheeled in a garden cart stacked with lumber. Nick went to hold the door. The person backing into the room nodded to thank him, and Nick recognized Nathan Swan, from Swan Lodge. A hammer hung from a loop on his tool belt.

"Oh, hi, Nick. I didn't know you were going to be here," Nathan said as he guided the cart toward the back wall. A woman Nick didn't recognize pushed the cart next to one already there filled with art supplies. "This is Skye Harper, the art teacher here. Skye, Nick is taking care of Max and Lyla."

"I know. I was at the field trip." Ms. Harper smiled at Nick. "Hi, Nick. Thanks for volunteering. We're going to need all the help we can get. I'm helping the fifth graders paint scenery today."

"And I'm building the supports to mount it," Nathan explained.

The principal stepped onto the stage, but the noise didn't stop. After a moment, she clapped her hands in a particular pattern. The teachers, and some of the kids, immediately clapped back, repeating the pattern. Then she clapped in a different pattern, and this time most of the kids clapped back. By the third time, conversations had stopped, and the students were ready to listen. Clever. Too bad Nick couldn't do the same when he needed to get passengers' attention.

"Good morning," the principal said. "And thanks to you parent volunteers. The Winter Jubilation Pageant is a big project, and we can't do it without everyone's help." The students started to shift, but she held up her hand. "Please wait until I've finished talking to take your places. Fourth graders, you will be joining Ms. Brooks right over there." She paused while the music teacher off to the right of the stage raised her hand. "Sixth grade, you're with Mrs. Kaiser up on the stage. Fifth grade today is backstage support. You're with Ms. Harper. Okay, everyone please report to your groups."

The room erupted as all the kids pushed past each other to their various groups. Nick spotted Lyla heading toward the chorus and Max jumping up on the stage. The principal said something to him, and he nodded and disappeared behind the curtains. A minute later, the curtains opened.

Nick had not been assigned to anything as far as he knew, but Lyla's teacher, Ms. Englund, came toward him and handed him a script. "We have you as prompter," she told him. "Keeping everyone on track with entrances and exits and helping if they forget their lines. Is that okay with you?"

"That's fine."

"Good. But we won't need you for that today, while we're doing tryouts, so if you'd like to help with building the scenery supports, I'm sure they would appreciate it."

"No problem." Working with his hands sounded more productive, anyway. He moved to the back, where the art teacher had taped large blocks of paper on the wall and was giving students instructions. A safe distance away from the students, Nathan measured a two-by-four. Nick went to him. "I've been assigned to help you build screens."

"Great." Nathan marked an *X* on the board and retracted the measuring tape. "I've cut the boards to length, but we'll need to drill holes for the bolts that hold it together, and to install casters." He waved a hand toward the students, who were putting on aprons and picking up paintbrushes. "The plan is that we build these rolling screens while the kids paint the scenery. Once the paint is dry, we'll clip the papers to the screens. That way, they can use the same screens in the future for whatever play they need."

"Makes sense to me. How can I help?"

Nathan handed him a measured drawing. "Take a look at the plans. If you can measure and mark the spots, I'll start drilling."

"I can do that." For the next two hours, Nick and Nathan worked together, first assembling a rolling wooden base for each screen, and then putting together a lightweight fabric-covered frame, not unlike a painting canvas, which would eventually support the paper scenes. By the time they had finished getting all the frames attached to the bases and installed clips around the edges to hold the paper, the students had finished painting scenery and were cleaning their brushes. The teacher was adding a few finishing touches. A shadow here, a highlight there, and suddenly the simple shapes became almost three-dimensional. While it was obvious the scenes had been painted by children, they were quite effective, with white birch trunks and spruce boughs giving a good impression of what it was like inside a forest.

The principal announced that it was time to go back to class, and once again pandemonium erupted, but within probably two minutes, the different grades were lined up and their teachers were leading them out of the multipurpose room. "That's actually pretty impressive," Nick said, as he swept up the sawdust they'd created.

"Yeah." Nathan packed his tools into his belt. "You know, I'd never been around kids much before this summer. I didn't realize how quiet and easygoing Paisley is until we had a family group with like eighteen kids staying at the lodge. It was like herding cats. Fortunately, Amanda knew how to keep them occupied."

"It must have been quite a change for you, from single guy in Arizona to married with a kid in Alaska."

"I never saw it coming. In fact, after a bad experience with a former fiancée, I'd made up my mind that I'd never marry." He laughed. "Never say never."

"So how did you learn to be a dad?" Nick asked, suddenly curious. "I mean, did you just do what your parents did, or—"

"Not really. My mom left when I was young, and my dad—well, he tried, but he was a busy man. I got my best life lessons here at the lodge, staying with my great-uncle and his wife every summer. They made time for me. Made me feel wanted."

Nick nodded. Janice and Coop had been like that for him.

"It's really not that hard," Nathan continued. "When you care for a kid, it comes naturally to want to be there for them. Just like you're there for Lyla and Max."

Filling in for a couple weeks was hardly the same, but it was nice to hear Nathan thought he was doing okay. Nick picked up a couple of spare bolts and handed them over.

"Thanks. And thanks for all the help today." The school bell rang, dismissing the students. Nathan picked up a bucket with leftover supplies.

"You're welcome," Nick said as they made their way from the multipurpose room to the parking lot. "See you here next week, I guess."

"Oh, I was just in charge of building the screens. But I'm sure I'll see you around soon. 'Bye, Nick." They went to their respective cars and Nick followed Nathan to get into the pickup line. Emily didn't go to the slope until Wednesday, but she had some sort of work meeting in the office in Anchorage today and wouldn't be getting home until around six, so Nick was handling kid pickup and dinner. When he reached the front of the line, Lyla and Max climbed into the car.

"Since Mom's working in Anchorage, are we getting pizza today?" Max asked hopefully.

"No. I'm making dinner," Nick replied.

Max groaned. "What are we having?"

"Chicken fajitas."

Max perked up. "With guacamole?"

"Of course."

"All right." Max sat back.

"How did tryouts go?" Nick asked. "I saw you up on stage, but I couldn't see what part you got."

Max shrugged. "We just read lines. They'll assign the parts next week."

"We learned a new song in chorus," Lyla said, "and we've got six more to learn. That's a lot."

"It is a lot." Nick pulled into the garage. "I didn't realize how much work goes into something like this."

They went inside. Max headed straight for the pantry, but Lyla stopped to look at a recipe Emily had printed out and left on the kitchen island. "What is *spitzbuben?*"

"Some kind of German Christmas cookie. Your Gramma sent the recipe."

"Ooh. Let's make it," Lyla suggested. "We can surprise Mommy."

"Why not?" Nick already had the vegetables sliced and the chicken marinating in the refrigerator. He looked at the recipe and then checked the pantry and cabinets. "We'll need to run to the store. I'm not sure if the mercantile will have almond meal or not, but we can check."

"We need more cheesy popcorn, anyway," Max said as he wadded up the bag he'd been eating out of. "Let's go."

Swan Falls Mercantile had a special display of Christmas baking supplies, and they found everything they needed there, including raspberry jam.

"Do you have cookie cutters at home?" Nick asked Lyla.

"Lots," she assured him.

Max showed up with three bags of popcorn, which seemed excessive, but considering how fast he went through food, Nick decided to go with it. Back at the house, Nick unpacked the groceries. "Why don't you two get your homework done and then we can bake the cookies?"

Max grabbed one of the new bags of popcorn and they both disappeared upstairs to their rooms, while Nick prepared to bake. He'd just read through the cookie recipe and set out all the ingredients when Lyla returned. "My homework is all done."

"Good timing. Let me check on Max." He found the boy on his bed reading the book propped on his pillow. Nick started to slip away so as not to disturb Max, until he noticed the book was a graphic novel. Not that there was anything wrong with that, unless Max hadn't done his homework. He stepped into the room and Max looked up. "All done?" Nick asked.

"Yeah," Max answered and then added, "Almost."

"Meaning?"

"I just have to write a paragraph about a book I want to read. In two weeks, I have to report on it."

"What book are you doing?"

Max held up the graphic novel. "This one."

"And your teacher okayed using this book?"

"Not yet. That's what the paragraph is for."

"What if she doesn't? Do you have a backup?"

Max shrugged. "Not really."

Nick remembered seeing a shelf of Alaska-themed books in his room, which had been Coop's office. "Have you ever read *The Call of the Wild*?" he asked.

"No. Is it good?"

"It was your dad's favorite book when he was about your age. I think there's a copy downstairs."

"Dad's favorite?" Max looked thoughtful. "Did you ever read it?"

"Yeah. It's good."

"Okay," Max said. "I'll check it out if this one won't work."

Nick nodded. "Lyla and I will get started on the cookies. If you want to help, you can come down when you're finished writing." He picked up the half bag of popcorn on the bed beside Max and carried it out.

Had mentioning Coop's favorite book been the right move there? Nick didn't want to make Max sad, but sharing his memories of Coop felt right.

When he got back to the kitchen, Lyla had pulled up a step stool and was already measuring ingredients into the bowl of the mixer Nick had set up.

"'Chill for one hour,'" Nick said, reading aloud after she'd mixed everything together.

Lyla scraped the dough off the mixing paddle

into the bowl. "We can put it in the freezer for fifteen minutes instead."

"Really? Does that work?" Nick asked.

"Mommy and me do it all the time," Lyla assured him. She opened one of the cabinet doors under the island. Then she checked the other one. "I know they're in here somewhere." She removed a stack of mixing bowls and crawled inside. "Oh, here they are." She backed out, carrying a plastic bin labeled "Cookie Cutters."

She sorted through the collection, looking at each cutter, before setting aside two sizes of hearts.

Once the dough was chilled, Nick used a rolling pin to flatten it. "These are sandwich cookies, so only half of them have holes."

"I know." Lyla cut hearts from the dough and used the small heart to create the openings. With Nick's help, she transferred the cookies to a baking sheet. "Me and Daddy used to make cookies together," she commented.

"Oh." Nick glanced over. "I didn't realize that was a special thing you did with your dad. I hope you don't mind that I'm the one making cookies with you today."

"No," Lyla set a cookie on the tray. "I like being with you, too. And besides, Daddy always said cut-out cookies are too fussy. He liked chocolate chip cookies, or those peanut butter ones with a chocolate piece in the middle. I had to wait until Mommy came home to make cut-out cookies."

"We could make chocolate chip or peanut butter later this week, if you wanted," Nick offered.

"I like these better. They're prettier." She beamed a smile his way. "Thanks for making them with me."

Nick could have sworn he could feel his heart growing inside his chest. If this was all it took to make Lyla happy, he would cheerfully bake cutout cookies with her every day of the year.

Max came wandering into the kitchen. "I'm all done." He leaned past Lyla and chose a shark-shaped cutter.

"That's not Christmassy," Lyla protested.

"As Christmassy as your hearts," Max argued.

"Max can use whatever cutter he wants," Nick ruled.

"Cool." Max used a small circle to cut a hole in the middle of his shark.

Lyla rolled her eyes and cut more hearts. Nick put the first batch into the oven.

While the kids finished cutting cookies, Nick started cooking the chicken and vegetables for fajitas. Once the cookies were cool, Max and Lyla sandwiched the baked cookies with jam in the middle, the holes they'd cut in the top cookies exposing the red filling.

The sound of the garage door alerted them to Emily's return. Lyla quickly arranged some of her heart-shaped cookies onto a tray with a holly border. Emily came through the laundry room and stepped into the kitchen. "What smells so good?"

"Cookies!" Lyla chanted, holding out the tray. "What are they called, Nick?"

"Spitzbuben," he said, no doubt butchering the pronunciation.

"Spitzbuben," Lyla repeated.

"They're beautiful." Emily's voice sounded a little raspy. Were those tears welling up in her eyes?

Before Nick could ask Emily what was wrong, Max stepped up holding one of the cookies he'd made. "Look, Mom. Sharks, with a harpoon hole in the middle."

Emily snorted. "Gross."

Max grinned as though she'd given him a wonderful compliment. "I know."

"You guys." Emily took the tray from Lyla and set it aside, then pulled them both in for a hug. As she pulled them close, her eyes met Nick's. They were definitely wet. *Thank you*, she mouthed silently. After a long hug, she stepped back. "Okay. Let me hang up my coat. I'm guessing that spicy smell isn't from the cookies."

"Chicken fajitas," Nick said. "They'll be ready in five minutes."

"Yum. Let's eat our fajitas and then we can taste your…what are they again?"

"Spitzbuben," Max and Lyla said in unison.

"Right. Max, you set the table, and Lyla, pour the milk. I'll be right back, and we can all have dinner together."

CHAPTER ELEVEN

SNOWFLAKES DRIFTED SOFTLY outside the kitchen window the next afternoon. It had been snowing on and off all day. Emily scrubbed a few Yukon gold potatoes as part of her dinner prep. She'd followed her usual last-day-before-work routine: catching up on the laundry, changing the sheets, scrubbing the bathrooms, making sure the calendar was up-to-date. Generally just making sure the household chores were done before Janice took over. Except this time, it wouldn't be Janice. It would be Nick.

She put her fists on her lower back and stretched. Today had been particularly hectic since she'd had to go into the office in Anchorage yesterday. The beauty of her current job on the North Slope was that normally after working full out for two weeks, the other two weeks were completely free to devote to the kids. But occasionally, something would come up. Yesterday, it had been an expert flying in to explain a new procedure they would be implementing for the first time during her shift rotation. The company had developed a promising new tool for cleaning mineral deposits that clogged the perforations inside the pipe of an oilwell, and this would be their first time to try it onsite.

And while she was excited about the new technology and eager to learn, it had pulled her away from home, away from her kids. And then, on the drive from Anchorage to Swan Falls, she'd started to worry. Could Nick really take care of two kids for two weeks with no experience? What if something went wrong? And it was so close to Christmas, with all the extra time and effort that entailed. Should she have hired a professional?

But then, she'd arrived home to find the house clean, dinner ready, and Nick and the kids making Christmas cookies, something she hadn't found time to do, and she knew she'd made the right choice. Nick loved those kids, and they loved him. Janice was having a blast on her river cruise. And Emily could report to work tomorrow with an easy mind.

The house seemed particularly quiet today. Nick was in Anchorage to have lunch with some pilot buddies, check in with his eye doctor, and run errands of some sort. She didn't expect him until dinnertime. Lyla had gone home with Paisley after school to play with the new puppy. And Max was at Ian's house, starting a team project they were working on together. She made a mental note to remind Max about getting supplies he might need before the project was due. Dina said she'd drop the boys at soccer practice later, so Emily just needed to pick him up at the school gym when she brought Lyla home.

Nala, who was curled up under the kitchen table, suddenly whimpered and paddled her feet, probably dreaming of chasing squirrels, or maybe running with the kids. Unexpectedly, the garage door sounded, and Nala opened her eyes and blinked.

A moment later, Nick came into the kitchen, carrying an armload of shopping bags. "Hi."

"Hi. What have you got there?"

He made a show of clutching the bags closer. "Don't you know not to be asking questions like that this close to Christmas?" He grinned and went to set the bags at the base of the stairs and shed his coat.

"I didn't expect you until later," Emily called. "Did you get all your errands done?"

"Pretty much." He returned to the kitchen. "I didn't want to be on the highway after dark."

Emily frowned. "Still seeing those halos around headlights?"

"A little bit."

"What did the doctor say about that?" she asked.

"He's still hopeful they'll clear up soon. The good news is my vision is now 20/20. The bad news is I still can't fly until these halos are gone." He gave a little shrug. "But there's nothing I can do about that except wait. By the way, I noticed a security pin pad in the laundry room. Is there something I need to know about that?"

She nodded. "The code is 0723."

"Your birthday."

"Right." Imagine him remembering that. "But we never use it as an alarm system. We got it when Lyla was four. One night, Nala was barking and then stopped, and when we got up to check on her, we found the front door open, and Lyla and Nala outside. For some reason, Lyla had decided to go for a walk with the dog at one in the morning. So we put sensors on the doors and set our phones to alert us if the doors open between ten and seven. But she never did it again."

Nick chuckled. "It might come in handy once they're teenagers, though. Just in case they decide to sneak out."

"I hope not. Did you sneak out when you were a teenager?"

He shrugged. "My mom didn't care when I came and went." He frowned momentarily, but then his face brightened. "How can I help with dinner?"

"I think I'm done. Potatoes are ready to cook. Chicken tenderloins are marinating in buttermilk, and I just need to roll them in panko crumbs before they go into the air fryer tonight. The beans are snapped and ready to steam. And we have those cookies for dessert. I thought about making biscuits, but Max won't want to wait that long after soccer practice."

Nick chuckled. "The way he eats these days, I figure he's getting ready to shoot up about a foot in the next few months. Oh, by the way, he's doing a book report on a graphic novel. Is that allowed?"

"Yes. I checked with Mrs. Kaiser."

"Okay, good." The dryer buzzed, indicating that the last load was dry. Emily started toward the laundry room, but Nick put his hand on her arm. "I'll get it. You keep on doing what you're doing."

"No, I've done all I can until time to cook dinner."

"In that case, why don't you relax for a few minutes?" Nick suggested. "I know you've been going full-steam all day. Put your feet up. I'll take care of this load."

She looked down at his hand, still resting on her arm. Despite the thick wool of her sweater, she swore she could feel his warmth on her skin. "You've had a long day, too."

He shook his head. "I sat in a restaurant, then sat in a doctor's office, then did a little shopping, and then I sat in a car. I need to move. You need to recharge." He brushed past her into the laundry room.

Bemused, she wandered into the living room and snuggled into the chair that directly faced the Christmas tree, spreading a fleece throw over her lap. Ordinarily, she never sat down in the middle of the day. But the twinkling lights caught her eye, and she took a minute just to admire the tree. That raven on top really was an inspired choice. As she sat, the cares of the day seemed to melt away, replaced by the peace of the season. Nala padded in from the kitchen and curled up on top of Emily's feet.

Nick walked into the living room, with a laundry basket balanced on his hip and a mug in his hand. He set the mug on a coaster on the table next to her along, with a tiny dish with Sip and Be Merry inscribed inside. "Let that steep for four minutes," he ordered, and then he was gone, carrying the laundry basket up the stairs.

She checked the tag on the teabag—peppermint. Nice. The book Nick had gotten for her still sat on the table. She opened it to the first page. Five minutes later—well, actually fifty-three minutes according to her phone—a chime went off to remind her it was time to pick up the kids. Nick had drifted through the living room a time or two while she was reading but she wasn't sure where he'd gotten to. "Nick?"

He didn't answer, but she heard a thumping noise on the porch. She crossed the living room to the front door and found him outside, shoveling the steps and front walk. He looked up. "Hi. You heading out to get the kids?"

"Yes. I should be back in about thirty minutes and then I'll make dinner." A flutter of black wings caught their attention, and a raven landed on the porch railing. The bird turned its head, studying them with a beady eye. "Can I help you?" Emily asked.

The raven squawked and then flew to the ground under one of the birdfeeders, where she'd spilled some peanuts while filling them earlier in the day.

"I think he's saying 'thank you,'" Nick said.

"You're welcome," Emily called and went back inside to grab her coat and bag. The weariness she'd felt earlier was gone. She'd long ago learned when working twelve-hour days on the slope that breaks were important to keep her operating at top efficiency. Why didn't she apply that knowledge when she was home?

Max was all packed up and ready to go when she arrived. She called a thank-you to Dina and they drove out to Swan Lodge. It took a little longer to disengage Lyla from Paisley and Willow, the puppy, especially after Max joined in the romp, but they arrived home at six forty-five, ten minutes later than she'd estimated to Nick.

"How long until dinner?" Max asked.

"About thirty minutes," Emily replied.

When they walked through the door, Nick was in the kitchen, mashing potatoes. The air fryer was running, the smell of fresh bread lingered in the air, and a pot with a steamer basket was on the stove next to the potato pot. "Dinner will be done by the time you hang up your coats and wash your hands," Nick told them.

But Emily had intended to make dinner. She always made dinner the night before she left. The kids ran off to put up their coats, but Emily lingered. "You didn't have to do this."

"I know, but I figured you'd all be hungry, and you already had everything prepared and ready to cook." He transferred the green beans from the steamer to a serving bowl, stirred in a small lump of butter, and set it on the table. Then he stopped to look at her, his head tilted to the right. "I'm sorry. Did I do something wrong?"

"No, of course not," she said quickly. Clearly, he'd just been trying to help. She put away her coat and washed her hands. When she got back to the kitchen, Max was pouring milk, Lyla was setting the table, and Nick was stacking chicken tenderloins onto a plate.

"Biscuits are in the oven keeping warm," he told Emily. She grabbed some hot pads and took the baking sheet from the oven, then pushed the biscuits into a napkin-lined basket Nick had set out. Meanwhile, he set a bowl of mashed potatoes and the plate of chicken on the table.

Everyone dug in. After tasting the chicken, Lyla said, "This is really good, Nick."

"Isn't it?" he answered. "I'm going to have to get your mom to give me the recipe for the marinade she used."

Okay, that was nice of Nick to share the credit for dinner. And the goal was to make sure the kids had a good dinner, not to score mom points. She should be happy he'd stepped in and had dinner ready to serve, so that Max didn't have time to fill up on junk while she cooked. She was happy. It just felt a little strange. Like she was losing control.

After dinner, homework and showers took up most of the evening, but Emily made sure to leave a little time for the whole family to sit in front of the fire and read aloud from the *Adventure Kids* book. Then she tucked Max and Lyla into bed. Lyla gave her a big hug and smiled when Emily kissed her forehead. Max squirmed a little at the kiss, but then he reached up for a second hug before she left him. This was the hardest part of her job, knowing that tomorrow she wouldn't be the one tucking them in at night. But after what she'd seen, she was confident they'd be fine with Nick.

When she went downstairs again, Nick was looking out of the living room window. Without turning, he asked, "Kids in bed?"

"Yep. Did it stop snowing yet?" If they were getting a lot more snow tonight, she would need to leave early to get to the airport tomorrow.

"It stopped, and the moon is out. Come see."

She walked over to the window. "Oh, wow." A coat of fresh snow covered the colored lights on the evergreen trees out front, diffusing the points of light so that the trees seemed to glow all over. Moonlight bounced off the snow and softly illuminated the whole scene with a silvery light. She opened the front door and stepped outside, onto the porch.

Nick followed her out, closing the door behind him, and stopped beside her next to the railing. The snow muffled all the usual sounds, giving the illusion that they were alone in this winter scene. "It's so quiet out here," Nick whispered.

"Peaceful," Emily agreed.

"Yeah. I confess, I had my doubts when you and Coop bought this place, but you were right. It's special."

"Mmm."

"Emily, um…" Nick paused, and then continued, "I'm sorry if I overstepped by making dinner. I didn't mean to upset your plans."

She turned to face him. "No, you did the right thing. It was just…making a special dinner for the kids the night before I leave is sort of my thing. It's really more for me than it is for them. Kind of a way to convince myself I'm a good mother."

"What? You're a great mother."

"But I'm only here half the time."

"But when you're here, you're engaged with them, and even when you're on the slope, you talk with them every evening. My mom was, in theory anyway, a stay-at-home mom, but I can't remember a single conversation where she asked about my day, or my friends, or what I was doing in school, or whether my soccer team won a game. She just didn't care the way you do. Your kids know you're there for them. They know you love them. Come here." He pulled her into a hug. "You're the best mom I know."

"Thanks." It felt so good, standing there in his arms. Neither of them had bothered with a coat, and Emily should have been cold, but Nick's words warmed her as much as his hug.

"Oh—" he said suddenly and backed off just far enough to look at her face. "Is that why you were upset when you got home yesterday and we'd made cookies? You wanted to be the one to make cookies with the kids?"

"No, just the opposite. I'd been fretting. Worrying that you'd be overwhelmed, that I'd made the wrong decision to leave the kids with you, and then I walk in and you're all working together. It was just so perfect it made me cry."

"So you're not worried anymore?"

"No." She grinned. "Well, maybe a teensy bit, but no more than I am every time I leave. You're a good man, Nick."

He smiled at her then. Their eyes met, and locked. And then, she couldn't say which of them leaned closer, but suddenly her arms were around his neck and his lips were pressed to hers, and something stirred inside her, something she hadn't felt in a long while. All her worries, her plans, her conflicted feelings melted away until it was just the two of them, holding on to each other. His lips were firm against hers, and yet soft. After a while, he leaned back just a bit and looked deep into her eyes, his face solemn, searching. And then he kissed her once again.

THE NEXT MORNING, Nick went through all the right motions of making sure the kids were up, checking the calendar to see if either of them needed a packed lunch and if there were any after-school activities, and slicing oranges for breakfast. But only half his mind was on his tasks. The other half was focused on Emily, on the way she moved, on the things she said, on each little expression that crossed her face as she went about her morning routine and got ready to head to the airport.

He'd give a lot to be able to read her mind right now. Had those kisses last night been a mistake? Probably. If nothing else, he'd made things awkward between them, which was the last thing he'd wanted to do. But at the same time, he couldn't summon up too much regret. Kissing Emily was like nothing he'd ever experienced before. They should probably talk about it, clear the air, but the kids were underfoot, and the morning rush was on. Private conversation would just have to wait.

Soon, everyone gathered in the kitchen. Nick set out the plate of oranges. Max went for his bagels and peanut butter, and Lyla took out her yogurt.

Nick got out a skillet and turned on a burner. "I'm making scrambled eggs," he said to the group in general, although he was looking at Emily. "Anyone want some?"

"I'm okay with this." Lyla opened her yogurt cup.

"I'll take one," Max said. "Extra protein."

"Eggs sound good," Emily agreed.

"I'm on it." Nick dropped a pat of butter into the skillet to melt. A few minutes later, he set a plate of golden eggs and buttered toast in front of Emily like an offering.

She took a bite. "Mmm. Tasty. Thanks."

Her smile made him feel like he'd been awarded a trophy. Mentally he rolled his eyes at himself, but he couldn't help it. He wanted to give Emily the world, but since he couldn't, he took pleasure in the small things. Like a nice breakfast. "You're welcome." He plated scrambled eggs for Max and then for himself.

"Max, your project with Ian is due Monday, right?" Emily asked.

"Uh-huh." Max took a big bite of bagel.

"Be sure to give Nick a heads-up if you're going to need any supplies. No waiting until the last minute. Okay?"

Max nodded his agreement and chewed. Eventually he said, "We're using Ian's Legos, but I'm not sure if we have enough."

Nick said, "Just let me know what you need."

"I will." Max peeled the rind off an orange slice and ate the rest in one bite.

Soon it was time to go. They all put on their coats and boots and went to the garage. Emily put her suitcase in her SUV and turned to the kids. "Hugs."

Max and Lyla each took a turn, and then Emily turned to Nick. She gave him an uncertain smile, but opened her arms. "Everybody gets hugs."

He wrapped his arms around her. She felt so good he would have liked to keep her there, but he made a point of letting go. "Safe travels."

"Thanks. Talk with you this evening. Love you, guys."

"Love you, too," Max and Lyla chimed as they climbed into the minivan.

Nick went around to the driver's seat, but he paused before he got in, looking over the roof at Emily. Their eyes met and held for a long moment before she turned and got into her car. Nick swallowed a sigh and did the same. He waited for her to back out first and watched in the rearview mirror as she turned and drove away.

"Are we going, or what?" Max's voice drew him out of his reverie.

"We are." Nick put the gearshift into Reverse. It was just him and the kids now. Time to earn his keep.

THAT NIGHT, EMILY lay on her bunk in the camp at Prudhoe Bay, staring at the ceiling. Ordinarily, she would be fast asleep by now, especially since she hadn't gotten a lot of sleep the night before, either, but her swirling thoughts kept her awake once again. She'd kissed Nick! Or he'd kissed her, she still wasn't sure. But either way, it had been entirely mutual and entirely unwise. And yet...

So many conflicting thoughts. Was it disloyal to Coop to kiss his best friend? Well-meaning people, including Janice, had assured her that Coop wouldn't want her to be alone. But Emily wasn't alone, she always said—she had the kids and Janice. And she was pretty sure they had in mind someone like Helen's nephew, someone with roots in the area, someone to build a life with. Not a confirmed bachelor like Nick, who was already committed to that job in Hawaii. But those kisses were amazing.

She loved Nick—as a friend, of course. He was great with Max and Lyla, and they adored him. So did Janice and Nala, for that matter. He'd demonstrated his willingness and ability to take care of everything while she was working. So why allow this attraction to muck things up?

On the internet call with the kids earlier this evening, she'd seen Nick milling around the kitchen behind them. Max talked about his school project, Lyla had chattered on about something she was creating in art class, but other than a general greeting, Nick hadn't participated in the call at all.

A two-tone chime sounded on her phone—the signal that a door had opened at home. Odd. She picked up her phone. A notice of the front door opening and closing was right on top. It was eleven thirty. Everyone should be in bed. She texted Nick. Door sensor open. Everything okay?

He texted back. All fine. I just stepped outside.

She could have left it at that, probably should have, but the urge to hear his voice overpowered her reason and she punched the dial icon. Nick picked up immediately. "Hi." Just one syllable, but the warmth in his tone felt like a hug.

"Hi. What are you doing up so late?" He was usually in bed by ten.

"I was watching some videos. Sorry I woke you. I forgot you'd get an alert if I open the door at night."

"I was awake," she admitted, but she didn't want to get into why she was awake. "What video? Something good?"

He laughed. "No, just videos on how to braid hair. Paisley called Lyla earlier. Apparently one of the girls in her class has proclaimed that all the girls should wear their hair in a braid tomorrow."

"What about the two girls with short hair?" Emily asked. "They shouldn't leave them out."

"Lyla was concerned about that, but Paisley assured her they've been consulted and are doing minibraids, whatever that means. Anyway, I watched a video, and that led to another, and another. I had no idea there were so many ways to braid hair. Some of them are like works of art. They should be on display in museums."

Emily smiled. "Just a simple three-part braid would be fine, I'm sure."

"Probably, but according to Lyla, Paisley is doing a French braid, and so I eventually found a really good video of French braiding for beginners and took some notes. I think I can duplicate that style, but then I saw the fishtail braids and they're pretty cool. I'm going to show Lyla in the morning and see which one she wants."

Emily's heart melted. How many men would go to all the trouble to learn to make fancy braids just to make a little girl happy? "You know what, Nick? You're far and away the best manny in Swan Falls."

He chuckled. "Since I'm ninety-nine percent sure I'm the only one, I think you're probably right."

"Best in Alaska, then."

"Now you're talking."

"Possibly best in the country? World? Universe?"

"Okay, enough with the flattery. It's just a braid, and I haven't even done it yet. It may be a complete failure."

"It won't be," she assured him. Nick was a capable man. When he decided to accomplish something, it got done.

"Fingers crossed, all the same." After a pause, he said, "Emily. About last night…"

Meaning those kisses that had been keeping her tossing and turning. "Yeah, maybe it would be better if we forget that ever happened."

"Um, okay. If that's what you want."

"I think it's for the best." And it would never happen again. Emily would see to that.

"Okay, then. I'll let you get some sleep. Good night, Emily."

"Good night, Nick." She put her phone on the shelf beside her bed and closed her eyes. The image of Nick braiding Lyla's hair played in her mind. She fell asleep with a smile on her face.

SATURDAY MORNING, Nick was running a little behind since he'd let the kids sleep in.

Lyla came running down the stairs, holding a comb. "Can you make two French braids today?" The fishtail braid had been such a hit that Lyla had demanded braids every morning since. In truth, the braid hadn't looked quite like the video. It listed a little to the left, and bits of hair kept slipping out, but Lyla loved it and that's what mattered. They'd sent a picture to Emily, who had showered them with praise.

Nick checked his watch. "I'm not sure we have time. Paisley's mom will be here to pick you up in ten minutes."

"Okay, just one, then. Ple-e-e-ease?"

How could he resist? "Sure." He picked up a comb from the coffee table, next to *Call of the*

Wild, which Max had started last night and seemed to be enjoying. "Max, have you got your stuff together?" he called, as he separated Lyla's hair into three parts.

"I'm ready," Max called back from the top of the stairs, wearing his blue soccer uniform and carrying his backpack.

"Did you remember to put your shin guards into your bag after I washed them?"

"Uh, yeah, I got them." But he pivoted back to his room. For some entirely different reason, no doubt.

Nick chuckled to himself and twisted the elastic around the end of Lyla's braid. "All done."

She ran to the mirror beside the front door and turned her head back and forth, trying to see the braid. Nick snapped a picture on his phone and showed her the back of her head. "Okay?"

"It looks good." She glanced out the front window. "There's Paisley. I'll get my stuff." She ran up to her room.

Paisley and her mom, Amanda, came to the porch. Nick opened the door before they could knock. "Come in. Lyla's just grabbing her backpack. I appreciate you taking her today. She wasn't really interested in hanging around Max's team's end-of-season pizza party."

"We're glad to have her." Amanda bent to pet Nala, who had come to greet the newcomers. "Peggy, our cook at the lodge, plans to put her and Paisley to work helping her bake Christmas cookies for the pageant on Christmas Eve."

"Lyla will love that."

Lyla came running down the stairs, backpack flapping from one shoulder. She dropped it, grabbed her coat from the closet, and ran to the door. "I'm ready!"

"Okay if I pick her up around four?" Nick asked Amanda.

"That's fine." Amanda told him. "We'll be home all day, so don't worry if you're late. Come on, girls. Peggy's waiting." She waved goodbye as she escorted the girls to her car.

Nick got Max rounded up and they drove to Wasilla, arriving at the gym just in time to watch the yellow team lose their game in a shootout.

Max pumped his fist. "That means if we win today's game, we win the season."

Nick smiled and put a hand on Max's shoulder. "You've got this."

He went to sit in the stands, purposely choosing a seat in an upper row after seeing Dina down front talking to one of the other moms. A minute later, though, Dina turned her head and saw him. She said something else to the mom up front and then came to sit beside Nick.

"Hi. Mind if I sit here? You look lonely by yourself."

"That's fine." He couldn't very well tell her to

back off. She was Max's best friend's mom, after all. He sat back to watch the kickoff.

It was a tight game. There were several good offensive runs from both teams, but by halftime, no one had managed to score.

While the kids gulped water and took a break, Dina turned to Nick. "So, I guess since Em's out of town, you've got the kids all weekend?"

"Uh-huh," he replied.

"Too bad. Ian's going to his dad's tonight, so I've got tomorrow free. I don't suppose you could get away?"

"Uh, no." Didn't he just say that? Besides, Nick would be leaving the state shortly, and even if he was interested in Dina, he wouldn't want to start anything knowing he'd be gone in a month.

And yet, he'd kissed Emily. If he truly cared about her—and he did—he shouldn't have been so careless about her feelings. She'd said to forget it, but did that mean it wasn't important to her, or that it was? Maybe he shouldn't have done it—but the way she'd looked at him, in that moment, in the moonlight, how could he resist? There was just something about Emily...

"Nick?" Dina was staring at him.

He blinked. "Sorry, I was thinking about something else. What did you say?"

"Never mind, the game is starting." With a little huff, Dina turned to watch.

Both teams struggled to score, until the goalie

kicked the ball to Max, who made a perfect pass, putting the ball right in front of Ian's feet as he dashed toward the goal. Two seconds later, the ball was in the back of the net and the parents from Max's team were on their feet, cheering.

The cheers changed to groans, however, when the sideline judge called the goal back, ruling that Ian had been offside when the ball left Max's foot. Dina made a megaphone with her hands. "Boo, bad call." She turned to Nick. "Can you believe that?"

Nick shrugged. "The line judge has a better view than we do."

Dina rolled her eyes and returned her attention to the game. Max managed to bring the ball down with his chest and pass it to the winger, who immediately passed to Ian, catching the defense flat-footed. Ian was able to basically tap it in.

This time, the score held. The two teams played hard but at the end of the game, Ian's goal was the only one scored, which made Max's team the league champions.

"Woo-hoo!" Dina yelled, and then turned to Nick. "Emily got the cake for the party, right?"

"I'm picking it up on the way," Nick assured her.

"Good. I'll see you there." Everyone made their way off the bleachers and met up with their kids.

Nick clapped Max on the shoulder as they followed the crowd to the parking lot. "You did great today. Especially that move when you chested the ball. Impressive."

Max looked around as if he didn't want anyone to overhear Nick's praise, but he couldn't hide his grin. "You showed me that move last summer, remember? I've been working on it since then."

"Well, you've got it down. Nicely done."

They stopped by the bakery, where a sheet cake waited for them. It featured a picture of a soccer ball in the middle, surrounded by the names of all the team members piped on in blue frosting. Nick set it in the back and got into the driver's seat. "Okay, the pizza place is on Knik Street, right?"

Max, who had been staring out the window of the car, looked up. "What?"

"Never mind." Nick checked the note on his phone for the address. He backed out and pulled onto the street. Max was staring straight ahead now. "Something on your mind?"

"Ian wants to move to a comp team. He's trying out this afternoon, after the party."

"Oh, yeah? He would probably do well in comp." But if Ian moved to a competitive team, that would leave Max without his best friend on his recreational team. It was understandable he was concerned.

Max nodded. After a long pause, he blurted out, "He says I should try out, too."

"Do you want to be on a comp-level team?" Nick asked. "It means more work. Possibly less playing time." Recreational teams usually tried to make sure all the players got roughly equal playing time.

In comp leagues, the less skilled players might sit on the bench for most of the game.

"Yeah, but the way to get better is to play with better players."

"True." Nick thought for a moment. Did Max really want to step up, or just be with his friend? "What if you made the team and Ian didn't? Would you still want to do it?"

Max looked puzzled. "Ian's way better than me."

"I'm not sure about that. Ian has certain skills, but so do you. But putting that aside, would you want to be on a comp team even if your friend wasn't?"

"Yeah. If I can get good enough, I want to try for a scholarship. Like you."

Huh, he hadn't realized that Max knew about his scholarship offer. "In that case, I think you should try out."

"Really?" Max gave Nick a hard look. "You think I have a chance of making the team?"

Nick honestly couldn't remember what the skill level was for twelve-year-olds in comp soccer, but Max was pretty good. "I don't see why not."

Max caught his lower lip in his teeth. "But what if I don't make it?"

Nick shrugged. "Then you'll do rec another season and try again when you're ready." Nick saw the sign for the pizza place, pulled in, and parked. He turned and nodded to Max. "It's up to you."

"What do you think Dad would say?" Max asked.

"Well, I'm not your Dad, but I know he'd be proud of how hard you've worked on your skills, whatever you choose."

Max only hesitated for a moment. "I want to try out."

"Then you should. I'll talk to Ian's mom. I don't know if you'll be able to do it today, or if you have to have signed up in advance, but I'll find out. In the meantime, let's go celebrate with your team. You're the champions!"

"Yeah." Max grinned, but he added, "Don't tell the coach or anybody yet, okay? In case I don't make the comp team."

"I won't."

Max got out of the car and waited for Nick to pick up the cake before walking with him to the restaurant and holding open the door. "Thanks, Nick."

"Anytime, bud."

CHAPTER TWELVE

THE TEAM HAD reserved a special party room in the back of the restaurant, a wise move for a group of noisy boys consuming massive amounts of pizza. Meanwhile, the parents gathered at different tables and chatted. Nick sat at a table with Dina so that he could ask about the tryouts, but he couldn't very well mention it in front of the other parents.

After pizza, the coach presented each boy on the team with a little speech and a special certificate. He branded Max "most versatile," mentioning that he'd played center midfielder in the summer, moved to wing when they changed to indoor, and then took the stopper position and was doing a smash-up job at it. "Not to mention that game where both our goalies got injured and Max filled in at goal for the last half. Great job, Max."

Everyone applauded. Max's cheeks were red as he accepted the paper and returned to his seat, but he looked happy.

The party broke up. Dina went to gather the leftover paper plates, and Nick finally saw his chance to talk with her alone. "Say, I wanted to ask you something." Oops, he should have worded that differently.

Indeed, Dina looked at him with a brilliant smile and brushed a lock of hair back from her face. "What's that?"

"Ian was telling Max about the comp soccer tryouts this afternoon, and encouraging him to try out, too. Are they open tryouts? Or would Max need an invitation?"

Her smile lost a few watts. "Oh, soccer. Uh, yeah, I think they're open. My friend's son is on the team, and she told me Ian could try out at their regular practice. Let me check with her." She texted something and a few seconds later got a reply. "She says Max is welcome. It's at the sports center at three."

"Okay." That would mean driving back to Swan Falls in the dark, which he'd been avoiding because of the halos, but this was important to Max. Nick would manage. "We'll be there. Thanks, Dina."

"See you." She hitched her bag onto her shoulder and walked out, calling for Ian to follow.

Nick checked his watch. It was one thirty now. Emily had given Nick an authorization document in case he needed to sign things like permission slips while she was away, so if they needed any liability papers signed or anything, he should be able to do that. He texted Nathan and Amanda about the change of plans, and received assurance that Lyla was welcome to stay as long as necessary.

Max walked over. "What did she say about tryouts?"

Nick gave him the good news. "So you've got an hour and a half to digest all that pizza and cake and be ready to work."

Max grinned. "I can do that."

"What do you want to do in the meantime?"

"We could go to the trampoline park," Max suggested.

"Since you've already played a full game and have a practice to get through, maybe we should stick to something a little less strenuous. Have you done your Christmas shopping?"

Max shook his head. "Christmas isn't for ages."

Nick hid a smile. "Two weeks." You'd think the Christmas music playing in the restaurant would have been a clue, not to mention the tree decorating and pageant practice over the past week, but sometimes Max lived in his own world.

"Oh. Okay. Let's go to the mall."

Nick drove them to the nearest shopping center. Inside, Christmas ornaments the size of yoga balls were stacked into a pyramid, and arrow signs pointed toward Santa's sleigh at the other end of the hallway. The stores seemed to be doing a brisk business.

They found a craft store, where, with a little prodding, Max chose a butterfly-themed jewelry-making kit for Lyla. Nick bought her a clay bead-making kit, and while Max was occupied with a model-train display, threw in a box of expensive but cool light-up interlocking blocks he'd noticed Max eyeing earlier. In another store, Max found a canvas tote bag with a picture of a girl holding a tottering pile of books. "For Gramma, to carry all the books she buys at Birdsong Books."

"Good idea," Nick agreed.

"Would Mom like this one?" Max held up another tote bag printed with a small flock of cedar waxwings on the branches of a tree.

"She'd love it," Nick assured him. He was still trying to think of what he could get for Emily for Christmas. He'd picked up a couple of little things, but he wanted something that would make her smile, to let her know how special she was. Not jewelry. Jewelry gifts sent signals, and after her insistence that they forget those kisses ever happened, he didn't want to give her anything that would make her uncomfortable. Besides, Emily couldn't wear jewelry on the job for safety reasons, and when she wasn't working, a Lyla original paracord bracelet meant more to her than a gold bangle ever could. But something...

"That's all my Christmas shopping." Max took both bags, and they went to stand in line for checkout. "Can we get root-beer floats?" Nick had introduced Max and Lyla to the treats summer before last, and Max had immediately become a huge fan.

"No." Nick laughed. "You don't want to be weighed down at the tryouts. Besides, it's time to head over there."

Max nodded, suddenly sober. "Do you really think I'm good enough?"

"You'll never know unless you try."

When they arrived at the rec center, Nick was surprised to find an indoor turf field inside. If he'd known, he would have had Max bring turf shoes, but his indoor shoes should work. Only four boys and their parents were there. Two of the boys juggled soccer balls on their knees, while the other two passed a ball back and forth between them. One of the moms greeted Max. "You must be Ian's friend. I'm Melissa, team manager. Max, why don't you join the others? Guys, this is Max," she called. "I'll get your dad to fill out these forms." She secured papers to a clipboard and passed it to Nick, along with a pen.

Max took his ball from his bag and hurried over. The other boys gave him a low-key greeting and continued what they were doing. Max hesitated for a second but then he set his ball down and started warm-up exercises. Nick took the clipboard and pen. "I'm not Max's dad. I'm Nick Bernardi, the, uh, nanny."

"For real?" Melissa blurted out, but then caught herself. "I mean, that's fine, as long as you have authority to allow Max to practice with us."

"I do. I don't have the papers with me, but I have a picture on my phone."

"That's okay. I believe you. Will you be the one bringing Max to practices and all?"

"No, I'm just temporary, until the end of the year."

"Okey dokey. Bring me that form when you're done."

Before turning away, Nick asked. "When and where do you practice, by the way?" It hadn't occurred to him until now that Max changing teams could mean extra driving for Emily and Janice. They probably wouldn't mind, especially if Ian was also on the team and they could carpool, but maybe he should call Emily. But they were already here, and he didn't want to disturb her at work for a nonemergency.

"Here. Tuesday and Thursday afternoons. Usually games are Saturdays, but since the season is over, we're practicing this Saturday and next."

Nick nodded and went to sit on the bleachers and fill out the form. Thanks to Emily's organizational skills, he had the answers to all the questions, right down to the date of Max's last physical exam, on the records she'd emailed to him. By the time he was done, the rest of the players had arrived, and so had Dina and Ian. Dina must have already filled out the required forms, because after greeting Melissa, she sat down on her right. The rest of the parents dropped off their kids and left.

The coach blew the whistle and had the boys gather around him. Nick handed the clipboard to Melissa, nodded to Dina, and chose a seat on Melissa's left.

The coach started practice with a passing drill. Unfortunately, Max was only the second player to receive a pass and, not being as familiar with the drill, missed where he was supposed to run until the coach whistled to stop the action and reminded him. Max's cheeks flamed as he took his place. Ian's turn came a few passes later, and he performed flawlessly. On his second try, Max did fine, but he still seemed stiff and uncomfortable. Maybe this hadn't been such a good idea.

They moved on to other drills, and while Max was often confused as to exactly where he was supposed to be going, his skills were fine and he seemed to be relaxing. He could certainly dribble as well or better than most of the other boys. Finally, the coach divided the team in half for a scrimmage, putting Max and Ian on opposite teams. Melissa handed out yellow pinnies to Max's group, who had gathered just in front of the parents. Max tried to pull his on, but somehow got his arm through the neck hole and the whole thing twisted around. He jerked at the fabric in frustration. None of his teammates stepped in, so Nick slipped over and helped him get it straightened out.

"Max," Nick whispered and waited until the boy met his eyes. "You've got this, okay?"

Max nodded and followed his team to take the

field. Nick settled on the bleachers once again. The coach assigned Max to the stopper position right in front of the goal. On the other team, he put Ian as right wing. He dropped the ball, and the non-pinny team took control. The center passed to Ian, who made a run about halfway to the goal and then passed back to the center forward. However, Max intercepted the pass, and, in a smooth motion, passed to his own winger, setting up a run that resulted in the first goal.

Yes! Nick clenched his fist. This was more like it. On the next drive, the clearly right-footed center forward dribbled straight toward the goal and then feigned to his left, his off foot. *Don't fall for it!* Nick was shouting in his head, but Max leaped to his right, leaving the player with a clear shot at the goal. Luckily, the keeper was able to deflect the ball outward. Max and the forward both scrambled toward it, but Max reached it first and booted it away.

On another drive, when Max moved to challenge the forward, the forward passed to Ian. Ian made a quick run and scored a nice corner shot, but that wasn't Max's fault. The other defender was out of position. Later, the coach moved Max to left wing and Ian to forward. Max managed one or two good passes to set his team up for some decent runs, but he clearly was better as a stopper than as an attacking midfielder. Overall, Nick felt like Max held his own.

At the end of practice, Melissa handed both Dina and him a folded brochure. "Here's the schedule and cost structure for the team. We have three or four more kids trying out at practice next Saturday and the coach should make a decision about which two to add to the team shortly after that. We'll give you a call, one way or the other. I have your cellphone number, right?" she asked Nick.

Nick nodded, having included both his number and Emily's.

"If they make the team, practices for the next session will start January eleventh."

Max and Ian came walking over, carrying their bags. Both boys looked like they were dragging a bit after a game and a full practice in one day. Hopefully, the coach would take that into account.

"Good job!" Dina told both boys. "You looked great out there."

"Yeah, you both did well," Nick echoed. The boys sat down to change their shoes. Nick turned toward Melissa and included Dina in his glance. "Thanks for setting it up so that Max could try out today."

"We're glad he came," Melissa replied. Her son, the center forward and clearly the team leader, came to join them.

He spared a glance toward Max and Ian. "You guys did okay," he said. They both sat a little straighter.

Melissa pulled on her coat. "We'll let you know

as soon as we can. In the meantime, merry Christmas."

"Merry Christmas to you," Nick replied along with Dina, Max, and Ian.

When Nick and Max were back in the car, the boy asked, "Do you think I'll make it?"

"Honestly, it's hard to say. You did well, especially in defense, but the manager says they have more kids trying out next week and they're only choosing two. I suspect a lot of it depends on what skills the coach is looking for, although, it seems to me they're a little short on defense, so I think you have a good shot."

Max nodded.

"You ready for that root-beer float?" Nick asked.

Max grinned. "I'm always ready for ice cream."

THAT EVENING, EMILY made her usual video call. The kids were at the kitchen table, and she could see Nick in the background, wiping the kitchen counters. As soon as Emily greeted the kids, Nala appeared from the laundry room and padded across the kitchen floor, disappearing from Emily's view as she got closer to the table. According to Janice, Nala often listened in on the calls.

Tonight, before Emily could even ask a question, Lyla started talking. "Mommy. Guess what? I was over at Paisley's today and her puppy Willow is so smart! We taught her to shake hands!"

"That's great," Emily said, but for some reason

Nick and Max were looking down at something under the table and laughing. "What's so funny?"

"Let me show you." Nick picked up the laptop and tilted it so that Emily would have a view of the dog, who was sitting between the two kids. "Lyla, say it again."

"What?"

"What you just said," Nick urged.

"That me and Paisley taught Willow to shake hands?" she asked. As soon as the words *shake hands* were out of her mouth, Nala lifted her paw and waved it. When Lyla didn't immediately take the paw, Nala set it on her leg.

Emily snorted. "She wants to show you she already knows how to shake hands. Lyla, shake her paw."

"Oh, you're a good dog, Nala." Lyla shook her paw and then rubbed her ears.

Nick grinned and set the laptop back in place. He crouched down so that his face was level with the kids and peered into the screen at her. "Nathan and Amanda say housebreaking is progressing well. How are things on the slope? I saw you got some weather."

There was something sweet about knowing Nick was keeping track of the weather eight hundred miles away just because she was there. "Yeah, windchill of minus sixty and convoy travel only, so we had to delay that new procedure until tomorrow. But that's okay, it gave us an extra day to go over everything one more time before we do it."

"Good. Hope it goes well." He smiled at her and then returned to the kitchen, leaving the kids to carry on the conversation.

"Max, how was the last game?" Emily asked.

"We won. And the yellow team lost so that means we were the champions."

"Wow! Congratulations! Did you have fun at the party?"

"They had six different kinds of pizza," Max told her, "and I tried them all."

"You ate six pieces of pizza?"

"They weren't big pieces," Max explained. "Everybody liked the cake you ordered. They ate it all. After that, me and Nick went to the mall and did Christmas shopping."

Lyla gasped. "You went to the mall, and you didn't take me?"

"I'll take you another day," Nick interjected from the kitchen.

"We needed to stay in town after the party," Max said, "so I could try out for the Glacier Bears."

"Wait, Nick let you try out for the comp team?" Without even talking to her?

"Yeah. Ian was doing it, and Nick said I could if I wanted, so I did."

"I see." But she didn't see at all. Dina had mentioned it, but Emily had made a conscious decision not to bring it up with Max. And yet, somehow, he'd found out about it and tried out, anyway. "How did it go?"

Max shrugged. "Okay, I think. We got scored on twice, but I made some steals, too." Max didn't act as though it was all that important to him. "Oh, and me and Nick got root-beer floats after."

"You got floats without me?" Lyla demanded, and once again Nick promised to make it up to her on another day.

Emily let Lyla change the subject, but inside she was seething. As soon as the conversation was over, she texted Nick. Call me once the kids are in bed.

Two hours later, her phone rang. Before she even had time to say hello, Nick spoke. "I'm sorry. When Max asked if he could try out, I didn't think about how you and Janice would have to drive him back and forth to Wasilla for practices and games."

"You think that's what I'm upset about?" Emily demanded.

"It's not?"

"No. I don't mind a little extra driving." Did he not get this at all? "It's Max. He's already going through this phase where he gets embarrassed at the slightest thing, and now you've set him up for failure. The last thing he needs is a blow to his confidence when he doesn't make the team."

"What makes you think he's not going to make it?" Nick seemed genuinely confused.

"Oh, come on." How could he not understand?

"The Glacier Bears were in the running for state champions this past summer. Ian tried out and didn't make the team last year, and Ian is way better at soccer than Max."

"I disagree," Nick answered. "Ian is flashier, but Max has skills. He's got quick reflexes and good spatial awareness. And his passing is as good as Ian's, maybe better now. He's also more of a team player, always looking for the open player instead of trying to do everything himself."

Huh. Maybe Max's skills were better than she thought. But still, the competition level was high. "That's nice of you to say, but the point stands that he's most likely not going to make the team. I can't believe you pushed him into this."

"Hey, I didn't push. Ian's mom had already set up a tryout and Ian suggested to Max that he should try out, too. I just agreed to take him there."

So Dina was in on this, too? "Dina told me Ian would be trying out and I specifically told her Max wouldn't."

"Hmm, she didn't tell me that." Nick muttered. "Maybe she thought you changed your mind."

Or maybe she was trying to do an end run around Emily. Practice and games would be a lot easier for her if both boys were on the same team and they shared the driving. "Well, I didn't, and neither of you should have acted without checking with me. I'm Max's mother. I should be the one making these decisions."

"You are and you should," Nick agreed. "I'm sorry. I should have called."

"Why didn't you?"

"I didn't want to disturb you while you were working."

On one hand, she appreciated that. It was awkward when her phone rang in the middle of a meeting. But was that really the reason, or had he taken the better-to-ask-forgiveness-than-permission route?

"But honestly," Nick continued. "I don't see why you're so upset. If Max doesn't make the team, he can continue playing on his rec team just like you'd planned. He doesn't lose anything."

Except for his self-confidence, which seemed to be in short supply. "He'll be devastated if Ian makes it and he doesn't."

"Hardly devastated. And besides, life is like that. You can't protect your kids from every disappointment."

"You think I don't know that?" she retorted. "You think I don't worry about my inability to protect them every single day of my life?"

"Ohhhh," he said slowly. "This is about Coop."

She started to deny it, but maybe it was. "Okay, yeah. My kids lost their father. So maybe that makes me a little overprotective, but I don't want them losing anything else if I can possibly prevent it."

"I get it." Nick's voice was gentle now. "I'm

sorry, Emily, I really am. I'll call and withdraw him from contention, and I'll tell Max I shouldn't have let him try out."

"And make me the bad guy?"

"No, I'll make up some excuse." Nick paused. "Maybe I'll tell Max there's some sort of paperwork problem, like I didn't have authorization to sign him up for tryouts. Which, actually, is pretty much the truth, I guess."

"It's too late now. He's already gotten his hopes up. If you withdraw him, it's just as bad as if they turn him down. No, just let it be." She sighed, thinking ahead on how to cushion the inevitable blow when it came. "When are you supposed to hear back?"

"They said some more kids are trying out next Saturday, and then the coach will make his final decision, so probably early in the week after next. I gave them your number and email as well as mine."

"Did they say how many kids they want to add to the team?"

"Two," Nick reported.

"And how many tried out?"

"Max and Ian today. Three or four next week. I'm not sure if they've had any before today."

So Max's chances were two out of five at best. "Not great odds."

"Not terrible, either."

"Okay." What was done, was done. "If you hear

back before I do, check with me before you tell Max. I don't want to be blindsided again."

"Understood. And Emily, I really am sorry."

"Yeah, I know. Good night, Nick."

"Good night."

She set her phone on the nightstand and stared at the blank white wall of her room. Janice would never have done this. Of course, she and Janice had already talked it over when Dina mentioned she planned to have Ian try out for the team again at the end of the season, and Emily had considered the matter closed. It had never occurred to her to bring it up with Nick.

Maybe she'd been too hard on Nick. From his perspective, he'd just been supporting Max's goals. If Coop was still alive, he'd probably be encouraging Max to try out at the next level. But if Coop was still alive, Max wouldn't be struggling with self-doubt. Or would he?

She'd assumed Max's recent awkwardness and embarrassment were related to losing his father, but maybe it was more because he was almost thirteen and the same hormones responsible for his enormous appetite were also creating chaos in his self-image. In their phone conversation, Max hadn't acted as if the tryouts were a big deal to him, but that didn't mean anything. When Max was worried about a test or a tricky situation, he'd often slip it into conversation casually, as though to gauge her reaction. The last thing she wanted was to make him think she didn't have faith in him.

Still, Dina should never have brought up the subject again, and Nick should have called before he agreed. Emily made the decisions in her kids' lives, not Dina, not Nick. Her.

CHAPTER THIRTEEN

NICK ARRIVED AT the school a little earlier than the scheduled time for practice the next Monday. He pulled his wallet from his pocket and stepped into the front office at the school to check in. The smiling secretary greeted him and waved away the offer of his identification. "Nick Bernardi, right? I've already got your information. Just sign in and go on back. The students will be there shortly. Oh, hold on." She stepped over to a box, retrieved a familiar black glove, and handed it to him. Max's initials were written in ink on the cuff. "Someone found this on the playground yesterday afternoon. I was going to drop it by Max's classroom, but you can give it to him."

"How did you know this was Max's?" Nick asked.

"MOC. Maxwell Oliver Cooper, right? Besides, I recognize his handwriting."

"Impressive. Thanks." Did the secretary really have the middle names and handwriting of all one hundred and fifty or so elementary students memorized, or did Max lose his stuff often enough to stand out? Nick suspected a little of both. He took the glove and made his way to the multipurpose room, where he found Nathan sawing a board in one corner.

Nick went to steady the end of the board. Nathan finished before looking up. "Thanks."

"You're welcome. What are you doing here? I thought you said you'd finished your volunteer task."

"I did, but one of the screens got broken, so I'm replacing the board." He jerked his thumb at the screen behind him, with a cracked board at the top.

"I see." Nick nodded toward the stack of papers he'd set on the floor against the wall. "Have you read the script?"

"No, but I know the gist. It's like all the Alaska animals are getting ready for a birthday party and figuring out what gifts they'll bring, right? One of the teachers wrote it."

"Uh-huh. It's kind of an odd story."

Nathan looked around although they were the only ones in the room and whispered, "Actually it's a surprise for Ms. Susanna."

"Ms. Susanna?"

Nathan nodded. "You know. The elementary school secretary."

"Oh." The lady who knew Max's handwriting. "I didn't remember her name. She seems good at her job."

"She's great. She's apparently worked there forever, but she's retiring at the end of this school year. Her birthday happens to be Christmas Eve, which is why they set the pageant date then, although they gave some other excuse. The play is all about the animals getting ready for a surprise party, but at the end they will call her to the stage and tell her the party is actually for her."

"That's really nice. It's not in the script, though."

"Of course not. It's a surprise for Ms. Susanna. There's no way this many kids could keep a secret for that long, so it's a surprise for them, too. Don't tell Max and Lyla."

"I won't." Nathan chuckled. "Now I feel like an insider. How come you know about the surprise?"

"What surprise?" Nathan grinned and pressed a finger to his mouth. "Loose lips sink ships."

"Gotcha."

Nathan picked up a sanding block and smoothed the cut ends of the board. "So how are things going now that it's just you and the kids?"

"Fine," Nick replied to brush off the question, but he changed his mind. "Well, mostly. I kind of messed up Saturday."

"Oh?"

"Yeah. Max asked if he could try out for a comp soccer team, which sounded reasonable, so I took him."

Nathan looked up. "Yeah, so? Did Max bomb or something?"

"No, he did okay. Problem is, I didn't check with Emily first."

"Oh." Nathan grimaced. "I can see that wouldn't go over well."

"It did not. She's furious with me."

"Because you didn't ask first, or because you took Max to tryouts?"

"Both. She feels like I set him up for disappointment. Apparently, this league is more elite than I realized, and she thinks he won't make the team, and that he'll be upset if he doesn't."

Nathan nodded slowly. "Why didn't you call Emily first?"

"I've been asking myself that. It crossed my mind briefly, but I knew Emily would be working and I didn't want to disturb her. But mostly, it just felt like a no-brainer. Max has come a long way in soccer the last year or so, and he felt like he was ready to move up to the next level. I guess it didn't occur to me that Emily wouldn't agree."

"So you made the decision based on your own evaluation of what was best for Max, instead of checking with his mother?"

"Yeah. Pretty arrogant of me, I guess." Just went to show that he was not cut out to be a parent.

"Maybe." Nathan carried the board to the screen, which Nick held while Nathan replaced it. "On the other hand, you're not just a hired babysitter. You're an old friend, and you care about Max and

Lyla. I agree, you should have talked to Emily first, but she left you in charge because she trusted you."

"A little less so now, I suspect."

"All done. Thanks for your help." Nathan set the nail gun in his tool bin and patted Nick on the shoulder. "Emily will come around. You crossed a line, but you did what you did because you thought it was good for Max. I get it. I've only officially been a dad for a few months now. Sometimes it's tricky to walk that line. But it's so worth it. Having Paisley in my life is…" Nathan grinned. "I don't even have words."

No words maybe, but Nathan's feelings were obvious. "Yeah, I can see that," Nick said. "But it's different for me. I'm just the nanny."

"Are you, though?" Nathan asked, but before Nick could answer, herds of kids came stampeding into the room.

Well, maybe *stampeding* was too strong a word. They were actually more or less walking in lines by class, it was just that they were excited, and excited children wiggled and chattered and stomped their feet. Lyla's class gathered on one side of the room, where the music teacher arranged them into three lines.

Paisley spotted Nathan and waved. Lyla turned to see whom she was waving to, and when she spotted Nick, she beamed him a wide smile that warmed his heart. Yeah, Nathan had a point. Nick wasn't just a nanny. He loved these kids. He'd loved them since they were born, but in these last few weeks of living with them, he'd gotten to know them on a different level. That didn't excuse him for taking Max to tryouts without Emily's permission, but it helped explain it.

He hated having Emily mad at him. There weren't a lot of people whose opinion mattered to him, but Emily's did. But what could he do? He'd apologized. He'd offered to call and withdraw Max from contention. He had to give her time and hope she eventually forgave him. In the meantime, he would make sure to keep her in the loop.

Max's teacher entered, pushing a cart piled high with papers, and led her class toward the stage. Nick said goodbye to Nathan, grabbed his copy of the script and Max's glove, and went to join them. The teacher had them all sit in front of the stage and motioned for Nick to come up and stand beside the cart, where he could see that the papers were copies of the script, each with a character name written across the top and that character's lines highlighted.

"As I call your name," Mrs. Kaiser announced to the class, "come forward and Mr. Bernardi will give you your script. Then go up on stage and tell Carly's mom, Ms. Moore, what size you wear." She waved a hand toward a lady standing on the stage with a clipboard. "She's volunteered to make all the costumes."

Wow. Nick didn't know anything about sewing, but that had to be a lot of work.

"Alissa, you're the pika," the teacher announced, and Nick handed the girl the pika script. "Ian, moose." Slowly they worked their way through the list until all twenty-three of the sixth-grade students had their scripts and parts. Some of them read the scripts silently, others read aloud in clusters, and several had laid their scripts on the ground and were talking and laughing. Two of the kids giggled and pushed the rolling scenery back and forth until the teacher reprimanded them.

Once they all had scripts, Mrs. Kaiser called for their attention. "Okay, about half of you are in the first scene. Those who aren't need to wait quietly off stage, over there." She pointed to a space at the edge of the stage behind the curtains. "Everyone else, come here and I'll tell you where you need to be standing when the scene starts. That's called your mark."

While the students were getting organized, Nick straightened the scenery screens. He pulled out his phone and texted Emily. Pageant practice. Lyla is singing her heart out with chorus. Parts assigned. Max is a caribou, and Ian is a moose. All good. There. She couldn't say he wasn't keeping her informed.

"Mr. Bernardi, could you come here, please?" the teacher called. "I need you to run lines with this group."

Nick pocketed his phone and went to help.

"How did your project with Ian go?" Emily asked during the video call that evening.

"We got an A," Max said. "We built the buildings out of Legos, and Nick took the map we made to a print shop, and had it blown up to poster size, so we could set the buildings on the map. They're going to display it at school until the night of the pageant so parents can see it."

"That's awesome." Emily was impressed. What a great idea, enlarging the map to the same scale as the buildings. "Good job. Nick said you're a caribou in the play."

"Yeah. Ian's a moose. Zoe's a squirrel." Max had mentioned Zoe a time or two. Emily only knew her from volunteering in the classroom, but she liked the friendly girl. "Ian called her 'Squirrelly,'" Max continued.

"That's not very nice."

"Zoe doesn't care," he said, clear admiration in his voice. "She just made that noise squirrels make, until he quit bothering her."

"Sounds like she knows how to handle teasing." Good for her. "Do we need to do something about costumes?"

Max shook his head. "Alissa's mom is making the costumes, and fifth graders are making the masks in art class. The fourth graders are singing."

"We have to learn six more songs for the pageant," Lyla announced. "We learned the first one today. Want me to sing it for you?"

"Of course." Emily listened while Lyla sang a verse of an unfamiliar song about snow. Unlike Emily, Lyla had a lovely singing voice and a knack for staying on key. She must have inherited that from Coop's side of the family. Nick hovered in the background. He kept throwing glances Emily's way, but he didn't say much. He had texted her several times throughout the day, telling her what the kids were up to. Nothing personal, though.

When Lyla completed her song, Nick handed the kids something from the kitchen desk. "Show your mom the postcards your grandmother sent."

They both held their cards up so that she could see the pictures. Max's was of a suit of armor standing in front of a wall of what looked like battleaxes and spears. Lyla's showed a half-completed striped blanket on a loom. The lengthwise yarns seemed to be weighted in place with rocks that had holes in the middle. "Isn't this cool?" Lyla said. "I want to try weaving someday."

"It is cool," Emily agreed. "So is that suit of armor. It doesn't look too comfortable, though, does it?"

They talked for a little longer, until it was time for the kids to get ready for bed. After she hung up, Emily did some Christmas shopping online, then a half-hour on the treadmill in the gym. After a shower, she returned to her room and picked up the mystery novel Nick had given her. She'd gotten so caught up in work and family in the last couple of years, she hardly ever read for pleasure anymore, and she'd forgotten how much she enjoyed this particular author. Such a thoughtful gift. She read for a while, but tonight she couldn't seem to keep her mind on the story. Her argument with Nick hung over her head like a thundercloud.

By nine o'clock, she couldn't take it anymore. She texted Nick. Are the kids in bed?

Yes, ma'am.

She dialed his number. He picked up on the first ring. "Hi."

"Hi." Where did she start? "I, uh, didn't catch you in the middle of something important, did I?"

"No. I was just picking up the living room." His voice sounded different, impersonal somehow.

"Oh. Okay. I wanted to let you know that I've ordered a bunch of stuff for the kids for Christmas. But now, I'm thinking I'll add some sort of weaving kit for Emily. I'm torn between a simple square loom with stretchy fabric loops, or a more complicated one that she could use to make long narrow things like a belt or a headband. What do you think?"

"You want my opinion?" He sounded surprised.

"Yes, I do."

"Okay. I'd go with the simpler one to start with, and then if she really likes weaving, you could get the other one for her birthday next fall."

"That's a good idea," she agreed. "I'll do that."

"When I was shopping with Max on Saturday, I got Lyla this kit where she can make her own beads from some special clay and bake them in the oven. I thought she might like to use them in her bracelets."

"Oh, perfect. She'll love that. The stuff I ordered is supposed to be delivered Thursday. Could you hide it from the kids for me?"

"Sure. You want it in the secret room?"

"Yeah." She smiled. "You remember when we found that space during the remodel, and we were joking about what to do with it?"

He laughed. "I still think it would make an awesome secret library for you."

"I don't read anything that needs to be kept secret. I have been reading that book you gave me, though, and really enjoying it."

"I'm glad," he said, but he still sounded tentative.

"Nick, I'm sorry. I overreacted about the tryouts. I don't think I was entirely wrong—you should have called me before taking Max—but it wasn't like you took him bungee jumping or something."

"I'm sorry I didn't call—I really am. I'm trying to make it up to you."

"Yeah, I got all the texts." She smiled. "You don't have to tell me every single time the kids eat or what their homework assignments are. We can save those things for them to tell me during the call."

"Well, I just wanted—"

"I know. You're trying to include me in all the decisions, so I don't yell at you again." She should have made this a video call so he could see her rueful smile. But maybe he would hear it in her voice. "I know I have a tendency to micromanage, but they're my kids, and when I'm not there—"

"You worry about them. I get it."

"It's not that I don't trust your judgment…" She trailed off, not sure how to finish that sentence. Truthfully, she didn't trust anyone's judgment completely when it came to her kids.

"I realized I overstepped," Nick said, "and it won't happen again."

"So…you and me. We're okay?" She held her breath, waiting for his answer. Why did it matter so much?

"Yeah, we're okay," he confirmed, and her heart swelled.

"Good. So what was pageant practice really like?"

"Organized chaos." Nick gave one of those soft, warm chuckles she liked so much. "But surprisingly productive. Oh, do you know about the big surprise at the end of the pageant?"

"What big surprise?"

"Never mind. I'm not supposed to say." His voice was teasing now.

"Hey, you can't start something like that and not spill," Emily protested. "What's the big secret?"

"Okay, but the kids can't know in advance, so keep it to yourself, okay?"

"I promise." Even though he couldn't see, Emily made a heart-crossing motion.

"Well, you know the school secretary, Ms. Susanna?"

"Of course." She was one of Emily's favorite people.

"Well, her birthday is on Christmas Eve, so..." Nick explained the plan for the surprise party at the end of the pageant.

"What a great idea! She totally deserves special recognition. I think she remembers the name of every kid that passed through that school in the past twentysomething years."

"Yeah, and she even knows Max's handwriting. She immediately knew a lost glove belonged to him."

"Sometimes, I've wondered if I should apply for an office job in Anchorage instead of working in Prudhoe Bay," Emily admitted. "But if I did, we'd have to move, and we'd lose all the people in Swan Falls like Ms. Susanna, and Helen at the bookstore—"

"And Nathan and Amanda at the lodge, and all the kids' friends," Nick added. "Yeah, when you and Coop bought this place, I had my doubts. But you were right. Once you fixed it up, the house is great, and Swan Falls is a special place. I'm glad Max and Lyla get to grow up here."

"Me, too."

"Since Max doesn't have soccer next Saturday, I was considering taking the kids cross-country skiing. Do you think that's a good idea?"

"I think that's an excellent idea." He'd definitely gotten the message about asking first.

"Should I let them invite Ian and Paisley along, or would that be too much?"

"By all means, invite their friends. Beach Lake Park at Chugiak has groomed trails, and afterward, there's a bakery across from the school—"

"Oh, is that the place with the caramel apple pie?"

"Yes, and the mocha fudge brownies."

"I'm sold." Nick chuckled again. "Emily," he said, but then he paused.

"Yes?"

"I, um, just wanted to say, thanks for calling. I feel better."

"So do I." A lot better in fact, as though a weight had been lifted and now, her spirits could dance again. "Good night, Nick."

"Good night, Emily." And just before she pressed the button to end the call, she thought he whispered, "Sweet dreams."

CHAPTER FOURTEEN

A WEEK LATER, the pageant was starting to take shape. At least half of the students had memorized their lines, and almost all of them understood their entrance cues and where to stand on the stage. While Mrs. Kaiser was busy working with some of the students on gestures and inflections, she had Nick running lines with another group. Max, Ian, and a few other kids were off to the side, talking. From what Nick could overhear, Ian was telling them about how they'd skied a marathon Saturday. In reality, they'd only skied about fifteen kilometers, but there were a couple of challenging uphills, and the kids had certainly earned their bakery treats.

And they'd taken full advantage, or at least Ian and Max had. Nick wasn't sure how much was appetite and how much was competition between the boys, but in the end, they seemed to enjoy it. Meanwhile, Lyla and Paisley sat on the other side of the booth and had a very civilized tea party with cinnamon-spiked cocoa and wreath-shaped sugar cookies while Nick enjoyed his apple pie and coffee.

Nick wouldn't have been surprised if Max was a little queasy later, but judging from his dinner consumption, he'd suffered no ill effects from bingeing on baked goods, and their report to Emily that evening was all positives. Even through the computer screen, the glow of happiness on Emily's face…

"Mr. Bernardi?" one of the kids said.

With a start, Nick came back to earth. "Sorry, what?"

"It's your line."

"Oh, right." He looked for the spot in the script. "Uh, here we go. 'What gift are you bringing?'"

"One of my wing feathers," said the girl, who was playing a bald eagle. "So that she can pretend to soar in the sky as I do."

At the end of the session, Mrs. Kaiser told the kids to line up, but while they were doing that, she took Nick aside. "Carly's grandmother in the lower forty-eight had a medical emergency, and Ms. Moore had to fly down to take care of her, so she won't be able to finish making the costumes. I thought maybe we'd just order natural-colored sweatpants and sweatshirts, but she says she's already cut all the pieces from fabric, so we can't return it, and we have no budget to replace the costumes. Do you know anyone who sews?"

"No, but I'll ask around." Nick wasn't quite sure

why she would think an outsider like him would know anyone.

Mrs. Kaiser nodded. "See you tomorrow."

Nick walked slowly to his truck. Janice used to sew occasionally, but since she and Helen were currently touring Croatia, that wasn't much help. She had another friend who worked at the lodge, though, who would know, but he couldn't remember her name.

He climbed into his truck, dialed Nathan's number, and explained the situation. "Do you know anyone who sews who might be able to help us?"

"No, but Peggy will. I'll ask her."

Peggy, that was her name. "Thanks."

A minute later, Nathan handed the phone off to Peggy. "Keisha Patterson sews beautifully," Peggy said. "But she's got a newborn, so her plate is full. Arne Meier sews custom outdoor gear, but he's just had shoulder surgery. Why don't you go by the arts and craft co-op, and talk to Kailee? She's the manager there. She'll know all the artsy people in town."

"That's the store on Main—"

"No, on Glacier. Wildwood Wonders."

"Oh, yeah, I've seen it. Thanks."

"Good luck," Peggy said. "Can't wait to see what the school comes up with for this year's pageant. I'm bringing cookies."

"I'll look forward to that. See you then."

He drove straight to the store. Inside, recessed

and pendant lighting, light wood floors, and white fixtures gave the space an open, airy feel. Tables displayed wooden toys, baskets, candles, and other crafty items. A pretty woman with short dark hair was polishing a glass display case filled with handmade jewelry. "Welcome to Wildwood Wonders. Can I help you find anything?"

"Actually I need advice. Are you Kailee?"

"Yes."

He introduced himself and told her about the situation at the school. "Do you know anyone who might be able to help with that?"

"Kristen O'Malley would be perfect if she has time. She's a quilter and also teaches sewing classes. That's her work, there." Kailee pointed to a quilted wall hanging featuring the classic view of Denali from Wonder Lake, all created from fabric and stitches. "She's supposed to drop off a couple of baby quilts this morning. I could ask her."

"That would be great. I'll give you my phone number." Nick pulled out his phone as the bells on the door jingled and a woman who was probably in her early fifties came in.

"Oh, Kristen. We were just talking about you." Kailee took the stack of quilts Kristen was carrying and repeated what Nick had told her about the costume problem.

"Oh, goodness. I knew Maisey Moore's mother had some health problems, but I didn't realize they were so serious. And just before Christmas, too.

I suppose Maisey's in-laws will step in and keep the kids while Doug is at work, but that doesn't solve your problem, does it? I wish I could help you." Kristen really did look as though it pained her to say no. "But I have a king-size double wedding ring quilt commission, and they need it before Christmas."

"I understand," Nick said. Now what?

"Although..." Kristen hesitated. "Do you sew at all?"

"Me?" Nick asked. "I've never even tried."

"Good, then you have no bad habits to break. I can teach you while I work on my quilt, and you can sew the costumes."

Nick blinked. "I could do that?" Learning a new skill that quickly seemed unlikely.

She gave a decisive nod. "I saw the pattern Maisey was using—supersimple. It would have to be if she's making costumes for the whole class in such a short time, right? We can find out in about an hour's lesson if you can learn to sew a straight seam, and if so, you'll be able to make the costumes. Are you willing to try?"

"Uh, yeah. Sure." The kids needed their costumes.

"Good. I was just on my way to grab lunch at the diner, before I spend the afternoon sewing. If you'll come over in about an hour—it's the A-frame four blocks down on Glacier—I'll give you a lesson."

Nick grinned. "Better yet, how about I treat you to lunch at the diner before we go?"

"Now, that sounds like a plan." Kristen linked her arm through his. "Let's go. Time's a'wasting."

AFTER A FORTIFYING lunch of a turkey club and cheesy potato soup, Nick followed Kristen's car and parked in front of a blue A-frame. Icicle lights dripped from the entire roofline and from the railing of the second-floor balcony that spanned the front. On the porch underneath the balcony, a half-barrel planter contained a cluster of greenery and berries, with a wooden sign rising out of it with painted letters *N-O-E-L* formed from holly leaves. A wreath with a trio of gnomes clustered at the bottom hung from the front door.

Inside, the bottom level of the A-frame was a kitchen and dining area against the back wall, two recliners and a television in one front corner, and the rest of the room devoted to worktables and wooden frames. Nick counted four sewing machines on tables around the perimeter. In the center of the room, a large table held grid-printed mats, scissors, rotary cutters, and other tools, along with templates and several bolts of cloth. Quilt squares were stacked off to one side.

Kristen hung her parka on a bentwood rack by the door. "Put your coat here," she told Nick, "and sit at that machine. It's a basic mechanical model." She pointed at the one nearest the window.

Nick sat in the chair and studied the controls on the machine. Kristen reached under the table and tugged a pedal attached to the machine with a long electric cord closer to his right foot. "This is like the accelerator in your car. Pushing makes it go, lifting your foot stops it. This—" she pointed to a dial "—is your stitch selector. Mostly, you'll just be using the straight stitch, possibly the zigzag. About a three is a good stitch length. Your presser foot—" she indicated the metal-bracket-looking thing on top of the main platform "—holds your fabric in place while the needle goes in and out to make stitches. A standard quilting seam allowance is one-fourth inch, which is the edge of the presser foot, but for the sewing you'll be doing, the standard is five eighths, which is marked on this guide."

Nick blinked. Stitch length? Seam allowance? Presser foot? He was in over his head.

Kristen smiled. "It will all make sense once you're actually sewing. Wait here a second." She went to the cutting table, picked up small pieces of fabric that had been pushed off to the side, used scissors to trim them, and brought them back. "So if we want to join two pieces of fabric, we arrange them right sides together—"

"Right side?" Nick asked. How could she tell left from right?

"Right side as opposed to wrong side. The right side is the printed side you want on the outside of your garment. So right sides together." She stacked a long yellow rectangle with white polka dots on top of a blue one with darker blue swirls. "Edges even. Then you pin it in place." She removed a straight pin from a nearby pincushion and joined the cloths together along the edge, repeating with three more pins about six inches apart. "To position it we raise the presser foot with this lever, set the fabric there, with the edge at the five-eighths line, and lower the presser foot to keep it in place."

Okay, now he understood what she meant by a seam allowance. It was the space between the edges of the cloth and the needle.

"You use your hands to guide the cloth through as you sew," she continued, "but keep your finger well clear of the needle. Put your hands here. Okay, press the pedal."

Nick did, and the machine roared into action, the needle flashing up and down, the fabric jumping forward, and everything clacking. Startled, he immediately took his foot off the pedal.

Kristen laughed. "Just like learning to drive, it takes a bit of practice. See, you've sown an inch. Now, before you sew the rest of the seam, you want to lock the stitches. To do that, hold down this reverse lever, which feeds the cloth backward. Hold down the lever and press the pedal gently for just a few stitches."

Nick did, and the machine backed up over the same area that he had already sewn. This time, the speed was more controlled, and he easily stopped when he reached the end.

"Good job. Now, stitch forward again. When you get to a pin, stop and pull it out before continuing. When you reach the end of the seam, reverse and forward to lock the stitches. Go ahead," she urged.

Nick pressed the pedal gingerly, and the stitches started forward. The fabric kept trying to drift left or right, but he would guide it back so that the edge of the fabric was next to the line Kristen had indicated. She watched until he reached the end and did the reverse, as she'd instructed.

"Good. Now, you raise the needle to its highest position using the wheel on the end of the carriage." She demonstrated. "Go ahead and lift up your presser foot with the lever. Now, pull the fabric away from the machine, leaving about six inches of thread tucked behind the needle, and cut it off near the fabric."

She unfolded the two pieces to show him how they were now sewn together. "Voilà, you've made a seam."

"How about that." Nick grinned at the unreasonable sense of pride he felt at this small accomplishment.

"Now." She refolded the cloth and pointed to the meandering line of stitches. "See how your seam wobbles back and forth? You need to practice until you can sew a straight line. Here, we'll just cut off the seam you made, and you can do it again. You practice a while. I'll be over here working on my quilt."

"Okay. Thanks." Nick repinned the cloth and sewed another seam. And another. She was right, learning to guide the cloth in a straight line through the machine was a lot like learning to drive and stay in a lane. Meanwhile, she was hard at work on her own machine a few feet away, which featured a computer display and hummed when she sewed, rather than clattering like his.

After a half hour or so, she came to watch as he completed his straightest seam yet, with only a tiny wobble at the end. "Very nice," she proclaimed. "I'll give Nancy a call."

Before he could ask questions, she'd already dialed a number. "Hi, Nancy, this is Kristen. I heard Maisey had to fly down south to help her mother. Uh-huh." She listened for a while. "Oh, that's good news. But still, a tough time to be away from home." Another long pause, and then she said, "Yes, that's what I was calling about. Nick Bernardi, you know, the man who's watching Emily's kids?... Well, I've just given him a sewing lesson and he's volunteered to take over sewing the costumes." A pause and then a laugh. "No, at my place. I'll be right here to guide him along... You will? That's wonderful. See you then. 'Bye-'bye." Kristen hung up the phone. "She's bringing everything over here."

"I could pick it up," Nick offered.

Kristen shook her head. "No, she says she needs to stop by the mercantile anyway, and she's thrilled that you're stepping up. Maisey's mom got through surgery just fine, by the way, but she'll need someone to stay with her for a week or ten days while she recovers, so Maisey will barely get back in time for Christmas. In the meantime, I'm going to show you how to wind a bobbin and thread the machine. We're safe going with medium brown thread, I think, for most of the costumes."

Ten minutes later, the front door opened, and a woman stepped inside, carrying a large plastic bin. "Knock, knock," she called. "It's me."

"Hi, Nancy," Kristin replied as Nick went to relieve her of her load. "This is Nick."

"So nice to meet you," Nancy replied as Nick set the bin on an empty table near the door. "Maisey will be so relieved. Yesterday, she was talking about having me ship all the costumes down so that she could work on them there, but now she can just concentrate on taking care of her mother."

"So you're Carly's grandmother?" As he recalled, Carly was playing the raven.

"That's right." She beamed. "You're the one who's been helping with the practices. You've certainly pitched in. Are you moving to Swan Falls?"

"No, he's just filling in while Janice is traveling," Kristen told her. "He's that pilot, the one who's going to Hawaii."

"Oh, the pilot. How are your eyes?"

Nick blinked. How did they know so much about him when he knew nothing about them? Close community, he guessed. "They're doing well, thanks." That was only partially true. The halos had been less bothersome when he drove Max home from Wasilla Saturday, but they were still a problem.

"Well, I appreciate all your work on the pageant and costumes. If you need me to watch Max and Lyla while you're at a doctor's appointment or anything, just let me know and I'd be glad to."

"That's kind of you to offer."

She waved her hand. "In Swan Falls, we like helping each other out. That's the beauty of a small town, eh, Kristen?"

"Yes," Kristen replied. "But if Nick is going to get those costumes sewn, he'd better get started. Thanks for dropping them off, Nancy."

"You bet." Nancy took the hint and retreated out the door.

Kristen opened the bin. On top was a pattern envelope, with pictures of kids dressed as a squirrel, a skunk, and an owl. The costumes themselves were loose overalls, sort of like a hazmat suit, with colors, tail designs, and in the case of the owl, sleeve design, creating the different animals. The rest of the bin was filled with gallon-size plastic zipper bags. Each cloth-filled bag was labeled with a child's name, size, and role. Kristen opened several bags and glanced inside. "You're in luck.

It looks like Maisey already put in all the zippers, which is the hardest part of the process."

"That's good."

"Very good." She opened the pattern envelope, removed what looked like an instruction page, and spread it on the table. Then she unfolded the pieces from the first bag, labeled Fox. It was a reddish brown and had a white chest patch already attached to the front on either side of the zipper. "She's already got the sleeves on this one, too. You'll just need to do the side and leg seams, and casings for the elastic in the wrists and ankles." She pointed to step six on the instruction sheet. "You're right here."

Nick had little idea what she was talking about, but he'd seen enough to know he could trust her to lead him in the right direction. "All right then. Let's get started."

EMILY WAS CHECKING her email during dinner that evening when she noticed a voice mail. She'd just assumed the unknown number earlier was spam, but if they'd gone to the trouble to leave a message, maybe not. She listened to the message. "Hi, this is Melissa Greer, manager for the Glacier Bears twelve and thirteen boys' team. I have news about Max's tryouts. Could you please call me at this number? Thanks."

Emily took a breath. If it was good news, the manager would have said so, right? Most likely, she wanted Emily to call so that she could say something encouraging, like that Max showed potential and if he worked hard, he might someday make the team. As though Emily would put him through the disappointment again. Should she break the news on the evening call, or wait until she got home and could be there in person to comfort Max? But she wouldn't be home until Christmas Eve, and she didn't want the bad news to cast a pall over Christmas. Besides, Dina would presumably have gotten a call, too, so it was quite possible Ian had already broken the news to Max.

Why, oh, why, didn't Nick consult her before taking Max to the tryouts? Yes, he'd apologized, and yes, she'd forgiven him, but the deed was done, and now she was going to have to deal with it.

She hesitated for a moment, and then pressed the icon to return the call. Four rings, and then a somewhat breathless voice answered, "This is Melissa."

"Melissa, it's Emily Cooper returning your call."

"Ah, Max's mom, right? Forgive my panting, I was in the kitchen, and I'd left my phone upstairs."

"Sorry." Emily shouldn't have called at dinnertime.

"No problem. Just loading the dishwasher. I'm glad you called back. Thanks so much for letting Max try out—"

But he's not good enough... Emily was already hearing it in her head.

Melissa continued, "The coach is really excited about adding Max to the lineup."

"I underst— Wait, what?"

"He thinks Max will be a terrific addition for our team. Boys this age tend to gravitate toward offense—they want to be the one to score—but he says Max has excellent defensive instincts and a solid foundation of basic skills. Coach feels like he has the potential to become an outstanding player. Practices start in January. I don't have the schedule in front of me right now, but I'll send it to your email."

"That sounds great," Emily said. "Thanks."

"No, thank you!" Melissa replied. In the background, two children seemed to be debating whose turn it was to take out the trash. "I have to go," Melissa said, "but save my phone number and feel free to call if you have any questions. 'Bye."

"'Bye." Emily ended the call. Wow. Max must have really impressed them. Nick was right. While she had been focused on playing it safe, making sure Max wasn't disappointed, Nick had seen that he was ready for the next level. That Max had the "potential to become an outstanding player."

She checked her watch. She was a little early for the evening video call, but she couldn't wait. She texted Nick. Could you get the kids and set up the computer call?

He responded immediately. No problem.

A minute later, the kids appeared on her phone.

"Hi, Mom," Max said. "Ian made the team for the Glacier Bears. Nick hasn't heard anything yet, though, so I don't think I did. But Nick's been showing me some dribbling drills to work on and I might be able to try out again for the summer session." He didn't even sound upset, just determined to work toward his goal. Such a mature attitude. Why had she been so afraid to let him fail?

"You won't be trying out this summer—" she tried to keep a straight face, but the corners of her mouth kept pulling upward "—because you're on the team! Congratulations!"

"I'm on the Glacier Bears? Woo-hoo!" Max yelled.

Lyla and Nick were cheering, too. Nick slapped Max on the back. "Congrats, Max!"

"She said the coach was impressed with your excellent defensive instincts," Emily told him.

Nick grinned. "I knew he was good." When Nick met Emily's eye through the screen, she expected to detect some level of smugness, but no, all she saw was genuine excitement for Max's accomplishment.

She smiled at him. "I'm glad you did."

CHAPTER FIFTEEN

CHRISTMAS EVE, EMILY'S second-favorite day of the year, was off to a great start. The new procedure had gone off without a hitch—her plane left the North Slope at exactly its scheduled time of 7:50 a.m., and the Anchorage forecast had called for light snow overnight, guaranteeing Christmas-card vistas all the way home.

As she buckled her seat belt, her thoughts slipped to Nick, and to those kisses on the porch just before she left. Would the attraction still be there? Did she want it to be? She had thought of him far too often, lying on her bunk at night.

With effort, she pushed those thoughts from her mind and instead focused on her plans for today and tomorrow. It normally took her twenty minutes to deplane and shuttle to the parking lot, then fifty-five minutes to drive home, but the snow might add a few minutes to her commute, which would put her at the house at about eleven. That gave her plenty of time to bake a batch of peppermint brownies for tonight's dessert, wrap the gifts she'd had Nick hide in the storage room, plant treasure-hunt clues, and change into her Christmas sweater before heading to the school for the Christmas pageant.

The pageant was always fun, but it would be even more special since Max was a sixth grader and would be up on the stage this year. And, according to the kids, Nick had sewn some of the costumes. She smiled at the thought. Nick Bernardi, confirmed bachelor, working as a nanny, baking cookies, sewing costumes—who would have guessed he could be so domestic?

This evening, she and the kids would use the clams they'd dug last summer to make clam chowder for dinner, along with cheddar drop biscuits. Then a treasure hunt to find the hidden early gifts—pajamas and new books—and a family read-in before the traditional Christmas prep at bedtime.

Tomorrow should be fun. All the gifts she'd ordered had been delivered. And Nick had picked up the ingredients she would need for their traditional Christmas foods. Janice would have moved the clams from the freezer to the refrigerator to thaw. But Emily wasn't counting on her for much more. Janice would no doubt be suffering from jetlag after flying all day yesterday and arriving late last night when Helen's nephew, uh, Peter—why couldn't she ever remember his name?—was to have picked the two of them up at the airport as planned and delivered them home. Emily couldn't wait to hear all about Janice's adventures.

Emily's flight landed, and she followed a man and an elderly woman out of the terminal. As they crossed the covered street of the loading zone to reach the shuttle stop, a snowplow powered past, clearing the street but creating a raised bank between the street and the sidewalk. She frowned. They must have gotten a lot more snow than the three inches predicted, and it was still falling at a steady rate. This did not bode well for her schedule.

The shuttle arrived and the doors opened, but the snowbank blocked the way. The man climbed on top of it, packing it down to form a flat surface, which took some doing. Meanwhile, Emily used her gloved hands to carve out a step on the side of the snowbank, and the driver did the same on the other side. Eventually, they managed to create a little staircase that went up, over the snow, and back down the other side to the shuttle step.

"All aboard," the driver called.

The man went first, and then turned to offer a hand. Emily helped the older woman climb up. Once she was safely inside, Emily scrambled in herself. She grinned at the driver and found a seat. "Hi, Fin. Looks like it's going to be a challenging day for you."

"This is my first run." He put the shuttle into gear and followed the path the plow had just cleared. "But nothing's getting me down today.

It's Christmas Eve, and one more semester is behind me."

"How did it go in Physics?" she asked.

"I got a B. Can you believe it?"

"Awesome," Emily said. "A B in Johnson's class is like an A plus anywhere else."

The shuttle pulled into the parking lot. Someone had obviously plowed recently, since there was only an inch or so covering the pavement. No one had shoveled the cars, however, and Emily found hers coated with a solid eight inches of snow. She pawed the snow away from the tailgate and pressed the button to open it, leaning in to reach the shovel she kept in the back. As the gate reached its uppermost height, a gap formed and a splatter of snow fell on top of Emily. She shook it off and shoveled the snow from her vehicle while recalculating her schedule. She could still make the brownies and wrap the pajamas and books, but she would have to do the rest of the wrapping after the kids went to bed. Then she noticed the woman who had boarded the shuttle with her trying to clear her car using only her hands.

She walked over, carrying the shovel. "Need some help?"

"I would be most grateful," the woman said. "I can't believe the brush I usually use is missing."

It didn't take too long to clear the small car, and soon, both of them were pulling out of the parking lot, only to find traffic backed up at the first traffic light. The plows had only cleared one northbound lane on Minnesota Avenue. The pattern continued throughout the city, with single lanes of traffic backing up to the point that it was taking Emily three or four cycles to get through each traffic light. It took an hour and a half to complete what was normally a thirty-minute drive across town to the Glenn Highway. Okay, no wrapping until tonight, just time to whip up the brownies and change into her sweater.

But the highway was no better. She joined a line of cars, following behind the snowplow at about twenty miles per hour. By the time she reached the exit to Swan Falls, it was past the pageant's start time. When she got close to the school, she began seeing cars parked along the street, hinting that the school parking lot was full. She took the first empty parking spot she saw, three blocks away, and ran as fast as she could through the snow.

Inside, she slipped into the back of the semidark multipurpose room and picked up a program from the table by the door. Janice was probably saving her a chair somewhere, but rather than disrupt the audience, she found an empty seat on the far edge of the room. Onstage, in front of a painted forest scene, an owl, a pika, and a squirrel were having a conversation that involved lots of melodramatic gestures. The costumes were simple jumpsuits. The owl's was a gray feather print, the pika's costume was a mottled taupe, and the squirrel wore reddish-brown with a white chest and a padded tail curled upward and attached to the back of the costume. Each of them wore a headdress with ears and had their faces made up to mimic the animals they were portraying. Ms. Harper, the art teacher, must have done the excellent makeup. Emily could barely recognize Zoe behind that squirrel face.

She used her phone to cast light on the program. They seemed to be in scene two, and she'd missed singing performances from the kindergarten/first graders and the second and third graders, plus the opening scene of the play, hopefully not the scene Max was in. A minute later, the trio finished the scene, the curtains closed, and the lights came next to the stage to highlight the fourth-grade class, who stood in three rows. After a short piano intro, they burst into a song about good neighbors. Lyla was right in the middle, standing next to Paisley, singing her heart out.

Once the song was completed, the curtains reopened to a new scene with mountains in the background. No one was onstage yet, but from her seat, Emily could see figures bustling around behind the curtains, and there was Nick, right in the middle, nodding to one of the kids who was dressed as a raven and setting a reassuring hand on their shoulder. A second later, four kids trooped onto stage. The porcupine delivered his line to the raven, who froze and looked toward Nick. Nick whispered the line, and, with obvious relief, the raven repeated it. At the end of their part, Nick offered silent high fives to each of them but saved a special smile for the raven with stage fright.

Meanwhile, a moose, a Dall ram, and a caribou entered from the other side of the stage. The elaborate antlers, horns, and makeup were so good, Emily almost didn't recognize Max and Ian. They did a terrific job delivering their lines, and even had a few dance steps when the chorus chimed in with a funny song. Max was grinning when he left the stage, giving Nick a high five as he passed him. The fifth graders sang, and then the final scene began.

All the animals came together for a birthday party, and they rolled out a huge sheet cake, but when they called Ms. Susanna up on the stage and announced the party was to honor her birthday, there wasn't a dry eye in the place. Certainly not Ms. Susanna's—she had tears of joy running down her face while all the "animals" took turns hugging her. Then, led by the chorus, the entire assembly sang "Happy Birthday" to her. A complete success.

Afterward, the school served punch, cake, and Christmas cookies, giving everyone a chance to congratulate the kids and wish Susanna a happy birthday. Emily wished she'd had time to change from her canvas pants, hoodie, and work boots, but nobody batted an eye at her ensemble.

"Mommy!" Lyla spotted Emily in the crowd and ran up to give her a hug. "Did you see me?"

"I did! You were great! You, too, Max," she added, as with studied casualness, he came to stand beside her. In deference to his sensibilities, she didn't give him a full hug in front of his friends but sneaked in a little shoulder squeeze. "Super job!"

Nick hurried over. "You made it! With all that snow, I wasn't sure you'd be able to."

"It was close. As you can see, I came straight here." She gestured to her work clothes. "Where's Janice?"

"Unfortunately, a late flight caused them to miss a connection, and the airline couldn't reschedule until today," Nick said. "So they put her and Helen up in a hotel in Atlanta."

"Oh, no."

"Actually, I think they enjoyed it. She said the hotel happened to be putting on a murder-mystery dinner event and they were able to join in. They flew out early this morning. I'm picking them up at eleven forty-five tonight."

"I thought Peter was picking them up."

"He was yesterday, but tonight he had a conflict, so since I knew you'd be home with the kids, I volunteered."

Max peered at the refreshments table. "They're cutting the cake. I'm going to get some before it's all gone." He and Lyla hurried off, leaving Emily with Nick.

He grinned. "So what did you think of the pageant?"

"I'm impressed." Emily spotted Maisey Moore pushing through the crowd toward them.

"You're Nick Bernardi, right?" Maisey asked.

"Yes."

"I'm Maisey Moore. I just got back into town yesterday, and I wanted to thank you for bailing me out on the costumes. I was afraid I was going to have to sew them on my grandmother's old pedal machine and ship them back while I took care of my mom."

"No problem," Nick said. "You'd already done the hard parts. How is your mother?"

"Much better. Healthy enough that she flew back with me and is going to spend a few weeks with us here. Anyway, just wanted to let you know I appreciate it. I'd better get back to the kids." As she turned, she almost bumped into Nathan Swan, who was coming toward them.

"Hi, Emily. Good to see you back home." Nathan turned. "Great job on the play, Nick."

"Yeah, it went well, didn't it? And the music was great, too." As they talked, a couple more people greeted Nick as they walked by. He was really getting to be a part of the community.

After a few minutes, Nathan excused himself and Nick smiled at Emily. "Birthday cake sounds good. Can I get you a piece?"

"No," she said with regret. "I have too much to do at home. But you and the kids stay and enjoy the party."

"What do you need to do?" Nick asked.

She ticked the items off on her fingers. "I need to get the clams out of the freezer, and make tonight's dessert, and wrap—"

"The books?" Nick asked, cutting in. "I already wrapped them. And the pajamas. Max told me about your traditional Christmas Eve treasure hunt. Lyla made peppermint brownies last night after dinner and we hid them from Max, so they're ready for tonight. The clam chowder is already in the slow cooker, all but the cream, which goes in at the end. We got out all the recipes and did an inventory to make sure we have the ingredients for tonight's biscuits and tomorrow's meals. The turkey has been thawing in the refrigerator for four days. Anything else?"

"Uh, no." She looked at him in wonder. "Sounds like everything is done."

"Well, not everything. I didn't quite grasp the whole treasure-hunt setup, but I figured you would have that covered—"

"I do." The clues were in her bag, ready to hide.

"Good. I also didn't wrap the Santa gifts…" He added in a whisper, "Because I wasn't sure if Santa wraps in your household or not."

"He does," she whispered back, "but with special wrapping paper nobody else gets to use. I can take care of that once the kids are in bed."

"Perfect. Now, how about some cake to celebrate your homecoming?"

"Sounds great." She smiled at him. "Merry Christmas, Nick."

He smiled back, and with a warmth that sent little tingles down her spine. "Merry Christmas, Emily."

NICK CHOSE TWO squares of carrot cake—Miss Susanna's favorite, according to the server. Since they would be eating brownies later, he almost skipped the cookie trays, but he spotted some lemon bars. Emily loved anything lemon. He added one to her plate, grabbed two cups of punch, and managed to transport the whole collection to the table where Emily sat, talking with Kailee from the craft store. But once he got there, he couldn't figure out how to put the cake down without spilling the punch. This must be why servers used trays.

"Here, let me get that." Emily took the cups, freeing his hands. "Nick, this is Kailee."

"I know Kailee. She's the one who hooked me up with Kristen O'Malley to teach me to sew. Can I get you some cake, too?"

"No, I've already had three Christmas cookies. Sit down. I was just telling Emily I'm thinking of holding children's craft classes after school, if I can get local artists on board."

"Lyla would love that," Nick said. "Max, too, if you did like a woodworking class, building something simple like a birdhouse. I could—" He stopped. He and Max had built a birdhouse together, a gift for Emily, and he'd been about to volunteer to teach a group of kids how to make one. But there was no time. On January second, he was due to start his new job in Honolulu. "That is, I could, uh, send you a link to a website with simple woodworking project ideas for kids," he said, finishing awkwardly.

"Okay. Thanks," Kailee replied.

"Nick." Nathan tapped him on the shoulder. "Could you give me a hand setting up more tables?"

"Sure." He jumped up, eager to extract himself from the conversation. For a moment there, he'd forgotten that this was all temporary. That his time here in Swan Falls was coming to an end. But he didn't need to think about that right now. Emily was home. The kids were excited. And today was Christmas Eve.

"Got all your Christmas stuff done?" Nathan asked as they set up the extra tables.

"Pretty much," Nick answered.

"We were nip and tuck there for a while." Nathan glanced around and then whispered, "We ordered a dollhouse for Paisley like a month ago and it didn't arrive until yesterday. Turns out it's more of a dollhouse kit." He rubbed his hands together. "I think we're going to be up all night assembling it so it can go under the tree tomorrow morning."

Nick grinned. "You don't look too upset about that."

"Nah, I'm kind of excited actually." Nathan chuckled. "It feels like a rite of passage or something."

"Good for you, Dad." Nathan might not have been a dad for long, but from what Nick could see, he was crushing it. While they set up the tables, people kept stopping by to talk. It was a while before he made it back to Emily.

"There you are," she said. "I was beginning to think you weren't returning and was debating whether to eat your cake."

"Don't you dare." He slid into the seat beside her and picked up a plastic fork. "Peggy, the cook at the lodge, made it." He took a bite. "So good."

Emily chuckled. "Do you know everyone in Swan Falls?"

"I doubt it, but the people I've met, I like."

"I'm glad." She finished her punch and set the cup on her empty plate. "I'm going to head home to arrange the treasure hunt. Give me at least a fifteen-minute head start before you bring the kids, okay?"

"Sounds good. The packages are in your secret wrapping room."

He watched as she crossed the room toward the trash cans, stopping to talk to Lyla's teacher, who looked delighted to see her. And who wouldn't be delighted? With her bright eyes and friendly smile, Emily was a joy to be around. Suddenly, fifteen minutes seemed like too long to wait to be with her again, but he filled the time finishing his cake and chatting with folks before rounding up the kids. "Time to go home."

As soon as Nick pulled into the garage, Max and Lyla jumped out of the car and ran into the house. Nick was right behind them. Nala met them at the door, and the savory aroma of clams, potatoes, and onions filled the kitchen, but Emily was nowhere to be seen.

"Mommy?" Lyla called.

"I'm right here." Emily, now dressed in a festive sweater, stepped out from behind the Christmas tree and opened her arms. "Hugs?"

Max and Lyla hugged their mom, and then it was Nick's turn. When he pulled her close, he caught the scent of lavender, just as he had that night he'd kissed her on the porch. He forced himself to let go after a moment. "Glad you're home."

"Me, too." She smiled at him.

"Do you have our joke?" Lyla asked eagerly.

Max halfway rolled his eyes, but Nick noticed he was waiting, too.

"A geologist told me this one," Emily said. "Which reindeer is a dinosaur's least favorite?"

"Uh, Rudolph?" Lyla asked.

Emily shook her head. "Comet."

Max and Nick burst out laughing. Those two little lines formed between Lyla's eyebrows, but then she grinned. "Oh, because of the comet that made them go extinct. I get it."

Emily slipped her arm around Lyla's shoulder. "Since Lyla made the brownies last night and Nick already has the clam chowder cooking, we have about an hour before we need to start on the biscuits. Do you want to go sledding?"

"Yeah. I'll get my snow pants on." Lyla took off upstairs, with Max right behind her.

Emily looked toward Nick, and their eyes locked. Without conscious intent, Nick found himself moving closer. She met him halfway, then he wrapped his arms around her, and they were kissing, there by the Christmas tree. So much for good intentions, but this felt right. Too soon, she pulled away. "The kids will be down any second."

"Yeah, we'd better get our snow gear on." But neither of them made a move. "Meet you in the garage in five?" Nick suggested.

She chuckled. "That's not going to happen unless we let go."

"Sadly, you're right." Nick dropped his arms and stepped back just as she did the same.

Emily laughed and trotted up the stairs to her room. Nick went to his own room and got dressed for sledding. Two weeks apart hadn't lessened the attraction he felt for Emily—if anything, it only made it stronger. They shouldn't be doing this, not with less than a week until he left for Hawaii, but right now that didn't seem to matter. And maybe that was the point. Right now, this Christmas was all they had, all they would ever have, so as long as they both understood, why not let it happen?

It seemed the sledding hill was the place to be that evening, and the kids had a wonderful time zooming down the hill with their friends. With so many kids taking turns, Emily and Nick didn't participate, just watched from the top of the hill until the hour was nearly up and Emily announced, "Last run for tonight."

Max dragged his sled over to them. "You guys have to try it. The snow is awesome. I'll ride down with Lyla."

"Okay," Nick replied. He sat down on the sled with his knees apart and Emily settled into the space in front of him. It seemed only natural to put his arms around her. Max gave them a shove, and they were off, flying over the slick snow. They hit a bump and both of them were airborne above the sled for a microsecond. Nick tightened his hold, and Emily laughed, the sound loud and joyous, and he couldn't help but join her. They slid to a stop in the deep snow at the bottom of the hill and giggled even more as they tried to untangle themselves and stand up.

Max and Emily came to a sliding stop beside them. "That was fun!" the kids said in unison.

"Yeah. Are you hungry?" Emily asked.

Despite Max having eaten two squares of cake and five cookies at the school—and that was only the food Nick knew about—Max declared, "Starving."

Making the biscuits and adding the final ingredients to the chowder took less than thirty minutes, by which time Max had consumed an apple, some string cheese, and half a bag of pretzels, but that didn't keep him from enjoying the soup and brownies with the rest of them.

As soon as they'd loaded their dishes in the dishwasher, Lyla declared, "Treasure hunt!"

"Yes!" Max added.

Emily grinned. "Okay. Look on the tree and find an ornament shaped like a penguin."

Both kids raced for the tree and began looking. "I found one!" Lyla held up a homemade ornament fashioned out of felt cutouts glued together.

"Oh, sorry, I forgot about that one," Emily said. "The one you're looking for is rounder."

"Got it!" Max held up a ball painted with wings and a white chest, with a penguin head attached to the top. A metal band went around the middle of the ball like a belt. "There's a latch." Max pushed something on the belt, and the ball hinged open to reveal a rolled-up piece of paper. Max read aloud, "'What's round like a bowl, smaller than a bathtub, but even the ocean couldn't fill it?'"

Lyla frowned in concentration. "It's smaller than a bathtub, but the ocean couldn't fill it. Why couldn't the ocean fill it?"

"Because it has holes!" Max cried.

"Yes! The thingy you use to drain spaghetti!" Both kids dashed to the kitchen. Max lifted the silver colander from its hook. Lyla reached inside and pulled out an envelope. "We were right." She opened the envelope and found another slip of paper. "Clue number two…"

Most riddles they got instantly, while others took some time. Before they were done, they'd visited every room of the house plus the front porch, where Lyla found the final clue hidden under the welcome mat, and read it aloud. "'My heart is cold, but I'm always ready to share my food.'"

"The birdfeeders," Max said. He and Lyla checked the two birdfeeders on the porch and then broke into a run to investigate every birdfeeder on the property.

Emily and Nick stood on the porch, watching. Emily had a bemused expression on her face.

"Not the correct answer?" Nick asked her.

"Not even close. If I'd realized they would be running around out here, I would have made them put on coats." She shivered.

"They'll figure it out soon." Nick put an arm around her shoulders, drawing her against him to help keep her warm. "It makes it more fun when it's a challenge."

But the kids, convinced that Max was right, visited each birdfeeder again, checking every surface. In the meantime, Emily snuggled closer against Nick. He decided he was in no hurry for Max and

Lyla to give up, but eventually they returned to the porch. "Can we get another clue?" Lyla asked.

"Sure," Emily answered. "But let's go inside first. It's cold out here."

Reluctantly, Nick moved his arm from Emily's shoulders, and they all stepped into the living room. Emily went to stand with her back to the fire. "Okay, first clue. No need to go outside again. It's in the house."

"O-kay," Max mused. "'My heart is cold—'"

"The refrigerator?" Lyla asked. "But we would have seen it when we got out the milk."

"The freezer!" Max shouted. Both kids raced to the laundry room. They came back grinning, each holding a stack of packages. Nick hadn't been positive which books went to who, so he'd wrapped each one individually in candy-cane paper and put a sticky note with the title on the outside. Emily had sorted them and tied a red velvet ribbon around each kid's bundle.

"Did you close the freezer?" Emily asked them.

"Uh—" Max looked back toward the laundry room.

"I'll check." Nick found the top sitting wide open. When he returned to the living room, Emily had pulled five packages from under the tree. Two, he recognized as the pajamas he'd wrapped, but the other three were new.

She handed one to him. "Here's yours, Nick."

"Don't we open packages on Christmas morning?" he asked. That's what Lyla had told him.

"All but this one." She distributed packages to Lyla and Max as well, keeping one and placing the last one on the coffee table. "This one's for Gramma when she gets home. On your marks. Get set. Go!"

The kids ripped into their packages. Nick opened his more slowly, beginning to suspect what might be inside. Sure enough, he found a pair of red plaid flannel pajama pants with dancing polar bears that matched the ones he'd wrapped for the kids. The coordinating long-sleeve T-shirt featured an ice-skating polar bear tangled in Christmas lights, with the legend Have a Beary Merry Christmas! underneath. Pure Emily.

He grinned at her. "Puns are the lowest form of humor, they say."

She snorted. "Only according to the person who didn't think of it first."

"Let's go put them on," Lyla shouted, "so we can open our books." She and Max grabbed their pajamas and streaked upstairs to their rooms.

Emily picked up Nick's pajamas and held them out to him. "We all have to be in our PJs for the family read-in."

"Yes, ma'am." Nick took the pajamas and went to his room to change. When he got back to the living room, Emily, already wearing her pajama set, was kneeling on the floor, slipping Nala's legs through a matching pajama top. The patient dog wagged her tail, happy to be included.

Emily nodded toward the bundles of books waiting on the coffee table. "I love how you wrapped each book individually so the kids will have the fun of unwrapping each one. I really appreciate all you've done to prepare for Christmas."

Nick shrugged. "I figured if Janice was here, she would have done all that."

Emily gave a wry smile. "Not that she wouldn't if I asked, but I've mostly had her leave things like this for me to do after I get home."

"Oh." Maybe Nick hadn't been as helpful as he thought. "Did I overstep again?"

"No, not at all. It's just that I don't want to make things any harder for Janice than they have to be."

He nodded. That explained all the frozen casseroles and the mammoth food-shopping expedition before she headed to the slope. Emily was devoted to her family, and considering the apathy Nick had experienced as a child, he admired that more than he could say. But Emily wasn't just a mom and employee. She was a woman, too, and as much as she loved doing things with and for the kids, she needed someone to take care of her once in a while. And maybe, during these last few days together, that someone could be him. He sat down on the chair behind her, pushed her hair forward, and began kneading the tight muscles of her neck and shoulders.

"Ahh, that feels good."

He continued to rub, slowly feeling the tension easing. He wanted to lean in and kiss that beautiful neck, but knowing the kids would be back any second, he contented himself with the massage. Seconds later, Lyla came flying down the stairs. "Mommy, can you cut off this tag?"

Emily pulled away from Nick and stood up. "Come with me to the kitchen for scissors."

Max appeared shortly after, laughing when Nala came to meet him wearing the pajama top. Emily and Lyla returned and settled onto the couch to unwrap their books. Judging from the excited squeals, Emily had done a fine job choosing.

"Which one should we read first?" Emily asked.

"The *Adventure Kids Arctic Mystery*," Lyla shouted.

Max nodded. Emily switched off all the lights except for the reading lamp beside the chair closest to the fire and the twinkling lights of the tree. She sat down and opened the book to the first page. The fire crackled softly in the background while she read. The lamp beside her chair highlighted the curve of her cheek, the graceful sweep of her hair. Beautiful.

The kids listened, throwing out an occasional laugh or comment. When Emily reached the end of the first chapter, she tucked in a bookmark and stood up. "Who's reading next?"

"Me!" Lyla volunteered.

"Can we make hot chocolate first?" Max asked.

"Sure." Emily started for the kitchen.

"I'll do it." Nick hurried to beat her there. "You've had a long day. Just relax."

She tossed him a surprised look, and then a smile. "Okay, I will. Thanks. Could you make mine peppermint tea, please?"

"Absolutely." He boiled water in the kettle while he heated the milk for cocoa. Ten minutes later, he carried a tray with four mugs into the living room. Lyla was in the chair now, reading her chapter. Max had moved to the floor in front of the fire, and was rubbing Nala's belly. Emily was on the couch, wrapped in a fleece blanket with her feet tucked up under her. Nick set the tray on the coffee table and distributed the mugs. He sat down at the opposite end of the couch from Emily and listened to the story.

At the end of that chapter, Max and Lyla changed places, involving a rearrangement of mugs, blankets, and the dog. While they waited for the kids to resettle, Emily shifted her legs out from under her. Nick reached for her sock-clad feet, set them on his lap, and rubbed the ball of one foot with his thumb.

"Mmm." Emily closed her eyes and then opened them. "You don't have to do that," she whispered.

"Shh," he said as Max opened the book. "Max is reading."

She didn't protest further, and by the time Max

had finished his chapter, Emily's eyes were closed, and she was breathing evenly. In the sudden quiet, she let out a tiny snore. Lyla giggled. "Mommy's asleep."

"Let's be quiet then," Nick whispered. With all the Santa presents to wrap, it would no doubt be a late night for Emily. "Lyla, you're up."

"But it's your turn to read," Lyla protested in a stage whisper.

He didn't want to risk moving Emily's feet. "I'll do it later."

Two chapters later, Emily awoke with a start. "Oh, wow. Did I fall asleep?"

"Yeah," Max said. "But don't worry. Nothing real exciting has happened, except they saw a polar bear. It's Nick's turn to read."

By bedtime, they'd made it halfway through the book. Then Emily announced it was time to prepare for Santa. Although, judging by their smirks, the kids knew, or at least suspected, the truth about Santa's visit, they happily played along, leaving carrots outside for the reindeer and a plate of cookies for Santa. Then Emily tucked them into bed.

Afterward, she came downstairs, where Nick had picked up the wrapping paper and was winding the ribbons into a roll. "All asleep?" he asked.

"Hardly." Emily chuckled. "But they will be soon. It's been a long day. They're tired." She gathered the empty mugs to carry to the kitchen.

"How about you?" he asked, as he gathered up

the kitchen trash. "It's been a long day for you, too."

"I feel pretty good. That catnap helped. I'll be filling stockings and wrapping gifts for a while."

"Want any help?" he offered.

She glanced his way. "After all you've been doing today, you're probably ready to hit the hay."

"You've worked just as hard. Besides, I'm picking up Janice and Helen at the airport, remember? The highway's been plowed. I've checked. That means I have a little over an hour before I need to leave, and I've never had the opportunity to play Santa before."

"Well, in that case, let's get wrapping." She took his hand and started toward the stairs, but he pulled her back.

"Before we go up, there's something I've been wanting to tell you all day."

"What's that?" she asked.

Instead of answering, he touched her face, and when she responded with a little smile, he took her in his arms and kissed her, slowly and thoroughly. Her hands pressed against his chest and then slid up to encircle his neck and draw him close. When they finally broke the kiss, she chuckled. "I thought you said you had something to tell me."

"I do." He kissed her once again. "Welcome home, Emily."

CHAPTER SIXTEEN

LATE AFTERNOON ON Christmas Day, the lack of sleep was beginning to catch up with Emily as she sipped her mug of *kinderpunsch,* a warm nonalcoholic fruit drink similar to mulled wine, which, according to Janice, was pretty much the official drink of European Christmas markets. The kids had been awake before six thirty this morning, champing at the bit to check their stockings. None of the adults had gotten to bed before two, but the kids' enthusiasm was both noisy and contagious, and by seven, they'd all gathered in the living room to unwrap their gifts.

Janice lavished them all with wool sweaters, candies, cookies, and new Christmas ornaments. She brought Max a scarf and autographed soccer ball from his favorite player from the Real Madrid team, Lyla got a carved music box, and both Emily and Nick received butter-soft leather belts. From the stories and photos she'd already shared, it seemed the cruise had been a great success. Emily vowed to herself to make sure Janice had the opportunity for many more trips like this one.

The kids were thrilled with their Santa gifts, both the ones they'd asked for and the surprises. Lyla had already made a microwave-set tie-dye shirt after lunch, and she and Max were currently in front of the television, playing the new soccer video game Max had requested. Janice had excused herself to take a much-needed nap right after lunch, and Nick was outside, filling the birdfeeders and installing her gift from him: a new birdfeeder with a built-in camera giving her a close-up view of the visitors there.

A chirp sounded on her phone. She opened the app to see a close-up of a redpoll gobbling up sunflower seeds. Sweet! She would even be able to see the birds when she was up on the slope. A second later, the bird flew away and she could see Nick's hand adding more seeds to the feeder and then a fish-eye view of his face, examining something. Even this distorted funhouse version of Nick was handsome. She smiled and pressed a finger against her lips, thinking about that kiss last night.

Welcome home, he'd said, and she'd certainly felt at home there, in his arms. Holding him close. Kissing his lips. And then they'd worked together to wrap the gifts and fill the stockings. The softness in his eyes whenever he looked at her, it made her feel...cherished.

It wasn't real, of course. In a few days, Nick

would be on a plane to Hawaii, starting a new life far away. But at least for today, for Christmas, she was just going to go with the flow. Another chirp sounded, and she watched a pair of chickadees feasting. A few minutes later, Nick came in through the back door and padded into the living room to see her on her phone.

"Is the camera working?" he asked, leaning against the side of the chair to look at the screen.

"Yeah, it's great." She tilted the phone so that he had a better view. A nuthatch had joined the chickadees, squabbling over the treats.

"Nick, Lyla wants to take a break," Max called. "Can you take her place and finish the game with me?"

"Okay, pause it and I'll be there in a minute," Nick called back. He ran his hand over the sleeve of Emily's new Nordic sweater. "Can I get you anything before I sit down?"

"Nope," she said, looking around the room at the twinkling lights on the tree and the kids playing happily together. She put her hand on top of his. "I have everything I need right here."

MIDMORNING THE NEXT DAY, Nick sliced leftover turkey. He laid out bread slices on the counter and built sandwiches, mayonnaise for Lyla and him, mustard for Emily and Max. No tomatoes on Lyla's sandwich, provolone instead of Swiss on Max's. After considering, he added another slice of bread and made Max a bonus half sandwich. No doubt the calories burned snowshoeing to Swan Falls would leave the boy ravenous. He tried not to dwell on the thought that this would most likely be their last family hike together.

The garage door rumbled and a minute later, Janice came into the kitchen lugging a reusable grocery bag. "They had what I needed at the mercantile!" She unpacked a package of bread flour, a bag labeled malted barley flour, and some packets of yeast. "Wait until you taste Vienna bread. It's wonderful."

"Can't wait." Nick returned the leftover turkey to the refrigerator.

She folded the bag and hung it on the laundry room doorknob to return to the car. "Where is everybody?"

"Getting into their winter gear," Nick replied. "Are you sure you don't want to go with us to the falls?"

"No, thanks. I've had enough steps in the last three weeks to last me for a while. I'm just going to spend the day baking bread and making soup from the turkey bones. It's good to be home." She pulled a big stock pot from the bottom cabinet. "How are your eyes doing?"

"Good. Twenty-fifteen at my last check. I had some halo effects for a little while, but they're gone now. My final appointment is tomorrow, and the doctor doesn't expect any problem certifying me to fly."

"I'm so glad to hear that." She ran water into the pot and set it on the stove. "When do you leave?"

"Three days, assuming all goes well."

"We'll miss you around here." She started the burner under the pot. "Patty Johanson at the mercantile was filling me in on the local news I missed."

"You mean gossip?"

Janice laughed. "Whatever you choose to call it. She says you sewed all the costumes for the entire pageant. When did you learn to sew?"

"A couple weeks ago, and I didn't sew all the costumes. Maisey Moore had already done the hard parts. I just finished them…well, most of them. Kristen O'Malley did the elastic on the last two so that they'd all be ready in time for the dress rehearsal."

Janice looked at him. "I never pictured you volunteering at the school, much less putting in all those hours at a sewing machine."

"Me, either, but the PTO had paid for the fabric and the kids had put in a lot of work getting ready for the play. I just wanted it to go right." Nick sealed the sandwiches into plastic bags, writing names on each bag.

"You've done a wonderful job. I confess, I was a little uncomfortable about leaving the kids alone with you for two weeks."

"You were?" Nick feigned amazement. "I never would have guessed."

She laughed again. "Maybe what I should have been afraid of was that you were trying to put me out of a job."

He gave her a brief shoulder hug. "No need to worry about that. You're irreplaceable."

Janice smiled and went to pull carrots, celery, and onions from the refrigerator. "Max told me he made the Glacier Bears team. How did you convince Emily to let him try out? She was dead set against it when Dina originally suggested it."

"I didn't," Nick confessed. "Max asked if he could go to the tryouts, and I didn't even think about asking Emily before I took him. She was not happy with me."

"But it's good you did. He made the team, so obviously he was ready." Janice washed the produce at the sink. "You know, for me, one of the hardest things about being a single mother was not having another parent with a different point of view to talk things like that over with. I imagine Emily feels that way, too, sometimes."

"She has you," Nick pointed out.

"Yes, but we're too much alike. Neither of us knows first-hand what it's like to be a boy."

"Seems to me you did a wonderful job raising Coop. Believe me, having you as a mom beats the pants off having a mom and dad who don't care.

Why do you think I hung around in your kitchen all the time?"

"I'm glad you did. It was nice having you around I'm proud of you, and I'm proud of the man Coop became." She patted the vegetables dry and set them on a cutting board. "But sometimes I still wonder about some of the choices I made." She sighed, pulled a chef's knife from the block, and cut the thick end from the celery stalks. "By the way," she said, as she chopped, "I ran into an old friend at the airport the other night." Something about the almost studied casualness of her voice made Nick look at her. Her cheeks seemed pinker than usual.

"Who's that?" he asked.

"Someone I used to work with, Dave Hernandez. He was flying in to visit his daughter's family for Christmas."

"Dave Hernandez." The name seemed familiar. Nick tried to think back. "Wait, didn't you date him for a little while when we were in, like, sixth grade?"

"I don't know that I'd say we were dating, exactly." She continued to chop, not looking at Nick. "We went out for dinner a couple of times. But then he got transferred to Miami and we lost touch. Anyway, his daughter lives in Anchorage now. He's recently retired and thinking of moving back to Alaska to be closer to the grandkids, but he doesn't want to be underfoot. I was telling him about Swan Falls. He said he might drive out this afternoon to see it, so I invited him to stay for supper tonight."

"I see." Nick chuckled. "Put a sock on the doorknob if something is happening that you don't want us walking in on when we get back from the hike this afternoon."

She grabbed a dish towel and threw it at him. "Nick Bernardi, what are you suggesting?"

"Kidding." He caught the towel and then leaned over to kiss her cheek. "I think it's great that you and your 'friend' are having a rendezvous."

"Who's rendezvousing?" Emily asked as she carried a backpack into the kitchen.

"Nobody," Janice said while at the same time Nick announced, "Janice has invited a friend for dinner tonight."

"Just someone I used to work with," Janice clarified. "Dave Hernandez. We ran into each other at the airport."

"Oh." Emily walked toward the pantry, but then she stopped and looked back. "Oh," she repeated in a different tone. "A 'friend.'"

Janice looked down but the corners of her mouth twitched upward. "Don't make this into more than it is."

"I won't," Emily replied. "But I will look forward to meeting him tonight."

Max and Lyla came barreling into the room. "We're ready," Lyla chimed.

Max grabbed one of the carrots from Janice's cutting board and munched on it. "Did you pack lunch?"

"Sandwiches and trail mix," Nick said. "Why don't you two grab apples and those little bags of chips from the pantry?"

Emily tucked the food into the top of her backpack, then mumbled, "First-aid kit, space blanket, food, extra socks." When the kids brought the apples and chips, she added them to the pack. "Max don't forget your hat. Lyla, you'll need your heavier gloves. It's only ten degrees outside today."

The weak winter sun had just risen high enough to make it through the kitchen window when the kids came running back. "Let's go," Max urged.

"We'll probably be home around four," Emily told Janice as they headed out the door.

"Have fun," Janice called. "Nick, take good care of them."

He patted her shoulder as he passed by. "I will."

LYLA HAD UNPACKED the contents of her bead-making kit onto the coffee table in the living room, while Max sat in front of the television, watching soccer. Meanwhile, Emily sat by the fire, reading, and had just reached the big reveal scene in the mystery Nick had given her last month when her phone rang. Probably spam. She glanced at the screen, planning to send the call to voice mail, until she saw Nick's name and her heart leaped. He'd gone into Anchorage that morning for his final eye exam. What if something had gone wrong? She answered. "Hi, Nick. What happened with your appointment? Is everything okay?"

"Everything is fine." Loud engine noises in the background almost drowned out his voice. "I passed the eye test, no problem. I was wondering if you, Janice, and the kids had any plans this afternoon."

She let out a breath. "Nothing special. Janice hasn't mentioned anything. Where are you? I can hardly hear what you're saying."

"I'm at Merrill Field in Anchorage," he said, speaking louder. "Just a second until this plane finishes takeoff." The roar increased and then faded away. "Better?"

"Yes."

"I was thinking, since I've now officially been cleared to fly, that I might take everyone up on a flightseeing trip. I just checked, and there's a plane available. The weather looks good. We could do Denali and back in three hours or so. What do you think?"

"Oh, wow." In all their years of friendship, she'd never been on a plane with Nick. She flew past Denali on her way to and from the slope every two weeks, but seeing it from a small plane would be different. "That sounds amazing. Let me ask Janice if she has plans." She walked toward the kitchen, where Janice was putting on the kettle for a cup of tea.

"The plane is a six-seater," Nick said. "So tell her if she wants, she can invite her boyfriend along."

Emily snorted. At dinner last night, Janice had gone to great lengths to act as though Dave was just a friend like any of her other friends. And yet, several times, Emily had spotted Janice looking at him with a special softness in her eyes that wasn't there when she interacted with Helen or Peggy. Dave, on the other hand, was clearly besotted with Janice, complimenting her on the turkey soup and homemade bread—which was quite delicious—and listening intently to every word she uttered. They were so cute.

"Hey, Janice. I'm putting Nick on speakerphone. He wants to celebrate getting his wings back by taking us all on a flightseeing trip over Denali this afternoon. He says he has room for Dave, too, if you want. Are you interested?"

Janice's eyes lit up. "Definitely. I don't know if Dave will be available, but I'm in. When and where?"

"Can you come now?" Nick asked. "I'm at the Yeil Aviation building near the Fifth Street entrance."

"I'll get the kids rounded up," Emily said.

"And I'll call Dave and see if he wants to meet us there." Janice turned off the stove under the kettle. "Can't wait."

"I'll make arrangements for the plane, then," Nick half shouted over the sound of another plane taking off. "See you in about an hour?"

"Sounds good." Emily hung up the phone, smiling. It had been one special treat after another since she got home, and a lot of that was due to Nick. He'd been the one to suggest the snowshoe trek to Swan Falls yesterday, which had been a blast. The kids were amazed at the fantastical shapes of snow over a frozen waterfall, something she hadn't been to see since before they were born. He'd also been the one to suggest they stop for ice cream on the way home—an odd choice after an outdoor adventure in the cold, but one the kids heartily endorsed. And now, he was taking them up in an airplane, to share his world with them. Emily couldn't think of a more fitting way of saying goodbye.

A flash of pain passed through her heart at the thought of him going. How, in such a brief time, had he become so important to her? To the kids? Granted, he'd always been part of the family, kind of an uncle for the kids, occasionally. But now, he seemed to be the very heart of the family. Maybe she should never have put the kids in this situation, where they would lose another man they loved, but how could she have known he would burrow so deeply into their hearts?

Regardless, it was too late now, and she wasn't going to tarnish their last few days together by brooding about what would happen next. For once in her life, she was going to live in the moment. Once he was gone, she could pick up the pieces. She'd done it before.

"Max, turn off the TV. Lyla, leave your things where they are. We're going to Anchorage."

"Aw, Mom," Max groaned, "this match is tied and we're in stoppage time."

"Record it. Nick is taking us all up in a plane to see Denali."

Lyla's eyes widened. "Nick's gonna fly the plane?"

"That's right. Everyone go to the bathroom and get ready to go. Bring your hats and gloves. It might be chilly on the plane." Not to mention they should always have winter gear when they ventured out.

"Is Gramma going?" Lyla asked.

"Yes, and she might bring Dave along, if he's not busy."

"Oh, good. I like him." Lyla looked up toward the ceiling. "I'm going to make him a bracelet. What colors do you think he likes?"

"I have no idea, but if he comes, you can ask. Hurry now, Nick is already at the airport, waiting for us."

They arrived to find Nick and Dave standing in the back corner of the parking lot behind the Yeil Aviation building, watching the airport through the chain-link fence. Emily parked the van nearby, and

Nick turned. "There you are, right on time. We're going to fly in a de Havilland Beaver today."

"Hi," Dave said to all of them, but he was looking at Janice. "Thanks for letting me tag along. I flew in a Beaver for a fly-in fishing trip once, but it's been years."

Janice smiled back at him. "Glad you could make it."

Soon, Nick was loading them into a yellow airplane equipped with fat tundra tires. He directed Janice and Dave to the back seats, the kids in the middle, and Emily up front beside him.

"Since he has experience, maybe Dave should be in the copilot seat," Emily suggested. "I've never even been in a small plane before."

A deep chuckle came from the back of the plane. "Everything I know about piloting I know from watching television," Dave replied.

"I've landed a plane in a video game," Max volunteered.

"Your mom will keep that in mind should the need arise," Nick told him. "Everyone buckle up and put these on." He handed out headsets. "That way we can talk to each other over the noise of the plane."

Once he'd checked that everyone was set, Nick settled into the pilot seat, and Emily could almost see him transforming into pilot mode. He sat up a little straighter, and his focus became more concentrated as he went through the preflight checklist. Then he grinned. "Okay, let's get this baby in the air."

He pushed several buttons and requested permission to take off. A few minutes later they were hurling along the runway before lifting off, clearing the shopping mall across the street from the field and then flying over the dark forest and snow-covered baseball fields of Russian Jack Park, gaining altitude until they were at the rugged Chugach Mountains east of Anchorage. The low winter sun lit the snow-covered ridges and created deep shadows in the valleys.

Emily turned in her seat to check on the kids, who seemed to be enthralled with the view out the windows. "There's Flattop." Dave's voice came over her headset. "My daughter and I hiked up there on summer solstice twenty years ago."

Passing by the Chugach Range, Nick turned the plane north, crossing the Knik Arm toward Point MacKenzie and then a little to the west. "That's the Susitna Glacier," Nick announced. Three winding pathways curved downward from the top of the mountains. Slopes too steep or windy to hold snow created dark patterns all around the flat surfaces of the glaciers.

"Wow," Emily said into her microphone. "From up here you can see how the glaciers really are just rivers of ice."

"But it only moves two millimeters a day," Lyla chimed in. "We studied it in class. The Susitna

Glacier and the Matanuska Glacier dug out the Mat-Su Valley."

"Good thing we didn't live there when it was covered with glaciers," Max commented. "That would make it hard to grow grass for soccer fields."

From there, Nick followed the Susitna River as it twisted and turned, separating into parts and then braiding back together. After a couple of miles, the Parks highway drew a thick line that paralleled the river northward. The sky was mostly clear, but clouds to the north blocked their view of Denali.

"There's Talkeetna," Nick said as they flew over the tiny town with a relatively large airfield that served as a base for flights to Denali to drop climbers who wanted to challenge North America's highest mountain, as well as tourists who just wanted a close-up view.

"Is that Denali?" Max asked as the clouds shifted, and a peak came into view.

"Foraker," Nick said with confidence. "But keep watching." He took the plane higher, and they rose above the clouds to see the famous peak of Denali shining in the sun. Clouds clung to the sides of the mountain below, making the peak appear to be rising out of a white, frothy sea.

"Oo-o-oh," Lyla said. "It's so pretty."

Nick took the plane in a wide circle so that they could admire the mountain from all sides. "Can we go higher?" Emily asked.

"Not in this plane," Nick answered. "We can't

go over ten thousand feet. But we can get closer." He turned toward the mountain. A red plane with skis was flying up from Talkeetna, and Nick fell in behind the other plane, following it along one of the glaciers on the south side of Denali. The red plane dropped lower, and then landed, sliding to a stop on the glacier below.

"Can we do that?" Max asked.

"Not this time," Nick told him. "No skis." But he did follow a different glacier down the mountain and circled over the red plane. The passengers from the plane were heading across the glacier, waving up at them. The kids waved back. Nick followed the loop through the glacial valleys, mountains rising up on either side of them.

"Dall sheep on the right," Dave reported. Emily didn't see them at first, but when Nick rose, turned, and made another pass, she was able to spot the white rams pawing at the snow for forage on the side of the mountain.

Emily turned toward Nick, intending to make a comment, but instead she was struck by his expression, the concentration as he maneuvered the plane through the passes, but also the joy on his face. Flying was what he was born to do. He glanced at her. "Having fun?"

"So much fun," she replied, and the kids chimed in, too.

Without taking his eyes away from the view ahead, Nick grinned. "Me, too."

THE NEXT MORNING Nick was the first one up. He went to the kitchen, greeted Nala, and let her outside while he made coffee, using the special blend from Italy that Janice had given him for Christmas. This time tomorrow, he would be on his way to the airport to begin his new life in Hawaii. Something he'd wanted to do ever since his first visit to Oahu when he was a teenager. So why wasn't he more excited?

Maybe he'd just been so busy, what with the eye surgery, and the pageant, and Christmas, that he'd stopped thinking about what life would be like when he started his new job. He looked out at the snowy landscape that wouldn't see sunrise for another four hours. Sea and sun would be a pleasant change from frozen darkness. And on his days off, he'd be free to snorkel among the tropical fish, or hike up one of the green mountain valleys, or just relax under a palm tree with a cold drink and a good book. It sounded…well, kind of lonely.

But once he was there, he was sure he'd be glad. In the meantime, he'd make the most of his last day in Swan Falls. Nothing too elaborate, he decided. Just family fun. After letting the dog back in, he dug out a waffle iron he'd found in the pantry, sliced strawberries, and waited for the rest of the house to wake up. When he heard voices upstairs arguing about who got to use the bathroom first, he plugged in the waffle iron and stirred the batter.

"Lyla, you can use my bathroom," Emily said, her voice carrying down the stairs.

After filling the waffle iron, Nick chose a Merry Christmoose mug, filled it with coffee, stirred in cream and sugar, and handed it to Emily as she came padding into the kitchen in the Scandinavian knitted slippers Janice had given her.

"Thanks." She took a sip. "Mmm, perfect. Waffles! What a great idea. I'd almost forgotten we had a waffle iron."

"You know what they say about waffles?" Nick asked. "They're really just polite pancakes."

Those two little lines formed between Emily's eyebrows. "How so?"

"They're like, 'Here, let me hold that syrup for you.'"

Emily snorted, barely covering her mouth in time to avoid spewing coffee all over herself. She set the mug on the island and grabbed a paper towel, mopping up her face. "I can't believe it. Nick Bernardi, telling a dad joke."

He grinned. "You've won me over."

"Welcome to the dark side. You're going to love it here."

The waffle iron gave a cheery beep, and Nick opened it and moved the first waffle to a plate, which he set in front of Emily. "Here you go. There are strawberries in the refrigerator." He poured batter into the waffle iron.

After setting her plate and mug on the table,

Emily gathered the bowl of strawberries and a can of whipped cream from the refrigerator, grabbed a bunch of forks from the drawer, swung by the pantry for a bottle of maple syrup, and carried everything to the table. Nick had two more waffles made and a fourth in the waffle iron by the time Lyla and Max stumbled into the kitchen.

"Waffles!" Max picked up a plate and carried it to the table. "Can I put peanut butter on mine?"

"You can put whatever you want on it." Nick grabbed the peanut butter and a knife and set them next to Max.

"Anything?" Lyla asked as she carried her plate over. "How about strawberries and chocolate chips?"

"Okay." Nick grabbed the bag of chocolate chips.

Lyla giggled. "Or what if I wanted candy canes and eggnog?"

"Or turkey and dressing," Max suggested.

"Or liver dog treats!" Lyla laughed louder.

Max snorted. "Or dog po—"

"Enough," Emily ordered. The kids stopped talking, but they giggled even harder.

"Sounds like a party in here," Janice said as she entered the kitchen.

"It's a waffle party!" Lyla announced.

"Sounds yummy." Janice accepted the waffle from Nick and carried it to the table. He set a cup of coffee beside her. "Thank you." She spooned strawberries over her waffle and took a bite. "Are you sure you don't want to stick around, Nick? You could open a waffle place here in Swan Falls."

Lyla gasped. "Oh, I forgot today is your last day."

Nick nodded. "So what do you want to do today? You want to try making the clay beads together with that new kit?"

"Yeah!" Lyla said.

"Will you play a video soccer tournament with me?" Max asked.

"Sure. And maybe we can go sledding this afternoon and get pizza at Raven's Nest for dinner."

"Yes!" Max pumped his fist.

"And then after dinner, we can try out that new board game you got for Christmas." Nick put a hand on Emily's shoulder. "Is that all okay with you?"

There was a definite trace of sadness in the smile she gave him, but her voice was cheerful. "That sounds like a perfect day."

CHAPTER SEVENTEEN

EMPTY CUPS AND stray bits of popcorn littered the top of the table with the new game board in the center. Max was in the lead, only a few spaces from the end, but Nick and Lyla were close behind him. Emily drew a card from the stack and turned to Nick. "The category is Fairy Tales."

"I'll take the question," he replied.

"'A curse has turned a prince into an animal, but it takes a princess's kiss to transform him back into himself. What is that animal?'"

"Hmm." He tapped his chin. "Well, there's that guy with the talking teapot who is some kind of beast." He grinned at Lyla, who had her hand over her mouth, wiggling with the effort to resist giving him the answer. "But I'm going with frog."

"Frog is correct," Emily announced.

Nick rolled the dice. "One. Well that doesn't help much." He moved his marker and handed the single die to Janice, then drew a card. "The category is Plants and Animals."

"I'm going to challenge Max," Janice announced, and gave her best impression of an evil laugh, which wasn't all that evil.

"Okay, Max," Nick said, "here's the question. 'Name a mammal that lays eggs.'"

"Ooh, I know," Lyla chimed.

"Shhh, don't tell him," Emily cautioned.

Max twisted his mouth around to the side, but then he gasped. "Duckbill platypus!"

"Correct," Nick announced. "Actually there are five, the platypus and four kinds of something called echidnas. They all live in Australia or New Guinea. Interesting."

"That backfired." Janice passed the die to Max. "Remember, you have to roll the exact number to get in."

"Come on, five." Max blew on the die, then shook it between his hands before throwing it on the table. It tumbled and skidded across the table and fell on the floor next to Emily's chair. She looked down at the die. "Wow, it's a five."

"I win!" Max shouted.

"Congratulations!" Nick high-fived Max.

Janice moaned. "I should have kept the question."

"Wouldn't have mattered." Nick grinned. "Max was on a roll."

"Good job, Max." Emily collected the game pieces and put them into their slots in the box. "I like that game. What do you all think?"

"It was fun," Lyla said, but then she turned to

shoot a look at Nick. "Except when you passed me that question about kings."

"Sorry," Nick told her. "But you were getting too far ahead." He gathered the cards, shuffled them, and returned them to their cases.

Emily checked the clock on the stove. "It's late. You two had better get to bed. You can do showers in the morning."

Lyla turned to Nick, who was busy gathering up the empty cups. "Will you be here when we wake up tomorrow?"

"I'm afraid not." Nick arranged the cups in the dishwasher and turned to her. "My flight is at ten, and I have to drop off my truck at an auction place before I go to the airport, so I'll be heading out early."

"But you'll come back to visit, right?" Max asked.

"Sure." Nick rested a hand on Max's shoulder. "But not too often. Hawaii is a long way from Alaska."

"Maybe we can come to see you, sometime," Lyla suggested.

"I'd love that," Nick said. "But for now, can I get a goodbye hug?"

Lyla threw her arms around him and squeezed with all her might. "I'll miss you, Nick."

Gently, Nick ran his hand over her back. "I'll miss you, too, sweetheart." His eyes were suspiciously shiny.

Max didn't say anything, but he gave Max a fierce hug. Then, at Emily's urging, both kids headed up for bed.

"Brush your teeth. I'll be by to tuck you in in a minute," Emily called.

Janice yawned. "I believe I'm ready for bed, as well." She took Nick's chin in her hand. "That airline in Hawaii is lucky to have you flying for them. I'm proud of you, and since I've known you since you were Lyla's age, I'm taking a little credit for the man you've become."

Nick smiled at her and blinked a couple of times. "If there's any credit to be had, it's all yours."

"Come here." Janice pulled him into a hug. After a long moment, she released him. "Fly away, but always remember, we're here, rooting for you."

"That means a lot. Good night, Janice."

After a smile and one last pat on his cheek, Janice went off to bed, leaving Emily and Nick alone. For a long moment, they looked at each other in silence, the tension between them almost humming. Finally, Nick glanced down. "You'd better go see about the kids while I clean the table."

She nodded and trotted upstairs, where she found Lyla already in her bed, holding one of her new books.

"Can I read for a little while before I go to sleep?" she asked, yawning as she did. "Since I don't have to go to school tomorrow?"

"Sure, go ahead." Emily kissed her forehead and

arranged the covers around her shoulders. "Happy dreams."

"Good night, Mommy."

Max was in bed, as well, but was staring at the ceiling. One of the gifts Nick had given him, a rebounding soccer net that he could use to practice shots and passes once the snow cleared in the spring, leaned against the foot of his bed. Emily sat down on the edge of his mattress. "Good job in the game this evening."

Max shrugged. "I got lucky."

"Maybe, but you knew the answers to your questions. Good night, Max." Knowing a kiss would embarrass him, she brushed a strand of hair from his forehead and stood up.

"Mom," Max said, before she reached the door.

"Mmm?"

"Do you think Nick will come back?"

"He said he would," she answered. "And I've never known Nick to break his promises." He would come to visit the kids, maybe take them out for the day. It wouldn't be like before, when he could be counted on for birthday parties, backyard cookouts, and the occasional performance or game, but they would still see him. But how long would that last? As he became involved in a new life in Hawaii, the time between visits might grow, until eventually he wasn't coming back at all. But she wouldn't tell Max that. He was hurting enough.

"I don't mean just to visit," Max clarified. "Do you think he'll move back to Alaska ever?"

"Oh. I kind of doubt it. Nick has wanted to move to Hawaii for a long time. Once he's there, I imagine he'll stay."

Max sat up. "What if you told him not to go? You could ask him to stay here and watch us."

"I couldn't do that. Nick was staying with you and Lyla as a favor, but he's not a professional nanny. He's a pilot. You saw how he flew the plane the other day. That's what he does."

"He could do that here, in Alaska, like he did before," Max said stubbornly.

"He could, but I would never ask him to give up his dream of living in Hawaii." She adjusted Max's blanket. "Someday when you're all grown up, if you want to move away, I won't try to make you stay. When you love someone, you want the best for them."

He looked at her sharply. "You love Nick?"

"Sure. He's like part of the family," she said, but was it true? Her feelings when she was around Nick hadn't been entirely the sort she would feel for a brother or a friend. She wouldn't kiss a friend the way she'd kissed Nick.

"Oh." Max seemed a little disappointed.

"Goodnight, Max. We'll do something fun tomorrow. Maybe go to a movie."

"Okay," he said, but with little enthusiasm. "Good night."

She shut the door and returned to Lyla's room, where she found her daughter already asleep, the book she'd been reading on the floor beside the bed. Emily put it on the nightstand, turned off the light, and tiptoed out.

She shut the door behind her and looked down the stairs, her heart aching at the thought that Nick wouldn't be there tomorrow. Maybe she should just go on to bed herself, forget about the pain of saying goodbye. But she couldn't do it. She found him in the kitchen, starting the dishwasher. Once again, their eyes met, but before either of them could say anything, her phone gave a bird chirp.

"That's odd. The birds should be roosting, not eating at the feeders." She opened the app to the feeder camera and backed up the video. "Oh, look."

Nick came to stand beside her, and she showed them the fleeting glimpse of huge eyes and pointed head feathers brushing by the feeder. "A great horned owl. I wonder if he's still there."

"Let's find out." They pulled on jackets and hats, and Emily grabbed a fleece blanket on the way out to the porch. A half moon shone between the clouds.

Nick sat down on the wooden bench next to the door and patted the space next to him. Emily sat down and he put an arm around her. She spread the blanket over their laps and pulled it up to their chins, creating a warm cocoon for the two of them.

The Christmas lights on the trees had automatically shut off at ten. At first, all Emily could see of the yard was the lawn area where the moonlight lit the snow and faint outlines of trees and bushes, but as her eyes adjusted, she began to make out the shapes of the mailbox and the various birdfeeders. A line of tiny tracks cut across the lawn between two of them, probably from a vole, which would explain the owl's presence. No breeze disturbed the exquisite silence of the scene. She rested her head against Nick's shoulder, feeling a contentment she couldn't explain. Something about the warmth of his body, the woodsy scent of the soap he used, the rhythm of his breathing—it all just felt like home. Family. Love. Oops, there was that word again.

"There he is," Nick whispered. "On Max's tree, second limb from the top on the left side."

Now that he'd pointed it out, the owl was quite clear, his distinctive "horned" head silhouetted against the winter sky. He turned his head, those enormous eyes scanning the area below while the rest of his body remained perfectly still. And then in a flash, he was off, streaking down on silent wings to strike at something in the shadows and then flying off into the forest. "Wow," she breathed.

"Wow, indeed." Nick shifted toward her. All she had to do was lift her face and then they were kissing, sending tremors straight to her toes. She reached up to stroke his cheek, to run her fingers over the bit of scruff on his jawline, and then she wrapped both arms around his neck and pulled him closer as they deepened the kiss, and her heart went into double time. When their lips eventually broke apart, they were both breathing fast.

He gazed at her as though he wasn't quite sure she was real, but even in the dark, she could sense an underlying sadness in his eyes. This was goodbye, and things would never be like this between them again.

Would he stay if she asked? He might, if he really thought she and the kids needed him. But she couldn't do that. What she'd said to Max was true. When you loved someone, you wanted the best for them, no matter what. Tomorrow he would be on a plane to Hawaii, chasing his dream, and she needed to let him go with no reproach, no reservations.

He had a long day ahead of him, starting early in the morning. She ought to get up and say goodnight, ought to encourage him to get some sleep. But their cozy little cocoon held her there, as though by magic. And so, instead of moving away, she leaned in for another kiss.

THE NEXT MORNING, Nick dragged his two suitcases from his bedroom as silently as he could so as not to wake the rest of the house, but when he got to the kitchen the light was on and coffee was brewing. Emily, in her Christmas pajamas, sat at the table beside the window, sipping from a mug. When she heard him, she turned and flashed him a smile. "Good morning."

"What are you doing up so early?" he whispered.

She shrugged. "I was awake, so I thought I might as well get up." She set down her cup and came toward him, her slippers slapping against the floor. "Need any help getting your stuff loaded?"

"No, it's just these two suitcases and my satchel."

"Want some breakfast?" she offered, but he shook his head.

"Too early. I thought I'd grab something at the airport."

"How about a coffee to go then?" she offered.

"Sounds good. I'll just put these in the truck and be back in a minute." He loaded everything and came back inside, where Nala had joined Emily in the kitchen. Emily held a souvenir travel mug decorated with a whale's tail.

"That's not my mug," he pointed out, as he stroked Nala's head.

"I know. You can return it next time you visit." She handed him the mug, but she didn't let it go until he met her eyes. "You are coming back to visit, right? I know you wouldn't lie to the kids about something like that."

"I'll be back," he promised. "But it might be a while. I don't get much vacation the first year."

They stared at each other for a moment, and then he set the mug on the island. "One last kiss, so I don't turn into a frog?"

With a snort of amusement, Emily rushed into his arms. The kiss was sweet, but it did nothing to lessen the ache in his chest. He held her tight, postponing the inevitable, but eventually he had to let her go. "You take care of yourself."

"We will," she assured him.

"Not we. You. I know you'll take good care of the kids, and Janice, and the dog, and the teachers, and the wild birds, and the people at work, but don't forget to be kind to yourself, as well. Okay?"

She sniffed and nodded.

"Goodbye, Emily." He kissed her on the forehead, ruffled Nala's ears, and then turned and left. The drive into Anchorage seemed shorter than usual. Part of him wished for an emergency that would block the highway and force him to turn around and return to Swan Falls, but that would only mean another round of painful goodbyes. Taking his truck to the warehouse and signing the title over so that they could sell it for him at their next auction took less time than he'd expected, which meant he arrived at the airport early, just as the sky began to lighten over the mountains. As the taxi drew close to the drop-off area, one of the lanes had been blocked off and the others were filled with cars.

"Which airline?" the taxi driver asked, but Nick could see a major traffic snarl near that gate.

"Just drop me here," Nick told him. "I can walk."

The taxi driver pulled to the curb and unloaded.

Nick paid him and rolled his suitcases along the walkway to the first door. Inside, Nick made his way around the crowd, passing next to the kiosk where he and Emily had gotten coffee together when she'd mentioned needing a nanny—was it really less than two months ago? It felt like a lifetime. "Excuse me," he said as he started to pass a man reading the menu board, but then he recognized him. "Nathan?"

"Nick! Hi."

"Hi. What are you doing here? On your way somewhere?"

"No, actually I'm here to pick up Amanda's mom and her husband, but their flight was delayed an hour, so I've been wandering around the airport," Nathan explained. "How about you?"

"Me? I'm going to Oahu to start my new job," Nick told him.

"Working in Hawaii, huh?"

"Yeah." Nick checked his watch. "Say, I have some extra time. How about if I check this luggage and we grab breakfast while you wait?"

"I'd like that."

The coffee kiosk didn't serve food, but one of the restaurants offered egg-and-sausage sandwiches and coffee at a take-out window outside the secure area. They took their breakfasts and went to sit on one of the nearby benches.

"So," Nick said as he opened his take-out box. "A visit from your new in-laws. Are you nervous?"

Nathan laughed. "Maybe a little. I want them to have fun, and I'm not sure how much they're into things like cross-country skiing. I think they're mostly here to spend time with Paisley, though, and we are a lodge, so it's not like we're unaccustomed to hosting visitors. But how about you? You're a pilot, right? Will you be flying jets back and forth from Hawaii to Anchorage?"

Nick shook his head as he finished chewing. "No, I'm working for a small inter-island airline. I'll be flying a Cessna Grand Caravan."

"That's a turboprop?"

"Right. Room for nine passengers."

"Nice. I've never been to Hawaii. Is it as pretty as they say?"

"Oh, yeah. The first time I ever visited was when I was twelve. It was late January, and we'd gotten a cold snap, so it was like minus twenty when we left Anchorage and about seventy-five when we landed in Oahu. Even the airport smelled like flowers. There were palm trees, and beach volleyball, and the ocean. I got to swim with sea turtles, and for once my parents were getting along. It was awesome. I found out later it was an unsuccessful last-ditch effort to save their marriage, but at the time it was great. I've wanted to live there ever since."

"Hmm. Like Jackson Hole syndrome," Nathan commented.

"What?"

"Oh, never mind. It was just something I read

once. Now that I think about it, it doesn't really apply to your situation."

"But what is it?"

"Well, this article talked about a family that spent their vacation in Yellowstone and Jackson Hole and they had such a wonderful time together that they decided life would be perfect if only they lived there. So they moved to Jackson Hole, only to find out that day-to-day, they're the same people in Jackson Hole as they were before, just in a new place. I was a little afraid Alaska might be that way for me. When I was a kid, I would have a blast visiting my great-uncle and aunt at the lodge every summer, so naturally I assumed living in the lodge in Alaska would make me happy. And it does, but it's really because of the people I'm with, not the place."

"Although, the place is pretty great," Nick pointed out.

"Yeah, I love Swan Falls, but it's the people that make it special. Like I said, Jackson Hole syndrome doesn't really apply to you. I'm sure you're not making your decision based solely on one happy family vacation."

"No. I've been back many, many times on my own since then. I just enjoy the sunshine and snorkeling and fresh pineapple."

"It does sound great. Maybe next year I'll plan to take Amanda and Paisley for a winter break. And speaking of family, I'm sure Max and Lyla are sad to see you go. Lyla talks about you all the time."

"She does?"

"Oh, yeah." He used his fingers to indicate quotation marks. "'Nick taught me how to play Go Fish. Nick took me Christmas shopping. Nick says rainbows are really circles and we just can't see the bottom because the earth is in the way.' She'll miss you."

"Yeah, I'll miss her, too."

"She's a special kid. Paisley is an introvert, and Amanda says she's sometimes had trouble making friends, but she and Lyla hit it off the first moment they ever met. They have so much fun together." Nathan smiled. "You know, it's funny. I planned never to marry, much less be a dad, and now I'm both and I can't imagine my life any other way."

"I can see that." Finished with his breakfast, Nick tucked his napkin and plastic fork into the empty box.

Nathan checked his phone. "Looks like the in-laws' flight just landed, so I'd better get down to baggage claim."

Nick threw their trash into a nearby bin. "Thanks for having breakfast with me. Have fun with your in-laws."

"I will. I hope Hawaii treats you well. If we do come next winter, I'll give you a call. Maybe we can meet for lunch or something."

"I'd like that. Take care, Nathan."

They parted ways, Nathan heading down the escalator while Nick got in line for security. He went through the scanner, put his shoes back on, and arrived at the gate without looking back. It was time for his new life to begin.

CHAPTER EIGHTEEN

ON THE TARMAC at the Honolulu airport, Nick walked around the plane to the tail section, completing his exterior preflight inspection. A welcome breeze ruffled his loose shirt, printed with hibiscus and tiny airplanes. Only in Hawaii would an aloha shirt be a pilot's uniform. A woman in a matching shirt came out from the terminal carrying papers. "Here's your flight manifest."

"Thanks, Susie." He glanced over the list of nine passengers, a full flight. Looked like a family of four, plus five women with different last names.

"They're all here now if you want to try to take off early."

"Let's do that. Go ahead and send them out." She went inside and a moment later, the passengers straggled out the door and across the tarmac. Nick went to greet them. A quick head count only revealed eight people: the couple with two kids, three women in matching hot pink T-shirts, and one wearing white. Finally, another young woman in pink emerged from the door, dragging a suitcase with a wonky wheel while juggling an oversize tote bag on her shoulder. As the women got closer, he saw that the pink tops had Bride Squad emblazoned on the front, while the white shirt read Bride.

"Aloha. I'm Nick, your pilot this afternoon," he announced. "You can set your luggage there. Hope you're all going to West Maui because that's where the plane is headed."

The kids snickered a little at the feeble joke, but one of the ladies in pink, the one wearing a flamingo-print ball cap, giggled loudly. "Maui, here we come!" she yelled.

"Great." Nick nodded acknowledgment and went to take the suitcase from the woman who was struggling. "I'll put this in the luggage hold."

"Thanks." She flashed him a vague smile. As she shifted her tote, he could hear glass clinking together, and he spotted the unsealed screw top of a bottle protruding from the top. She and the bride squad must have picked it up after clearing security.

"You're welcome," he told her as he set the suitcase next to the plane to load. "I'm going to need those bottles, too."

She opened her eyes wide. "What bottles?"

"The ones in your bag. You can't take open alcohol containers on the plane. Federal regulations."

"Oh, come on," She hugged the bag closer. "I'll share."

"Thanks, but no thanks. It's only a fifty-three-minute flight. You'll be fine." He held out his hand and she handed over a bottle of vodka. "And the rest," he persisted. With a pout, she passed him bottles of whiskey and tequila, which technically weren't open, but he didn't trust her to leave them that way. He wrapped them in a towel for padding and stashed them in the hold. "Anyone else have any liquor I should know about?"

The giggling bridesmaid in the cap raised her hands above her head and gave a little shimmy. "Want to search me?"

"That won't be necessary. Anyone else?"

The bridesmaid with a messy bun shook her head, but the bride and the pink-haired bridesmaid were whispering together and didn't meet his eyes. He walked over to them. "Any liquor bottles for me to stow?"

"No, thanks." They seemed a little glassy-eyed, but not drunk.

Nick nodded and opened an ice chest. "Okay then, let's see if we can get you out of here a little early today. Help yourselves to some soft drinks or bottled water if you like." Nick looked over the manifest at the weights the passengers had provided and then again at the group. The dad looked like he might have been an offensive lineman at some point in his past. Nick suspected the weight he'd given came from his official playing weight, probably ten years and fifty pounds ago. No problem—with the kids and the women they had plenty of weight capacity, but that meant he needed to put the dad in the back to balance the load, and he liked to keep families together. Unfortunately, that meant the bridal party would be up front.

"Kevin Johnson, you'll be in the back row, along with your younger daughter. And in the next row, mom Rebecca Johnson and older daughter."

He got them settled into the plane and then appraised the rest of the group. "Ashley Andrews?"

The giggler jumped up and down as though she'd been selected to win a prize. "That's me!"

"You're in three-A. Ashley Smith?" The bridesmaid with the messy bun, who seemed to be the most sensible of the group, waved her hand. "You're up front, next to me. Samantha in three-B, Sarah two-A, and Stephanie in two-B. Let's go, ladies."

He spotted the two Ashleys conferring as they climbed the steps to the plane while he finished loading their luggage. When he came aboard, Ashley-with-a-bun was in row three and Ashley the giggler was in the front seat. He considered making them change but decided against it. "Is everyone buckled in?" He checked all their seat belts and made sure their carry-on items were secure. "Okay, then. Let's fly."

After going through his checklist and receiving the go from the tower, Nick took off, ten minutes early. Once they'd gotten airborne, the Ashley next to him said, "We're staying at the Mau Loa condos on Maui."

"Oh, those are nice. Close to the beach, and they have good tennis and pickleball courts," Nick replied.

"And a swim-up bar," she added.

"That, too."

"You should come hang with us tonight. It's going to be awesome."

Nick nodded. "I'm sure it will be."

She leaned closer. "Then you'll come?"

"No, sorry."

Her lower lip protruded. "Why not? Are you married?"

Maybe he should start wearing a ring just to forestall these conversations. "No, but, you know, company rules." Actually there weren't any rules against socializing with guests, but it sounded better than telling her the truth: that he'd prefer a root canal to hanging out with a group of tipsy bridesmaids. Maybe fifteen years ago, when he was their age, it would have sounded appealing, but now his perfect evening was much different.

"Humph." She turned to look out the window.

About twenty minutes into the flight, Nick spotted a heartwarming sight, and announced, "If you look out the window on the left side of the plane, you can see a humpback whale with her calf."

"Ooh." The passengers all leaned forward to look.

"Humpback whales nurse their calves, but they

don't feed the whole time they're in Hawaii," the girl in row four announced. "They live off the fat they stored while they were feeding in Alaska over the summer."

"That's right." Nick was impressed. Lyla would love this girl. "I'm going to circle once, so you all can get a better look before we go on." He dipped the left wing to fly in a circle. As they watched, the calf drew closer to nuzzle its head against the mother's. A collective "ah" sounded throughout the cabin.

Nick straightened the wings and resumed his flight path. A few minutes later, he heard a tinkling sound. He looked back just in time to see the woman in two-B pulling a tiny bottle from her purse. "Stephanie, put it back."

"I was just going to pour—"

"I know what you were going to do, and it will have to wait until you get to Maui."

She rolled her eyes. "Yes, Dad."

Nick restrained a laugh. He flew along for another minute before he realized Ashley the giggler hadn't had any reaction to that exchange. When he glanced her way, the greenish hue of her face told him they had a different problem. "Ashley, look straight at the horizon," he said gently, "and press your thumb against the middle of your other wrist."

She turned toward him. "I feel sick."

"I know. There's a bag in the rack beside your seat if you need it. Don't look at me or at anything inside the airplane. Focus your eyes on the horizon and breathe slowly. Four counts in. Four counts out. Try it."

Obediently, she stared where the sea met the sky, took a deep breath, and let it out. "That's a little better."

"Good. Just keep doing that. We'll be on the ground in another twenty minutes."

All went well for another ten minutes, and Nick had received clearance to land, when Ashley clasped one hand over her mouth and grabbed the bag from the rack, but then she recovered without using it.

"Ashley, are you okay?" Stephanie unbuckled and leaned forward.

"Keep breathing, Ashley. Everyone make sure your seat belts are securely buckled. You, too, Stephanie. We'll be landing shortly."

Once they were on the ground and he'd brought the plane to a stop, he dug out a few moist towelettes and handed them to Ashley. She tore open a package and wiped her face.

A few minutes later, after allowing another plane to take off, he taxied across the runway to the gate. "Thanks for flying with us. Have a great stay," he told the passengers as they deplaned and he reunited them with their luggage and liquor bottles.

"Which way to the rental-car place?" Stephanie asked as she collected the wonky suitcase.

Nick hesitated. "Um, you're not driving to your

condos, are you?" He looked pointedly at the liquor bottles she'd stashed in her tote.

"I'm the designated driver," the second Ashley, the one with the bun, volunteered. "I haven't been drinking."

"She's preggers," Ashley One said with a giggle, apparently recovered now that she was on solid ground again.

"Congratulations. Okay, then, turn right when you get inside the terminal and follow the hallway to the end."

They started off, with Ashley Two lagging behind the group, shaking her head. "I thought I was getting a vacation, but they're harder to wrangle than my fourth-grade students," she muttered to Nick.

Nick nodded with sympathy, but at least the Bride Squad wasn't staging a sit-in at the end of the boardwalk at Swan's Marsh. On the other hand, Ashley Two had no one to call for backup like Nick had. "I see that. Good luck."

"I'll need it." She extended her suitcase handle and followed the others.

Nick took the last suitcase from the hold, and Kevin came to take it from him. "Thanks for the extra time to watch the whales. We all enjoyed that, especially my youngest. She's really into science and animals."

"Yeah, I know a girl just like her."

"Your daughter?" Rebecca had come to help

with the luggage. "Maybe we could arrange a play-date while we're here."

"No, a friend's daughter, and she's in Alaska, where I used to live."

"Oh, wow, Alaska." Kevin grinned. "We definitely want to go there someday."

"You should. It's beautiful." Nick closed the luggage hatch. "While you're on Maui, you might want to check out the aquarium. I've heard good things."

"You haven't been?" Rebecca asked.

"Not yet. I've only been here for a month."

"And before that you were in Alaska? Big contrast."

"Definitely. Hope you have a great time in Maui." Nick waved to the kids as the family went inside.

That was his last flight of the day. As he drove to his apartment, the sun was setting, the fiery orange ball dropping quickly into the water without lingering the way sunsets did in Alaska. He parked and made his way toward the door. Poinsettias formed a hedge in front of the building, the showy blooms reminding him of the pot of poinsettias on Emily's hearth.

He went inside and checked his mailbox. Nothing but junk mail and a flyer from his apartment complex about a social event tomorrow. Tomorrow was his day off, but he wasn't really into hanging out by the pool all day. He could go snorkeling, but he'd done that last week, taken a boat to Molokini crater to swim among the colorful tropical fish, and the colorful tourists as well. The week before, he'd gone hiking in 'Iao Valley, where waterfalls cascaded from emerald-green mountains, and the 'Iao Needle, a volcanic tower, stretched toward the sky. But all he could think of as he hiked was how much Emily and the kids would enjoy seeing all of this. He'd sent a picture, but it wasn't the same.

Maybe tomorrow he should take his own advice and visit the aquarium. He'd kind of been saving that for when Lyla and Max came to visit someday, but would that ever happen? Now that he was gone and their lives were back to normal, Lyla would likely forget all about visiting him, like she'd suggested. Or maybe he'd just have a lazy day at home, do some laundry, read a book.

"Hi, Nick." Shelby, his neighbor from across the hall, walked by, flip-flops slapping against her heels. Judging by the bikini, she must be going to the pool. "Will I see you at the get-together tomorrow?"

"No, I'm afraid I have plans," he told her, eliminating the choice of relaxing at home, since she was sure to pressure him into attending the party if he did. So the aquarium it was. After that, who knew? He was a single man, free to spend tomorrow afternoon any way he wanted. Living the dream in Hawaii. So why did his thoughts keep running back to Swan Falls?

February might have the fewest number of days, but to Emily, it always felt like the longest month, this year more than ever. With the glow of Christmas far behind and summer just a promise in the distance, the only way through was to just keep taking every day as it came. Today, she'd volunteered to assist at an after-school carpentry class Nathan and Amanda Swan were leading. Dinner would need to be ready as soon as they got home after the class, because Max had a soccer game in Wasilla tonight at eight, and Janice was spending the day with Dave.

Emily smiled to herself as she pulled out her binder of favorite recipes and turned to the slow-cooker section. Janice was still pretending she and Dave were just friends, but who were they fooling? The way Dave's eyes softened whenever he looked at Janice, the way he would touch her back or her hand at every opportunity or hold her coat for her to slip her arms through—it all added up to more than friends. Not to mention that the moment Dave heard about a home in Swan Falls coming on the market, he'd jumped on it. The closing had been last week, and now he and Janice were furniture shopping before having dinner with Dave's family in Anchorage.

And speaking of couples, last Saturday, Emily had run into Dina and Peter having dinner together at Raven's Nest Pizza, so her introduction must have sparked something. Everyone seemed to be pairing off.

Nala came rushing into the kitchen, looking over her shoulder toward the laundry room, which meant the washing machine had entered its spin cycle. Emily crouched down to rub the dog's ears. "It's okay, girl. That mean old washing machine isn't really after you." Nala gave a sheepish wag of the tail. When the sounds stopped, Emily went to transfer the clothes to the dryer, including Max's soccer uniform, which she'd discovered under his bed when it was missing from the hamper. He would need it for the game tonight.

Soccer was another bright spot this February. Max was thriving on his new team, learning new skills and starting in about half of the games. Ian was having a little more trouble, adjusting from being the star player to just one of several, but he seemed to be settling in. Every time Emily saw Max grin after successfully blocking a pass or stealing a ball, she was grateful that Nick hadn't called her before taking him to tryouts.

Really, things were going pretty well, and if certain parts of her life felt empty, well, it wasn't anything she hadn't been through before. Yes, Nick was gone, and she missed him, but she knew how to handle loss. Her kids deserved a positive and cheerful mom. She saved her sadness for those times when she was alone, and even then, she never let herself wallow.

She paged through the recipes. Beef stew. Barbecue chicken legs. Pulled pork. Salmon chowder. Nothing caught her fancy today, until she turned the page to see Nick's recipe for five-alarm chili, although he'd marked out the five and written in a two. Broth substituted for beer, jalapeños had been changed from four to one, and a note in Nick's handwriting at the bottom suggested substituting fire-roasted tomatoes for the kind with hot peppers. He'd completely changed his recipe to suit her family's taste, just as he'd changed his lifestyle during his time with them. Volunteering at school, learning to braid hair—good grief, the man had even learned to sew just to make sure the pageant could proceed. He really cared.

That empty spot in her heart ached. Nick had been in Hawaii for longer than he'd been there with them and still, nothing seemed quite right without him. Food didn't taste as good. Family reading time wasn't as cozy. Even sledding wasn't as fun.

When Emily would go shopping at the mercantile, or volunteer at the school, or take the kids for pizza at Raven's Nest, people would ask about Nick. She would tell them he was flying airplanes in Hawaii now, and they'd laugh and say "lucky him."

But it wasn't luck. Ever since she'd first met Nick, he'd talked about moving to Hawaii someday. He'd researched the airplane models most commonly flown by the inter-island flying services there and, on his days off, he would often rent one of them to log flight hours in that particular plane. He'd watched for job postings and networked with pilots he knew from flight school. And he'd visited the islands often, taking time out of his vacation to drop by and fill out job applications. All that time and effort had finally paid off. The dream job was his, and he deserved it. She was happy for him. Really.

Granted, she'd never quite understood the why of Nick's dream. She'd been to Hawaii twice, once on spring break when she was in college and another time with Coop after they'd married but before the kids came. Hawaii was lovely, not too hot but never cold, with beaches and mountains and tropical plants everywhere. A wonderful place to visit, but at the end of vacation, she'd always been ready to go home. But obviously to Nick, Hawaii felt like home, and so she had to be glad he was there, and never let him know it broke her heart to let him go.

Chili it was. She gathered the ingredients, browned the meat, chopped the vegetables, and pretended the tears in her eyes were only from the onions. The dryer buzzed, and she washed her hands, went to the laundry room, and folded the clothes, separating out Max's soccer stuff. She was carrying the laundry basket upstairs when the robin's chirp sounded on her phone. She set the laundry on her bed and checked her phone to see what kind of bird was dining at the feeder now. Except it wasn't a bird. Instead, the camera showed a purple flower lying on top of the birdseed. What in the world?

She ran to the front door and opened it, only to find a familiar figure waiting on the porch. She blinked. "Nick?"

"It's me."

"Oh, wow, I was just..." But instead of completing that thought, she threw her arms around him and hugged him with all her might. Chuckling, he embraced her, but after a long hug, he let her go. Reluctantly, she stepped back.

"Aloha." He raised his hand, and she saw that he held a purple orchid lei that matched the flower in the birdfeeder. He draped it over her head.

"Aloha, yourself." She stared, still not sure she wasn't imagining this. "Why aren't you in Hawaii?"

"Maybe we should talk about it in the house?" he suggested, nodding at the open front door.

"Good idea." She stepped inside and he followed, closing the door behind him and kicking his boots onto the tray. He shed his coat and pulled off his hat, revealing new golden highlights in his hair that contrasted with the deep tan on his face. Emily would have sworn Nick couldn't get any more good-looking, but she would have been wrong. Nala came running up and he bent over to rub her ears, crooning sweet words to the dog.

Why was he here? She couldn't wait any longer to find out. She threw his coat over the back of a chair, took his hand, and led him to the couch in front of the fireplace. They both sat down, angled to face each other. "Okay, talk."

"All right. Let me get this right." Nick looked at her, with just a little smirk on his lips. "What's red and blue, and has wings?"

"Uh, a parrot?"

"No." He chuckled. "Well, yes, but not the answer I'm looking for."

"Okay, I give. What's red and blue, and has wings?"

He pointed toward himself. "A sunburned, homesick Alaskan pilot in Hawaii."

She snorted and reached for his hand. "What do you mean homesick? You've always wanted to live in Hawaii."

"Yeah, I have, but it turns out it was Jackson Hole syndrome."

She shook her head. "What in the world is Jackson Hole syndrome?"

"Nathan explained it to me. It's when you attach a certain feeling to a place and think if you live there, you'll keep that feeling all the time, but it doesn't work that way in real life."

"I still don't understand."

"It's like this. The first time my parents ever took me to Hawaii—"

"You were twelve," Emily said. "And you fell in

love with snorkeling and beaches and everything about Hawaii. You've told me that story."

"But what I didn't tell you, what I didn't really realize until later, was that that my parents planned that trip to try to save their marriage, and so they were being extra nice to each other. And to me. Everything fell apart shortly afterward, but for that week I had the happy family I'd always wanted."

"And so you associated that feeling with Hawaii," Emily squeezed his hand. "I get it."

"Yeah. But it turns out that living in Hawaii doesn't automatically create that feeling. Sure, I still like snorkeling, and beaches, and tropical flowers, but I discovered what makes me genuinely happy is being part of a happy family."

"You mean—"

"Yes. Being here, with you, and Janice, and the kids. Getting involved in your lives. Cutting Christmas trees, volunteering at school, hiking, sledding, even driving the kids to practices and play dates. That's what I want." His eyes met hers. "But is that what you want? We went into this agreement, knowing it was temporary." He leaned closer. "I wasn't supposed to fall in love with you. But I did."

Emily gasped. "You're in love with me?"

"Deeply, truly, head-over-heels in love," he affirmed. "The question is, do you love me? I think I've seen signs, but we've been friends for a long time. Maybe I'm misreading—"

But he couldn't continue, because Emily threw her arms around his neck and pulled him in for a kiss. A long, deep, highly satisfying kiss. And when they finally broke apart, just in case he hadn't gotten the message, she said, "I love you, too."

"That's a relief," he said, "because otherwise, I quit my job for no reason."

"You quit your job in Hawaii?"

"Put in my notice, I should say. They've asked me to stay until May, when one of their pilots will be back from maternity leave, and I agreed. Considering they held the job for me while I had my eye surgery done, it only seemed fair."

"And then what?" Emily asked.

"And then, I'll be back in Alaska, hopefully working. Tomorrow, I have to go to Talkeetna to interview for a job."

"Doing those flightseeing tours and glacier landings in Denali?"

"Exactly. It's just a summer job, but I think I'll be able to find something permanent by fall."

"That sounds amazing. We'll be counting the days until you get back."

He grinned. "About that. If I remember correctly, spring break falls between your hitches. How about if you and Janice and the kids come to visit me on Maui? I've been scoping out all the best things for you all to see. Beaches, aquarium, pineapple plantation tours. I've even found a couple of really good hole-in-the-wall restaurants the tourists don't know about. One has this incredible moo shu pork, and the other makes coconut shrimp like you've never had before. What do you think?"

"I think that is a brilliant idea. I'll check into tickets ASAP."

"Actually..." He pulled a paper from his pocket. "I already did. Saturday travel out was all booked up, so you'll have to fly on Sunday and return the next Saturday evening."

"You didn't!" She looked at the printout in her hand showing flights from ANC to HNL. "You did. You bought us tickets to Honolulu!" She looked up at him. "But what if I'd already booked us somewhere else?"

"I checked with Janice first."

"Oh, so Janice is in on this?" Janice hadn't dropped a single clue, at least none that Emily had picked up on. "Is that why she arranged to be gone for the day?"

"No, she knew I was buying tickets, but I didn't tell her I was flying back to see you. Where is she, anyway?"

"She and Dave are furniture shopping for his new home in Swan Falls."

"Furniture shopping, huh?" Nick raised his eyebrows. "That sounds promising."

"It does, doesn't it? Maybe we're all going to live happily ever after." She reached up to smooth a strand of hair away from his forehead. "You're not sunburned, by the way."

He blinked. "Why would I be?"

"Your riddle. You said sunburned, but you don't burn. You tan."

"That's true," he said with a shrug, "but red and blue made for a better riddle."

She scoffed. "So now you're a connoisseur of riddles? You always groan at my puns and jokes."

"That's because they're awful," he said with a smirk, laughing when she hit him with a pillow. "But secretly, I love them. And not so secretly, at least from this point forward," he whispered as he leaned closer for another kiss, "I love you."

CHAPTER NINETEEN

EMILY PEERED THROUGH her goggles at the curly shapes of coral on the ocean floor below her. A pink sea star clung to a rock. A yellow-and-black-striped fish with a long top fin swam by, and then another, followed by a whole group of flat brownish fish with big eyes and tiny mouths. Although she was surrounded by people, the only thing she heard was the sound of her own breathing through the snorkel she wore. It was like being inside an aquarium. All it would take would be a little kick with her fins to move across the surface, but there was something so relaxing about just floating along in the warm salt water. No wonder Nick loved it here.

But then a turtle passed beneath her, flippers flowing in a supple ballet move, almost as though it was beckoning her to follow. And so she did, swimming along just behind the creature. How could an animal that seemed so awkward on land pass through the water so gracefully?

Something brushed her foot, and Emily looked

back in alarm, but it was only Lyla trying to get her attention. Emily stopped and raised her head out of the water. Lyla popped up beside her, her snorkel flapping against her orange flotation vest and her eyes wide behind the goggles. "Mommy, I saw a turtle. He swam right up and looked at me!"

Emily spit out her snorkel. "Wow. I saw one, too, but it was swimming the other way."

A second later, Nick joined them. "Did you see it, Nick?" Lyla demanded. "The turtle who looked at me?"

"I sure did." Nick shoved his goggles up onto his forehead and pointed to the camera attached to his wrist. "I got a picture."

"Cool. I thought snorkeling was going to be hard, but it's not. All you have to do is float and breathe. Ooh, Max and Gramma are looking at something. I'll go see what it is." She popped the snorkel back in her mouth and took off toward her brother, her pale legs thrashing the water with the fins on her feet. Emily made a mental note to reapply sunscreen to everyone once they were back in the boat. She wouldn't let sunburn spoil their first full day in Hawaii.

"She's having fun," Nick commented, watching her with a fond smile on her face.

"We all are. When we left Anchorage yesterday, with sky overcast and snow covering everything, it seemed like the entire world was in shades of gray. Here, it's like a rainbow of colors—the blue ocean, the green palm trees, the magenta and purple bougainvillea blooming in front of our condo. Not to mention the sunshine, the warm water, and swimming with the turtles—Hawaii doesn't even seem real."

"I know what you mean." Nick looked up at the sky. "It does sort of feel like magic."

"Just one amazing thing after another. Like when we passed over all those whales when you flew us from Oahu to Maui yesterday. I counted nineteen. I had no idea there were that many humpbacks in a pod."

"Well, that was what they call a competition pod. It's when a group of males chases after a female, each one trying to catch her eye."

Emily chuckled. "Maybe they should take her and the kids to cut a Christmas tree. It worked on me."

"Is that so?" Nick paddled closer, but before he got to her, a whistle blew. Nick looked toward their charter boat. "I guess our time in Turtle Town is up. I'll get Janice and the kids. Meet you at the boat." With a few easy strokes, he was on the other side of the little bay, rounding up the rest of the family. She watched him cut through the waves. The man swam like a fish.

Emily made her way to the ladder of the tour boat, handed up her flippers and snorkel equipment to the crew member there, and pulled herself aboard. Most of the others on the tour had settled into the seats on the sides of the boat, under a canvas boat shade. Emily gathered her things and stood near the ladder, wrapping the kids in towels as they climbed onto the boat. Janice followed, accepting the towel with thanks.

"Let's find a place up front," Max suggested. "They said we might see porpoises on the way back to the harbor."

"Fine with me," Janice agreed, setting a wide-brimmed hat on her head. "It's in the sun, but the breeze should keep us cool."

"Are there any snacks?" Max asked.

Emily handed her bag to Janice. "There are some energy bars in there, and you'd better dig out the sunscreen."

"Good idea." Janice followed the kids around the cabin toward the other end of the boat.

Nick came up the ladder last. He shook his head, sending a spray of water from his hair. Droplets ran down his toned chest. Emily handed him a towel.

"Thanks." He used the towel to wipe his face and threw it over his shoulder. "Where are Janice and the kids?"

"Up in the front, I mean the bow."

Nick waggled his eyebrows. "I love when you talk nautical."

Emily snorted. "Belowdecks. Port. Starboard. Had enough?"

"Oh, baby." He swooped in and literally swept

her off her feet, leaving her toes dangling as he kissed her.

Someone applauded and several people laughed, but she couldn't do anything but grin as he set her back on the deck. "Wow. Maybe I should buy a nautical thesaurus. I could drive you wild."

Nick put his lips close to her ear. "Let me tell you a little secret. You could recite a grocery list, and it would drive me wild. It's your superpower."

"My superpower, huh?" She nodded solemnly. "I'll try to only use it for good, never evil."

Nick laughed and took her hand. "Come on." He brushed one more kiss across her lips. "Let's go find Janice and the kids."

THAT EVENING, MAX and Lyla were in the water again, this time in the pool at the complex where they were staying. The three-bedroom condo would normally be way out of Nick's price range, but a coworker who had a sister who was friends with the owner had set him up at a reasonable price. While the kids swam, Nick manned the grill, arranging pieces of chicken that had been marinating all day in the refrigerator in a tangy soy-and-ginger sauce.

Emily sat back on a chaise lounge next to the pool. After the snorkel trip, she'd put up her dark hair in a messy bun, exposing her slender neck. The lights around the pool bounced off the water to cast a soft glow on her lovely face as she watched the kids. But were those little lines between her eyebrows back? What could she be worrying about?

Janice came out of the condo, bringing a container of macaroni salad Nick had picked up from his favorite take-out place, along with red pepper strips and slices of fresh pineapple he would add to the grill just before the chicken was done.

"Thanks," Nick said.

"No bother." She looked up at the sky and breathed in the scent from the plumeria tree blooming nearby. "It's such a treat to be able to eat outside in March." Her phone chimed, and when she looked at the screen, a little smile lit her face.

"Text from Dave?" Nick asked.

"Uh-huh. I sent him a picture of the sun setting over the ocean with palm trees from the beach. He says he's jealous."

"Maybe you should come here on your honeymoon," he said in a teasing voice.

She scoffed, but then she raised her chin. "Right now, we're thinking of going on a different trip together. You know that river cruise Helen and I went on? Well, the company also offers a cruise on the Mississippi River, and Dave says he'd love to do it with me."

"That sounds fun." Nick turned the chicken pieces with his tongs. "When would you go?"

"We're trying to pin that down. They're offering a nice discount in September, but it might conflict with Emily's schedule."

"You know, my contract with the flying service in Talkeetna ends after Labor Day, and the job I've applied for with that regional airline wouldn't start until October, so I'll be free to stay with the kids anytime in September. You should book it."

"That would be wonderful."

Emily walked over, carrying her water bottle. "What are you two talking about?"

"Nick was saying he's got a month between jobs coming in September, and so that would be a good time for Dave and me to take that Mississippi River cruise," Janice explained. "Maybe I'll book next week when we're home."

"Great," Emily replied. "And even if Nick's plans should fall through, I'm sure we can work something out so that you can go."

"Why would Nick's plans fall through?" Janice asked.

"Yeah, why?" Nick repeated.

"Well, you know. You said that regional airline job doesn't start until October, but what if they want you earlier? Or what if you don't get it and have to work somewhere else and your schedule changes? But, like I said, if that happened, I could always take some vacation days."

What was this about? Did Emily not want him there in September? When they'd talked on the phone just before the flight to Hawaii, she couldn't wait for him to return to Alaska, and they were already making plans for summer and fall. Now, she seemed to be making excuses. Nick tried to read her face, but she gave nothing away. "What's going on?" he asked her.

She nodded at the grill. "Your chicken is burning."

"Oh." He snatched the chicken off the grill and replaced it with the peppers and pineapple he'd forgotten to add earlier. "Kids," he called. "Better get out and dry off. Dinner's almost done."

Janice went to hand them towels, leaving Nick and Emily alone next to the grill. "Is there some reason you don't want me staying with the kids in September?" he whispered.

"Of course not, just..." She glanced toward the kids. "We'll talk later. Max, don't forget your flip-flops. This chicken smells amazing. Come on. Let's eat."

Nick turned off the grill and transferred the peppers and pineapple to the platter with the chicken, but his mind wasn't on his cooking. Had Emily changed her mind about being with him? After so many weeks making do with phone calls and texts, they were finally together again. Everyone was having fun. And there was that kiss—the one he and Emily had shared on the boat after snorkeling at Turtle Town. He hadn't imagined the passion they'd both been feeling. No, something must have happened after that. But what?

No one else seemed to notice anything wrong. After a day outdoors, the kids were famished, especially Max, who managed to down two servings of macaroni salad and three chicken thighs. Janice loved the chicken and demanded his recipe. But Emily just nibbled, and Nick couldn't get much food past the knot in his stomach, either. Was he losing her?

Finally, Janice offered to take the kids up to the condo for showers. "I'll be back for the dishes," she said, but Nick waved her away.

"We'll get them. Why don't you give Dave a call while you have a minute?"

"Good idea. Come on, Max, Lyla. You need to wash the salt and chlorine out of your hair."

As they headed up the stairs to the condo, Emily began stacking the plates and silverware, but as soon as she heard the door close, she turned to Nick. "I love you."

He put his hand on his heart, which felt like it had been trying to beat its way out of his chest. "That's a relief. I love you, too."

"I know. That's why—" Emily turned away from him and walked a few steps stopping under the plumeria tree.

"What is it?" Nick followed. "Did I do something wrong? Whatever it is, you can tell me."

"Nothing's wrong." She turned to face him. "Everything is perfect. After spending time with you here, I can see how much you love everything about Hawaii." She touched his face. "Am I a terrible person to ask you to give it up for me?"

"Is that all?" He laughed, despite the fact that Emily looked so miserable. He plucked a fragrant white-and-yellow flower from the tree and tucked it into her hair. "Emily, I would give up the stars in the sky to be with you. But in this case, I'm not giving up anything at all. I do love Hawaii, and yes, I think we should make it a point to vacation here every year or two, but the life I want isn't here. It's in Swan Falls, with you and Janice and the kids."

"Are you sure?" She looked happier now, but still uncertain. "Because I was thinking. A lot of people who work on the North Slope live out of state and fly in for their two-week hitches. Theoretically, we could live here in Hawaii, and I could commute to my job."

"No way." Not only would it be hugely inconvenient for her, but it would also be hard on the entire family. "Take the kids away from their home, their school, and their friends? I'd never do that. Not to mention Janice and Dave, and their growing relationship. Besides, I love Swan Falls."

"You do?"

"Of course I do. I've loved it since you and Coop first bought that ridiculous ramshackle house and turned it into an amazing home. I love the bird sanctuary, and the falls, and all the hiking trails. I love how the whole town turns out for an elementary school pageant. And don't get me started on the Raven's Nest. I've been mourning the loss of their Blizzard Pizza ever since I got here."

She laughed. "Maybe we'll have a joint pizza party for Max's birthday and your homecoming in May."

"That would be awesome." He pulled her closer and whispered in her ear, "Can I tell you a secret?"

She put her arms around his neck and those amazing blue eyes gazed into his. "You can tell me anything."

"Here goes, then. Emily, I love you. There's nothing I want more than to be part of your family. And as soon as we're living in the same state again, I plan to make it official with a ring and a date. Do you have a problem with that?"

She grinned. "I do not." And without another word, she rose up on her tiptoes and pulled him into a kiss. The scent of plumeria and sea salt filled his nose, and champagne bubbles of happiness filled his soul. This, this was what living was all about. When they finally broke the kiss, she sighed and leaned her head against his shoulder. Suddenly she snorted. "Nick?"

"Mmm?"

"What happened when a cider maker fell in love with a lumberjack?"

He chuckled in anticipation. "I give up. What happened when a cider maker fell in love with a lumberjack?"

"They lived pineappley ever after."

Nick groaned, but then he planted a kiss on her forehead. "And so will we."

* * * * *

*For more charming Alaska romances
from Beth Carpenter and
Harlequin Heartwarming,
please visit www.Harlequin.com today!*

Get up to 4 Free Books!

We'll send you 2 free books from each series you try PLUS a free Mystery Gift.

FREE Value Over $25

Both the **Harlequin® Special Edition** and **Harlequin® Heartwarming™** series feature compelling novels filled with stories of love and strength where the bonds of friendship, family and community unite.

YES! Please send me 2 FREE novels from the Harlequin Special Edition or Harlequin Heartwarming series and my FREE Gift (gift is worth about $10 retail). After receiving them, if I don't wish to receive any more books, I can return the shipping statement marked "cancel." If I don't cancel, I will receive 6 brand-new Harlequin Special Edition books every month and be billed just $6.39 each in the U.S. or $7.19 each in Canada, or 4 brand-new Harlequin Heartwarming Larger-Print books every month and be billed just $7.19 each in the U.S. or $7.99 each in Canada, a savings of 20% off the cover price. It's quite a bargain! Shipping and handling is just 50¢ per book in the U.S. and $1.25 per book in Canada.* I understand that accepting the 2 free books and gift places me under no obligation to buy anything. I can always return a shipment and cancel at any time by calling the number below. The free books and gift are mine to keep no matter what I decide.

Choose one:
- ☐ **Harlequin Special Edition** (235/335 BPA G36Y)
- ☐ **Harlequin Heartwarming Larger-Print** (161/361 BPA G36Y)
- ☐ **Or Try Both!** (235/335 & 161/361 BPA G36Z)

Name (please print)

Address _____ Apt. #

City _____ State/Province _____ Zip/Postal Code

Email: Please check this box ☐ if you would like to receive newsletters and promotional emails from Harlequin Enterprises ULC and its affiliates. You can unsubscribe anytime.

Mail to the Harlequin Reader Service:
IN U.S.A.: P.O. Box 1341, Buffalo, NY 14240-8531
IN CANADA: P.O. Box 603, Fort Erie, Ontario L2A 5X3

Want to explore our other series or interested in ebooks? Visit www.ReaderService.com or call 1-800-873-8635.

---

*Terms and prices subject to change without notice. Prices do not include sales taxes, which will be charged (if applicable) based on your state or country of residence. Canadian residents will be charged applicable taxes. Offer not valid in Quebec. This offer is limited to one order per household. Books received may not be as shown. Not valid for current subscribers to the Harlequin Special Edition or Harlequin Heartwarming series. All orders subject to approval. Credit or debit balances in a customer's account(s) may be offset by any other outstanding balance owed by or to the customer. Please allow 4 to 6 weeks for delivery. Offer available while quantities last.

Your Privacy—Your information is being collected by Harlequin Enterprises ULC, operating as Harlequin Reader Service. For a complete summary of the information we collect, how we use this information and to whom it is disclosed, please visit our privacy notice located at https://corporate.harlequin.com/privacy-notice. Notice to California Residents – Under California law, you have specific rights to control and access your data. For more information on these rights and how to exercise them, visit https://corporate.harlequin.com/california-privacy. For additional information for residents of other U.S. states that provide their residents with certain rights with respect to personal data, visit https://corporate.harlequin.com/other-state-residents-privacy-rights/.

HSEHW25